ECHOES OF THE OUTBACK

OUTBACK QUEENSLAND ROMANCE

RHONDA FORREST

Valeena Press

*The Outback Queensland Romance Series
has captured hearts both here in Australia
and overseas. If you love romance,
memorable characters and the Australian
outback, settle in and enjoy.*

Thankyou for your
support of an Aussie
author!
Happy reading ♡
Rhonda Forrest

PROLOGUE

They travelled across the red heart of a continent that was not their own. Men from distant lands and ancient trade routes who left behind families and familiar ground to walk beside their camels over a land that mirrored their homeland in its harshness and beauty.

They faced the sun's fury and the bitter cold of night. They endured suspicion from those who saw their darker skin and foreign tongue as a threat rather than a gift. Yet they persisted, loving this brutal country with its endless sky and unforgiving earth because it spoke to something in their bones. Their camels are gone now, replaced by motors and sealed roads. Most of the Afghan camel drivers returned to their own country, but some remained. They had sailed an ocean to walk a desert, and now they carried their echoes of hope forward. Those who remained with their families built lives in the spaces between acceptance and exile, despite being told they didn't belong. They were the Afghan cameleers.

CHAPTER 1

$\mathcal{E}$lla checked the time, calculating how long until she had to meet Cass at the pub. Three hours, she told herself. Enough time to sit for a while and then walk back to where she had parked. She always ended up in the same spot. It wasn't because it offered the best view or provided the deepest shade against Queensland's outback heat. Rather, an invisible thread drew her back, time and time again to this small clearing on the rise, on a property that belonged to someone else, where weathered rocks formed a circle around a larger flat stone that seemed deliberately placed for sitting.

It had always been this way. When she was younger and wrestling with decisions that felt too big for her young shoulders, this was where she'd always come to think. Years ago, the question had been, should she leave Matfield for Melbourne to study astronomy at university, chase stars and pursue career prospects? Or should she stay and carry on the family tradition, working at Patterson's Produce like her grandfather and father before her?

She'd sat here for hours, turning questions over until answers emerged that felt right, even if they turned out to be wrong, years later. Her dad had been patient with her indecision back then, never pushing, just reminding her that the store would always be there if she wanted to come back and work there. Her mum had been the opposite, encouraging her to spread her wings, to see what else the world had to offer beyond the dust and heat of outback Queensland.

She remembered one particular afternoon when she'd ignored rare heavy rain pounding against her waterproof jacket as she sat in the same spot, staring out across the plains. Puddles had formed on the edge of the clearing and small animals scurried for cover. A feeling washed over her that she couldn't quite articulate. A presence, perhaps. An echo of lives lived here before hers. Whether it was spirits from the past or simply her own thoughts finding clarity in the silence, she always felt guided when she came to this place. Her grandmother used to tell stories about the Aboriginal elders who could read the land, who knew its moods and memories. Ella had never met those elders, most having passed before she was born, but she understood what her grandmother meant about listening to the country.

There was, however, more to this place than what her grandmother talked about. The old-timers in town shared other stories about the family who had once lived here, on what the records showed had been called Pazhvak Station. That name had long since disappeared from official use, but some locals still referred to it as the Ghan Place or Camel Camp. They said the original name was related to the echoes and traditions of the Afghan cameleers who opened up the outback with their patient beasts. The stories and details had grown hazy with time and the telling, but they said the woman who first lived there was a descendant of those men.

Because it had been so long since anyone had lived on the property, it was difficult to envisage what it once had been. The crude house made of split logs had long since fallen down and been eaten by termites. The only parts still even remotely intact were a stone section at the bottom of a wall and a crumbling stone chimney that rose like a broken finger against the sky. An old shed had also nearly disintegrated, and apart from a couple of old rusty pieces of farming machinery and a windmill left in the paddocks, there was barely a trace that anyone had lived there. Yet the careful arrangement of the rocks, and the way the land seemed to hold its breath around this particular clearing, was as if the place was waiting for someone to remember what or who had come before.

Her gaze wandered to the low hills nearby. A blurry haze hugged the base of them and dust from a whirlywind twirled across the plain. It was so different from the city she had moved to in her early twenties. This was the place she had missed the most. The spot that she dreamt about at night as she lay in her unit listening to the traffic in the street below, cars beeping in impatience and the sound of music coming from a restaurant across the street.

Melbourne had been everything she thought she wanted. Her mind had been filled with lectures on celestial mechanics, late nights at the observatory and a studio apartment where she could pretend to be someone other than Colin Patterson's daughter from a town most people had never heard of. The city dazzled her at first, the sheer volume of opportunity overwhelming after Matfield's quiet limitations. She'd thrown herself into student life with determination, joining astronomy clubs, volunteering at the planetarium, dating a series of forgettable boys who seemed sophisticated compared to the farm kids she'd grown up with. But she'd missed this spot desperately. She'd missed the sweet scent of eucalyptus blossoms from the trees bordering the gully further down the ridge and the profound silence broken only by birdsong and wind through dry grass. There had been no room for this kind of peace in the traffic and chaos of the city. When everything fell apart with Trent, the one serious relationship she'd had, her carefully constructed city life began to crumble, and it was this place she'd dreamed about. This exact spot she longed for when she finally admitted that the career and lifestyle she'd fought so hard to achieve weren't what she wanted after all.

Still, coming back to Matfield felt like failure at first. Twenty-eight years old and she was back in the one place she'd longed to leave. Moving into the cottage behind her parents' house and working at the family store completed the circle. Her friends from university were politely confused when she told them, their expressions suggesting they thought she'd given up on herself. Maybe she had, in a way. But the first time she walked back out here, following the familiar path through scrub and over dried creek beds, she'd smiled when the rock circle came into view. Some things remained constant even when everything else changed. The rocks had weathered another decade, but the familiar flat stone was still warm in the afternoon sun, and the view across the plains still made her chest expand with an emotion close to joy

She'd always searched for clues about who might have sat here before her. The rocks were too deliberately arranged to be natural, and the flat sitting stone showed signs of human shaping, although weathered almost smooth by decades of exposure. It would have been wrong to disturb anything or to dig around looking for artefacts or answers. Her feet were walking on history itself, and that deserved respect. Perhaps this had been an Aboriginal meeting place, sacred ground where stories were shared and ceremonies performed. Or maybe it had been created by that first family, the ones connected to the Afghan cameleers, perhaps marking a place to rest and survey a land that may have reminded them of distant homelands they'd never see again. There might also have been shepherds or drovers who made camp here, or farmers who paused in their work to rest and survey the land they were trying to tame.

She would probably never know the truth, but that didn't bother her as much as it might have when she was younger, believing every mystery could be solved with enough research and determination. The tranquility of her special spot and the entire abandoned property that surrounded it had become more than just a peaceful refuge. It had become her dream. It was what she thought about when she couldn't sleep and what she aimed for with every dollar she saved.

The property had been abandoned for as long as anyone in Matfield could remember. Decades of neglect had left fences collapsed and paddocks overgrown with scrub and weeds. Outside contractors appeared on occasion to get rid of some of the weeds that the council had probably sent notices about. No one in town seemed to know much about the owners who had just up and left without anyone realising. The rates were always paid on time though, and whenever the council served a weed control notice, someone took care of it. But no one ever visited, no one ever inquired about developing it, and the whole property sat like a ghost waiting for someone to remember it existed. Her father had made inquiries years ago, back when she was still in high school, thinking he might buy it himself. The same people who owned Pazhvak Station, owned the block that was next to Ella's family produce store in town. Another block her father had his eye on and was keen to buy if it ever came on the market. Whoever owned them though, wasn't interested in selling, and eventually people stopped asking.

Ella was determined to buy the station. She had been busy saving her money since returning to Matfield, building her deposit, researching property values, and working with the local real estate agent to communicate with the owners. Her plan was simple but deeply felt. She would buy the property, build a modest house right here near her special spot, and create a life that honoured both her need for solitude and her connection to this place. She'd sketched rough plans in notebooks, calculated costs, and researched sustainable building materials that would suit the climate. In her mind she could already see it; a simple homestead with wide verandahs, water tanks to catch what little rain fell, and solar panels to make her independent of the grid. She'd restore some of the fencing, clear the worst of the scrub and maybe run a few head of cattle or some sheep. Nothing ambitious, just enough to keep her busy. She would also sit in this exact spot watching sunrises and sunsets, and finally put down roots in soil that felt special in ways she couldn't explain.

She imagined her grandmother would have understood and approved of her plan. When Ella spoke to her for the last time before she passed and told her that she was thinking about coming back home, Granny had told her that some people were meant to stay close to where they came from, that there was no shame in choosing homeland over wings.

Her plan to purchase the property was getting closer to reality. In the next few months, if everything went according to plan with the connections and information Phil, the local real estate agent, had mentioned he was following up on, this place might actually become hers. Not just in dreams, but in deed, title and her daily life. It felt like destiny, like everything she'd been through, all the false starts and disappointments in Melbourne, had been leading her back to this spot. Phil had been cautiously optimistic when she spoke to him last week, mentioning that the latest information was that the owners were getting ready to sell. He said it was looking very promising, and he'd try to get confirmation and even a contract ready to go for her. She hadn't dared to hope too hard, but the possibility hummed through her veins whenever she came here.

She just had to make it happen before someone else discovered what she already knew. This land was special and held endless possibilities for her future. Anxiety knotted in her stomach at the thought of losing it, of someone else buying it and putting up a building that didn't honour its history. She couldn't let that happen. This place was meant to be hers.

Standing up, she brushed red dust from her jeans and took one last look across the valley before heading back to her car. Cass would be waiting, and Friday nights at the pub were important for maintaining the social connections that made small-town life bearable. Even if she'd rather stay here watching the sunset, some obligations couldn't be avoided.

*E*lla showered quickly when she got home, washing away the dust from her walk and trying to scrub off the melancholy that always followed her visits to the property. Wanting a place so badly, yet having no control over whether she could actually get it, was exhausting. The uncertainty gnawed at her, making her irritable and restless. She pulled on her favourite jeans and slipped into a simple green top that Cass insisted brought out her eyes, then grabbed her keys and walked the short distance to the pub. The evening air was still warm, dry heat lingering long after sunset, and she could hear the distant sound of someone's television through an open window, typically the most exciting entertainment in Matfield other than the pub.

Friday nights at the Matfield Pub were the social highlight of the week for most locals under forty. The back bar filled up around seven, the music started by eight, and by nine the small dance floor would be packed with people letting off steam after a long week. Ella usually avoided the rowdier nights, preferring quieter midweek visits when she could actually hear herself think, but Cass had been persistent. Her friend had called three times today alone, insisting that Ella was in danger of becoming a hermit and needed to get out more. She would not allow her to spend every Friday night at home with a book and a glass of wine. Eventually Ella had given in, if only to stop the nagging.

'About time!' Cass called out when Ella pushed through the front door. Her friend was already at a table with others from their year group; Jenny from the post office, Sarah who worked at the chemist, and Rod who managed his family's sheep station. This was the usual crowd. These were the ones who had stayed or come back, choosing Matfield over whatever else the world might offer. 'We were starting to think you'd bailed on us.'

'Just running late. Had to finish some stock work at the store.' Ella slid into the empty seat left for her and accepted the glass of wine Cass had already ordered. The pub was filling up nicely, the after-work crowd mixing with early diners, conversations rising in volume as the alcohol flowed. 'What did I miss?'

'Nothing yet, but the night's young.' Cass's eyes sparkled with mischief, and Ella recognised that look. Her friend was plotting. 'I heard those new builders might show up tonight. Oscar mentioned they needed to unwind after a big week.'

Ella felt her mood dampen. The last thing she wanted to do was spend her Friday night watching every single woman in town throw themselves at a couple of tradies from Melbourne. She'd already heard enough about them from her father, who'd been impressed by their work ethic when he stopped by the pub to check on the renovations. 'How exciting for everyone.'

'Don't be like that. You haven't even met them yet.'

'Don't need to.' Ella took a long sip of her wine. She could already picture them. No doubt they'd be overconfident, probably covered in tattoos. The kind of men who knew they were attractive and used it to their advantage. She'd met enough of that type in Melbourne to last a lifetime.

'You're such a cynic,' Jenny chimed in, leaning across the table. 'What if they're actually nice? Not every good-looking man is a dickhead, you know.'

'Experience suggests otherwise,' Ella muttered, but she smiled to take the edge off the remark. Jenny meant well, even if she had terrible taste in men herself.

* * *

THE EVENING PROGRESSED PLEASANTLY ENOUGH. The wine was chilled, the conversation easy, and the music loud enough to discourage serious discussion. Rod told a long, rambling story about a stubborn sheep that had half the table in stitches, and Sarah shared gossip about the new worker at the chemist who apparently caused quite a stir by being both competent and attractive. By ten o'clock, Ella had relaxed considerably, the stress of the week melting away under the influence of good company and a second glass of wine. Maybe Cass had been right about getting out more.

Then the atmosphere shifted.

It was subtle at first. A few heads turned towards the door, conversations paused mid-sentence, then there arose the kind of collective awareness that always seemed to accompany someone noteworthy entering a small-town pub. Ella looked up to see two men walking towards the bar with the casual confidence of people who had no idea they were being watched, or perhaps were so used to being observed that they no longer registered it.

The blonde one was attractive in a conventional way. He was tall, broad-shouldered, with an easy smile he flashed at the bartender. His hair was sun-bleached and slightly too long, falling into his eyes in a way that probably looked artfully casual but was more likely just laziness about getting a haircut. But it was the dark-haired one who made Ella's breath catch. He moved with a confident grace, his olive skin and strong features striking even in the dim lighting. Dark hair fell across his forehead, and when he turned slightly, she caught the line of his jaw and the intensity in his dark eyes. He was the kind of handsome that led women to do stupid things, the kind that came with danger signs she'd learned to read too late with a couple of casual boyfriends and then again with Trent.

'Oh my God,' Cass whispered beside her, her voice heightened with appreciation. 'That's them. The builders.'

Every woman in the vicinity had noticed. Ella watched with detached amusement as her friends suddenly became very interested in refreshing their drinks or positioning themselves for a better view. It was predictable and slightly pathetic, although she couldn't entirely blame them. The men were undeniably attractive and Cass had already found out they were single. Single men were in short supply in Matfield.

The blonde one, Eli she heard someone call him, was quickly surrounded by a group including Cass, who'd wasted no time making her move. Ella watched her friend laugh at whatever he'd just said, saw the way she touched his arm with calculated casualness, and shook her head. Cass fell in love hard, usually with spectacularly bad results. The dark-haired one stood slightly apart, surveying the room with an expression that suggested he was assessing the situation.

Then he moved towards the bar, and Ella realised with dismay that the only empty space was directly beside her. Of course it was. The universe had a terrible sense of humour.

She kept her eyes on her wine glass, determined not to be another gawking local, but she was acutely aware of him settling beside her. Up close, he was even more striking. His shirt was rolled up at the sleeves, revealing forearms marked with the kind of muscle definition that came from hard physical work rather than gym sessions. A pleasant scent surrounded him. Soap, maybe, a clean and masculine smell that made her want to lean closer even as her brain screamed at her to keep her distance.

'Evening,' he said, his voice pitched low enough that she had to turn to hear him properly over the music and conversation.

Warmth flooded through her. It was an immediate reaction, a physical response she hadn't felt in years and certainly hadn't expected from a complete stranger. His eyes held hers for a moment longer than strictly necessary, and she saw surprise flicker across his face as though he'd felt it too. For a second neither of them moved, caught in that moment of unexpected connection that sometimes happened between people and usually led nowhere good.

She looked away, angry at herself. This was exactly the kind of surface attraction she'd promised herself to avoid. Pretty faces and confident smiles had led her astray before, causing her to ignore red flags that she wouldn't miss again. She wasn't going to make that mistake, no matter how fast her pulse was racing.

'Evening,' she replied curtly, giving him the briefest nod before returning her attention to her wine. If she were cold enough, maybe he'd take the hint and leave her alone.

'You from around here?' he asked, seemingly unbothered by her cool response. There was amusement in his voice, as if he found her attitude entertaining rather than off-putting.

'Born and raised.' She didn't elaborate, failing to offer the opening that he was clearly fishing for.

'Lucky you. Beautiful country.' He ordered a beer from the bartender, then turned back to her, clearly not ready to give up despite her obvious lack of interest. 'I'm Dusty. Dusty Camilleri.'

'Ella. Ella Patterson,' The name came out reluctantly. She could feel Cass watching them from across the room, probably already planning their wedding.

'Pleased to meet you, Ella.' The way he said her name, with a slight emphasis that made it sound almost intimate, sent another unwelcome rush through her system. He had a nice voice, deep and warm, with just a hint of a foreign accent in the cadence. Not quite Australian, but not quite anything else.

'You're one of the builders working on the pub.' It wasn't a question, and she didn't try to make it sound like one.

'Guilty. How did you guess?' That amusement again, playing around the corners of his mouth.

'Small town. Word travels fast.' She took a deliberate sip of her wine. 'Plus, everyone's been talking about the two blokes from Melbourne who showed up to renovate Todd and Oscar's place.'

'All good things, I hope.' There was a note of genuine curiosity beneath the teasing. Maybe he cared what people thought.

'Depends on who you ask.'

'And what would you say?' He was watching her intently now, his eyes fixed on her face.

She finally looked at him properly, meeting his gaze with deliberate coolness. Time to make her position clear before this went any further. 'I'd say the jury's still out. We don't know you yet.'

'Fair enough.' He accepted his beer, paid, then raised it slightly in her direction. The gesture was casual but somehow charged with meaning. 'Here's to changing your mind then.'

Before she could formulate a response that would definitively shut down whatever was happening here, Eli called his name from across the room, and he moved away to join his friend. Ella released a breath she hadn't realised she'd been holding, her shoulders dropping from the tension that had gripped them.

'What was that about?' Cass materialised beside her, eyes wide with curiosity and no small amount of glee. She looked like she'd just witnessed a momentous event.

'Nothing. Just small talk.' Ella drained the rest of her wine.

Cass placed a glass of champagne in front of her. 'My shout. Get that into you.'

The two of them clinked their glasses together before raising them to their lips. The refreshing liquid went down quickly and they locked eyes while tipping their glasses up high. When they stopped at the same time, they laughed before finishing the rest of the drinks.

'Right,' Cass said. 'That was for old times' sake. Now, give me the lowdown. What did you and the hot builder talk about?'

Ella placed her empty glass down on the bar. Her head spun a little and she remembered she hadn't eaten very much that day. Drinking on an empty stomach was not a good idea. Her reply was short. 'Nothing.'

'That did not look like nothing. That looked like serious chemistry.' Cass was practically bouncing with excitement, and Ella wanted to throttle her.

'Don't be ridiculous.' But even as she said it, Ella knew Cass was right. She couldn't explain or dismiss what had happened during that brief moment. The air between them had felt charged, electric, dangerous. And judging by the way her pulse was still racing, her body had registered what her mind was trying to deny.

The music shifted to a slower song. It was more rhythmic, and people began drifting towards the small dance floor. Ella stayed put, trying to focus on the conversation around her. She was doing well, deliberately not looking in his direction, until she felt someone's presence behind her. She knew who it was before he spoke, felt it in the way her body tensed and her breathing changed.

'Dance?' Dusty's voice, close enough that she felt his breath against her ear, warm and intimate.

She should say no. Every rational part of her brain screamed that getting closer to him was a terrible idea. He was exactly the type she needed to avoid. He was too attractive, too confident, too temporary. He'd be gone in a few months, back to Melbourne and whatever life he had there, no doubt leaving chaos in his wake. But when she turned and met his eyes again, excitement overrode her common sense. Maybe it was the wine, or maybe it was the way he was looking at her, as though she was worth discovering rather than just another small-town girl in a pub. Maybe she was just tired of being sensible.

'One dance.' She stood, ignoring Cass's delighted gasp behind her, and let him lead her to the floor.

The dance floor was crowded enough that they were pressed close together almost immediately. He took her hand in his, his other hand settling on her waist with gentle confidence, and they moved together to the music. Ella was shocked by how natural it felt, how her body seemed to know instinctively how to match his rhythm. The heat of his palm through her thin shirt sent awareness cascading through her. They fit together perfectly, her height just right for his, her body aligning with his.

'You're a good dancer,' he said, his face close enough that she could see the gold flecks in his dark eyes. She inhaled sharply. She could count his eyelashes if she wanted to.

'You sound surprised.' She tried to inject some coolness into her voice, some distance, but it came out huskier than she intended.

'Not surprised. Impressed.' His thumb traced a small circle against her waist, and she felt it like a fire, like his touch was burning through the fabric. 'There's a difference.'

They moved through the song in silence, charged with tension that made breathing difficult. Every point where their bodies touched seemed to generate heat, and Ella found her senses heightened. She noted the strength in his arms, the way he smelled and the slight scruff on his jaw that would feel rough against her skin if she reached up to touch it. His hand tightened slightly on her waist, pulling her closer, and she didn't resist. Couldn't resist, really, because her body seemed to have ideas completely independent of what her brain was telling it.

When the song ended, neither moved apart immediately. They stood there, swaying slightly even though the music had picked up pace It was as if they were caught in a trance neither seemed willing to break. The pub fell away, the crowd disappeared, and there was only his hands on her and the thundering of her pulse in her ears.

Then he leaned down and kissed her. At first, the kiss was brief, barely more than a brush of lips, but it sent shockwaves through her entire system. His mouth was warm and surprisingly soft, and for that split second, everything else disappeared. No carefully constructed walls to protect herself, just sensation, pure and overwhelming. She leaned in and let herself go, her lips pushing firmly and passionately against his.

When they pulled away from each other, she saw surprise in his expression mirroring her own, as though he hadn't planned that any more than she had, as though it had simply happened beyond either of their control. The air between them felt electric, charged with possibility and danger in equal measure. She could see his chest rising and falling rapidly, matching her own breathlessness.

'I should go,' she said, her voice not quite steady. The words felt wrong even as she said them, but panic was setting in, reality crashing back with uncomfortable force.

'Should you?' There was a tone in his voice that sounded almost like disappointment.

'Yes.' She stepped back, breaking the spell, putting necessary distance between them. Her hands were shaking and she clasped them together to hide it. 'This was a mistake.'

She turned and pushed through the crowd, finding Cass at their table. Her friend's knowing smile was more than she could handle right now. 'I need to leave. Now.'

'What? Why? What happened?' Cass reached for her arm, but Ella pulled away.

'I've had too much to drink. I need to go home.' The lie came easily, necessary to escape the confused look in Cass's eyes and the questions she wasn't ready to answer.

'I'll walk with you.' Cass was already reaching for her bag, ready to abandon her own night to play caretaker.

'No. Stay. Enjoy your night. I'm fine, just tired.' Ella grabbed her bag and headed for the door without looking back, terrified that if she turned around, she'd see him watching her leave, and then she might lose her nerve and go back to him.

Outside, the cool night air hit her like a slap, clearing her head slightly. Trying to process what had just happened, she walked quickly towards her cottage, her footsteps loud in the quiet street. She'd spent the entire day at her special place, making plans for a future built on independence and careful decisions. Then one dance with a handsome stranger had called her choices into question again, leaving her shaken and confused.

By the time she reached her cottage, locking out the events of the night along with the door behind her, she'd made a decision. Whatever 'that' had been at the pub, it couldn't happen again. Dusty was exactly the kind of complication she'd come back to Matfield to avoid. Attractive, confident, and temporary. A recipe for disaster and a path she'd walked before with painful results. He'd be gone in a few months, back to Melbourne and whatever life he had there, leaving her with nothing but regrets and a small town full of people who'd witnessed her fall.

One impulsive kiss didn't have to mean anything. It could be written off as a moment of weakness, too much wine and too long since she'd felt anything resembling attraction.

But as she lay in bed that night, unable to sleep despite her exhaustion, she kept touching her lips and remembering the way he'd looked at her. She wondered if that kiss had affected him as deeply as it had affected her. She could still feel the imprint of his hands on her waist, and remembered him watching her with an intensity that made her forget every lesson she'd learned the hard way.

This was going to be more difficult than she anticipated.

CHAPTER 3

Sunlight filtered through a slender sash window, highlighting dust specks that danced lazily in the air. A whiff of fragrant soap accompanied the dull padding of rubber-soled boots across timber floorboards, an oddly pleasant contrast to the smell of fresh sawdust that threatened to fill the space. There remained, though, the mustiness of old wood and age, that particular scent of buildings that had stood for generations and held stories in their walls.

Dusty positioned himself on an old timber crate behind one of the walls that remained intact, grateful for the break his partner Eli had suggested. He pulled out his thermos and esky, both filled with sustenance for what had already been a gruelling morning. After Friday night at the pub and that inexplicable kiss that had kept him awake half the night, he'd thrown himself into work with renewed intensity. Physical labour was good for clearing your head, or at least that's what he'd been telling himself. So far it wasn't working. He kept replaying the moment she walked away. He thought about how she looked at him just before she left, panic flashing in those green eyes.

The past two days had seen them systematically dismantling walls in one of the back rooms at the Matfield Pub, the first stage of extensive renovation plans. The owners, Todd, Oscar and Patricia, were determined to restore the grand building to some semblance of its former glory, and due to the lack of available builders in this outback area, they'd searched further afield to recruit the workers they needed. The job was bigger than they'd originally thought though, layers of dodgy repairs and quick fixes hiding structural problems that would need proper attention.

It had been somewhere different for him and Eli to relocate to, and they had been ready for a country change. At that time, there was nothing to keep him in Melbourne. There had been a few girlfriends over the years and the last one, Tanya, had lasted the longest. But the relationship had ended badly when he realised it wasn't right and he didn't want to commit to her timeline. After that he'd felt like he was drifting and not really striving for anything in particular. His mother had always said a person should have an aim, even if it was small. Just a purpose. It's what keeps you going. She'd said it in Portuguese, the way she said most important things, her native language carrying more colour and emphasis than English could match.

A purpose, he mused. A project to aim for. At thirty-two, Dusty Camilleri had inherited his father's tall build and his mother's Brazilian practicality. The physical demands of construction work had left him broad-shouldered and lean, with calloused hands that spoke of years of wielding tools. His olive complexion darkened easily in the sun, and his dark hair constantly fell into his eyes, no matter how often he pushed it back. After years of Melbourne crowds and traffic, the quiet of the outback suited him perfectly. Right now, with Eli off collecting supplies from the hardware store, he was savouring this rare moment of solitude and the chance to eat his lunch without any interruptions.

The sound of approaching voices made him tense. These voices were distinctly female, and one of them he recognised immediately. That smooth, confident tone of a beautiful woman with long blonde hair. A woman who had said his name in the pub before she'd kissed him back with an intensity that had knocked the breath out of him, but then fled like he was contagious. Ella.

'What a mess!' a young woman's voice echoed through the empty space, followed by a fit of coughing. 'They're certainly getting stuck into it.'

'It's a large room. Hard to believe it's been left unused for five years. Oscar and Todd will be thrilled to see it restored.' That was definitely Ella's voice, and hearing it again made his chest tighten. He should announce himself, step out and face her. But he kept still, waiting.

'It's a blessing for the entire town that Oscar came into that inheritance. Even better that he decided to spend it here in the pub instead of retiring like everyone thought he would.'

'Perfect timing for Todd and Penny too, with another baby to look after. They can take over more of the day-to-day running while Oscar focuses on the renovations.'

Dusty stayed perfectly still behind the wall, caught between revealing himself and staying hidden. After

Friday night, after the way she'd looked at him and then ran, he wasn't sure what kind of reception he'd get. Part of him wanted to see her reaction. He wondered if she'd been thinking about that kiss as much as he had.

'I wonder where the builders are,' Cass mused. 'Every single woman in town was getting an eyeful of them at the pub on Friday night, that's for sure. Talk about good-looking.'

Dusty's jaw tightened. So, they had been the topic of conversation. That tracked with how the entire pub had stared and the way conversations had stopped when they walked in.

'I tell you what, Cass, you need to think more carefully about your choices in men. Especially men who look like that. I wouldn't touch either of them with a ten-foot pole.'

The words hit him like a physical blow. Only a few nights ago she'd been in his arms, kissing him back with an intensity that had obviously shocked them both. Now she was standing fifteen feet away, telling her friend she wouldn't touch him? The dismissal stung worse than it should have.

'Are you serious? Did you have a good look at them? Tell me why, Ella. Because from where I was standing, they both looked pretty spectacular.'

'Too good-looking for their own good. Especially the dark-haired one. Dangerous, obsessive, probably misogynistic and controlling. I can pick the type from a mile away. Believe me, I know.'

Dusty felt his face flush with anger and hurt. She'd kissed him. She'd looked at him like he was worth knowing. And now she was categorising him as dangerous and misogynistic based on nothing but his appearance? Based on one dance and one kiss, she'd seemed to want as much as he had? He gripped his thermos hard enough that his knuckles went white.

Cass laughed, clearly not taking her friend seriously. 'Speaking from experience?'

'Unfortunately, yes. Never getting caught again like I was with Trent. Same thing. He was good-looking, muscular and confident. A walking red flag wrapped in an attractive package. Took me six months to realise what everyone else could see from the start.'

So that's what Friday night had been about. She'd projected some ex-boyfriend's issues onto him and decided he was a threat before they even had a proper conversation. The kiss had probably terrified her and made her run straight back to her protective walls. Her words should have made him annoyed or made him think she was someone not worth the effort. But instead, he felt something else. Understanding, maybe. He'd been burned, too. He knew what it was like to build walls after someone hurt you.

'Well, I prefer the blonde one anyway. He smiled at me. And you were too busy dancing with the dark-haired one to notice me trying to talk to Eli. You looked like you were enjoying yourself, by the way. Very cosy.'

Dusty tilted his head, straining to catch every word now.

'Don't get sucked in, Cass. They're just a couple of city blokes with no idea about life out here. Probably here for a good time and to make a quick buck, no doubt charging a fortune because they know they can get away with it. We don't exactly have local builders lining up for work.'

'Crikey, you're a bit harsh. You looked pretty cosy

dancing on Friday night. And then you practically ran out of there like you'd been spooked.'

There was a pause, and Dusty could picture Ella's expression. Probably that cool, guarded look she'd given him before the kiss, before everything changed after those few charged minutes.

'That was a mistake. Too much wine and poor judgment. It won't happen again.' He listened harder. She didn't sound conflicted or uncertain. More like her mind was made up that he wasn't worth the risk. She'd reduced their kiss to a drunken mistake, as if it had meant nothing, as if she hadn't felt what he'd felt when their mouths met.

'Shame we don't have our own tradesmen to handle jobs like this. At least you'd know what you're getting then. Same story with all the other essential workers we desperately need out here.'

'And teachers. They've got the principal covering classes again at the high school. Same old story. Nobody wants to live out here. I can't really blame them when there's no cinema, no decent shopping, nothing for young people to do.'

'I do.' The conviction in Ella's voice was unmistakable, and despite his anger, Dusty registered it. Her words were genuine, like she really did love this place and the community. 'I love it here. I tried Melbourne and hated every minute of it. It's the people who make a place. You won't get this sort of community in a big city. Now I've been away, I appreciate living here even more.'

'I know you do. You came back, but most don't. Only a few from our year group are still here. Not many. Everyone else scattered to Brisbane or Sydney or Melbourne the second they finished school.'

'Well, they don't know what they're missing. I've never been happier since returning. Speaking of which, I've been talking to Phil at the real estate office again.'

Dusty's attention sharpened.

'And?' Cass's voice lifted with interest.

'He reckons the property just outside town and the block next to our store might come on the market soon. Apparently, the people who own them have been doing some council searches and making moves like they're going to make changes to them. Phil has it on good advice that they're preparing to sell both, and he's going to investigate whether I could make an offer for them before they list publicly. You know how long I've wanted that place out of town.'

'Yes, but what would you do with the one next to the produce store?' Cass asked.

'Dad's obsessed with creating a men's shed for some of the older blokes who get a bit lost once they retire. You know how it is. The women have their bridge games and coffee mornings, but a lot of the men need somewhere other than the pub to gather and support each other. Somewhere they can tinker with projects and just be together without the pressure of having to drink or spend money.'

'That's a brilliant idea. I love it. Your dad would be perfect to run a project like that. He's so good with people.'

'He is. And it would give him a purposeful, voluntary job to do when he finally decides to step back from the store. You know how restless he gets without a project.' Ella's voice was warm now, animated in a way it hadn't been when she'd been talking about him. 'The corner block would be perfect for it. Close enough to town that the older men could walk there and big enough to build a decent shed with room for woodworking benches and maybe a small kitchen.'

Their voices began to fade, and Dusty exhaled slowly, processing everything he'd just heard. She thought he was dangerous and controlling based on a dance and a kiss. And she'd looked him in the eye Friday night, felt what he'd felt, and then decided to pretend it meant nothing.

'I wonder if they're working in one of the other rooms?' Cass's voice drifted back, closer now as though they were circling back through the space.

'Who?' Ella replied, and he could hear the disinterest in her tone.

'The builders. I'd like to talk to Eli again. He seemed really nice. And funny.'

'Get your mind off them, Cass. They'll be dickheads for sure. City dickheads with oversized egos to match their bank accounts.'

'But you really looked like you were enjoying yourself. More than enjoying it, actually. You looked like you were about to throw yourself at him right there on the dance floor.'

'I told you that was a mistake. Now, can we drop it?' There was a defensive edge to Ella's voice now. 'I came here to look at the renovation progress while there isn't anyone else here, not to gossip about a couple of tradies who'll be gone in a few months anyway.'

Dusty heard their footsteps fade and then the sound of a door closing. He remained frozen behind the wall, his face tight with anger and hurt. He massaged his temples, replaying the words in his mind. After Friday night, after that kiss that had felt so genuine, hearing her dismiss it all as a drunken mistake cut deeper than he wanted to admit. When he finally stood and stretched, brushing sawdust from his work shirt, he made a mental note to remember this conversation. She'd made herself clear. Whatever he'd felt on Friday night was one-sided. She thought he was dangerous, temporary, and not worth her time.

Fine. He could work with that. He'd keep his distance, do his job, and forget that for a few minutes holding her had felt like coming home.

* * *

ELLA LINKED her arm through Cass's and steered her friend out through the pub's heavy door onto the wide footpath. The afternoon sun cast long shadows across the main street, and she was grateful for the fresh air after the dusty interior. Her heart was still pounding from being in that space, knowing the builders were somewhere nearby, terrified that she might run into him again.

At twenty-eight, Ella had inherited her mother's blonde hair and her father's determined green eyes. Her hair fell in loose waves down to her waist, constantly escaping the ponytail she tried to keep it in at work. Years of country sun had given her a natural glow that no amount of Melbourne living had diminished, and her high cheekbones were a family trait she shared with her grandmother. She was taller than most of her friends, which had made her self-conscious as a teenager, but now she appreciated. At least she could reach the high shelves at the store without needing a ladder.

An elderly man moving slowly with his walking stick

approached them, his weathered face breaking into a smile when he spotted them. 'Afternoon, girls,' Ernie called out, his voice carrying that particular rasp of someone who'd spent decades smoking.

They paused for their usual chat about the weather, the hope for rain that never seemed to come and the state of various crops struggling in the dry. Ella was nodding along to Ernie's concerns about the dam levels on his son's place when she noticed movement behind them. The blonde builder stepped up, and she felt Cass practically vibrate with excitement beside her.

Ernie shuffled around on his walking stick, his face lighting up with genuine pleasure. 'G'day, young Eli. How're the renovations coming along? Oscar tells me you boys are making good progress.'

The fair-haired man flashed them a quick grin that had Cass straightening her posture and smoothing down her shirt. Ella gripped her friend's arm, recognising the warning signs of Cass about to make a fool of herself.

Cass thrust out her hand with barely contained enthusiasm, practically bouncing on her toes. 'Pleased to meet you! I'm Cass, and this is Ella.'

'Pleasure to meet you both.' Eli's handshake was firm and friendly, his smile easy and genuine. He had nice eyes, Ella noticed, blue and warm. 'I briefly met you last Friday night at the pub.' He looked up at the building. 'We've certainly got our work cut out for us. We found the place in worse shape than we thought once we started pulling back the layers. Enough to keep us busy for months, maybe longer.'

'Where are you from?' The words practically gushed from Cass's mouth, and Ella fought the urge to roll her eyes. This was exactly how her friend operated. Meet a cute guy and lose all sense of dignity.

'Melbourne. Well, I'm originally from Daylesford. About an hour and a half out of the city. Country town, green and lush. Lots of trees and rain.' He gestured up the street, his expression thoughtful. 'Bit different from here, but we've come to make some good money and have a bit of fun while we're at it.'

The word 'see?' nearly escaped Ella's lips, but she clamped her mouth shut and maintained her polite smile. Here for money and fun. Exactly what she suspected. Temporary, uncommitted, and out for themselves.

Eli addressed Ernie with genuine respect, asking about the weather and how his day had been so far. He then turned back to include both women. 'You should come in and have a look around. It's a mess at the moment, but it's good to see the before stage of a big renovation. Makes the after so much more impressive.'

Cass moved faster than Ella could intercept, already steering them back towards the pub. 'Oh, we'd love to, wouldn't we, Ella? Come on, Ernie. A private tour!'

Before she could voice any objection, before she could make up an excuse about needing to get back to the store, Cass steered them all back through the doorway and into the very room they'd been in just minutes earlier. Ernie tottered along beside them, delighted by the attention, and soon they were all listening to Eli explain the restoration plans with genuine enthusiasm. He was good at this, Ella had to admit. The way he talked about the building's history, about respecting the original architecture while updating it for modern use, showed a depth she hadn't expected from someone she'd written off as just another good-looking tradie.

'And here's my partner in crime,' Eli announced, gesturing towards the back of the room. 'I think you met him Friday night also.'

From behind a partially demolished wall, Dusty emerged with a hammer in his hand. Ella's stomach dropped. The doorway they'd just entered through was currently the only way in or out. He'd been here the whole time. He'd heard everything she'd said. Every nasty word, every dismissive comment, and her justifications used to convince Cass and herself that Friday night had meant nothing.

Cass must have realised the same thing because her face flushed bright red, and she shot Ella a look of pure panic, her eyes wide with horror.

He sauntered directly towards them. Up close, in the better light near the door, he was even more striking than she remembered. His dark hair was slightly messed from work, and there was a smudge of dust on his jaw that she wanted to reach up and brush away. When he smiled, the corners of his eyes crinkled in a way that made her pulse race despite everything. But it was his eyes that held her attention. They were dark, knowing, and currently dancing with unmistakable amusement.

'Pleased to meet you all again,' he said, extending his hand. When his eyes met hers, with a grin that told her everything she needed to know, Ella's body stiffened defensively. He'd heard. He'd heard every word. And he was enjoying her discomfort.

'We're down from the big smoke to stir up some dust,' he added with deliberate emphasis, his voice carrying a note of irony that made her cheeks burn. He threw a cheeky wink in Cass's direction before crossing his arms and positioning himself beside Eli, the two of them presenting a united front.

Ella stood in mortified silence as Ernie peppered both men with questions about the renovation, about their plans, about their experience with heritage buildings. Cass, seemingly recovered from her initial panic, chimed in whenever possible, practically glowing under their attention. She laughed too loudly at their jokes, touched Eli's arm with calculated casualness, and generally made a spectacle of herself. Meanwhile, Ella tried to shrink into the background, mentally replaying every word she'd spoken earlier. Misogynistic, controlling, dangerous, dickheads with oversized egos. Oh God.

She kept her eyes firmly on the floor, studying the worn boards with intense fascination, but she could feel Dusty watching her. When she finally risked a glance up, she found him looking directly at her. The corners of his mouth curved upward, suggesting this was the most entertainment he'd had in weeks.

Eli seemed genuinely taken with Cass's bubbly personality, and Ella's heart sank when her friend arranged to meet him for drinks after work. 'I can introduce you to some of the locals,' Cass offered brightly, her voice pitched slightly higher than normal. 'We're a friendly bunch. You'll come too, won't you, Ella?'

'I've got an appointment this afternoon. Maybe another time.' The lie came easily, born of pure self-preservation. There was no way she could sit across from Dusty knowing what he'd heard.

Dusty's smile widened at her obvious reluctance, and

she wanted the ground to open up and swallow her. He was probably used to women throwing themselves at him, not trying to avoid him. Except that wasn't fair, was it? He was covered in sawdust and clearly had been working hard all morning. And the way he'd talked to Ernie had been respectful, kind even.

She was the first one out the door, practically fleeing into the sunlight. As they said goodbye to Ernie and continued down the street, she felt a tightness in her chest that had nothing to do with the dust they'd been breathing. It had everything to do with the way Dusty had looked at her, with amusement and something else. Disappointment, maybe. As though she'd confirmed exactly what he suspected about her.

'Do you think Dusty heard what we said earlier?' Cass whispered, her confidence evaporating now that they were out of sight. She grabbed Ella's arm, her fingers digging in. 'Oh God, Ella. It was a bit harsh. I feel terrible.'

Ella drew herself up tall and tried to look nonchalant, even though her mind was whirling. 'I don't particularly care if he did. I'd say my summary of him was pretty spot on.'

Cass did a little twirl, her distress forgotten in an instant, her eyes widening with delight. 'Oh my God, Ella! How gorgeous is Eli? I think I've just experienced love at first sight. Did you see the way he smiled at me? And he's funny and he listened when I talked. Most blokes just stare at my chest.'

Ella steered her friend down the street, needing to put distance between herself and the pub. 'No, Cass. Don't base everything on looks. You need to be smarter about your choices in men. Sure, they both look good, but that's as far as it goes. Think sensibly.'

Cass practically skipped along the footpath while Ella struggled to keep pace, her mind still reeling from the encounter. She could feel how he looked at her and saw right through her. His amused smile and the way he'd watched her squirm with obvious enjoyment were etched in her memory.

'Hopeless,' she muttered under her breath. 'Absolutely bloody hopeless.'

But she wasn't sure if she was talking about Cass or herself.

CHAPTER 4

'Are you right to pass me up those bales?' Colin called out from the back of the delivery truck.

'Hang on, Dad. I just need to get these other bags out of the way.' Ella glanced up at him, his weather-tanned face looking down at her, waiting with the patient impatience of someone who'd been doing this work for forty years and knew exactly how long everything should take.

Ella carefully lifted ten bags of dog food, one at a time, creating space to reach the hay bales behind them. Each bag was twenty kilos, and by the eighth one her shoulders were protesting. She'd been doing this for over a year now and her muscles had adapted, but there were still days when she felt the burn.

Her father called out again from the back of the delivery truck, his calloused hands still outstretched impatiently. At sixty-eight years of age he could still work as hard as any younger man, and his huge hands lifted the bags as if they weighed nothing. It was both impressive and slightly irritating. Although her strength had improved vastly over the previous year, she was still no match for him, her brother or her nephew. The Patterson men were built solid, broad-shouldered and strong-backed from generations of farm work.

'We could have used the forklift,' he pointed out, watching her manoeuvre around the stacked supplies with the critical eye of someone who'd been running this business since before she was born.

'It's fine. There's only a dozen or so. By the time I get the forklift going, we'd have it done.' She hoisted the first bale up to him, feeling the familiar strain in her shoulders and arms. This was the kind of honest physical work she'd missed during her years in Melbourne.

City life had been a novelty at first. She'd originally loved the bars, restaurants, concerts, gallery openings and the constant hum of possibility. Most importantly, university. Her astronomy degree had kept her mind engaged and allowed her to pursue a lifelong fascination with the stars and planets that had started when her grandfather had given her a telescope for her tenth birthday.

The small studio apartment she rented in a towering high-rise had felt like freedom at first, like she was finally becoming the person she was meant to be, and she'd thrown herself into discovering the city with a growing circle of friends and eventually a boyfriend. The friendships had endured and strengthened over the years, which was more than she could say for the toxic relationship that had nearly derailed her life.

The memory made her shove the next bale with unnecessary force, almost knocking her father off balance.

'Oi! Watch what you're doing.' He steadied himself, giving her a sharp look.

'Sorry. My mind was elsewhere.'

Trent. Horrible, nasty, controlling Trent. How had she been so blind to what everyone around her could see? It had taken two agonising years to recognise the manipulation. The way he'd slowly isolated her from her friends, undermined her judgment, and convinced her that his jealousy proved how much he loved her. Another six months to finally break free, to find the courage to pack her things while he was at work and never look back. Thank God he'd moved to London and from what she'd heard through mutual friends, was now married with a child. She shuddered at the thought, genuinely pitying whoever had ended up with him. A narrow escape that had taught her everything she needed to know about trusting her instincts when it came to men. Or not trusting them, as the case may be.

She helped her father secure the tailgate before grabbing a broom and sweeping the concrete floor of Patterson Produce. The astronomy degree had been everything she dreamed of, opening her mind to the vastness of the universe and the intricate movement of celestial bodies. She loved every lecture and every late night at the observatory, mapping star positions. The work itself had been everything she'd hoped for. But the reality of turning that passion into a career had been an entirely different scenario.

The few academic positions available required a PhD. That meant another four years of study, living on a stipend that barely covered rent and competing with hundreds of others for the same handful of postdoctoral positions. Positions that might, maybe, lead to a permanent role. The alternatives were either buried in government bureaucracy at the Bureau of Meteorology, where her supervisor during an internship had spent his days writing reports about cloud patterns rather than studying the cosmos, or tied to mining companies using astronomical data for GPS coordinates and geological surveys. One interviewer had seemed confused when she'd expressed an interest in research, telling her bluntly that they needed someone who 'understood this was about practical applications, not stargazing.'

None of it fed her soul the way she'd hoped. The stars were still beautiful, but the career had become about politics, funding, and proving yourself worthy rather than about wonder and discovery. After her third soul-crushing job interview, she'd sat in a café watching people rush past and realised the truth. She'd rather come home and look at the stars on her own terms than spend the next decade fighting for the privilege of studying them professionally.

Grain dust from the lucerne bales swirled in the afternoon light streaming through the open roller doors, creating golden shafts that reminded her of childhood, of playing in this very space while her grandfather served customers.

The produce store had occupied this corner of Matfield's main street for nearly fifty years, built by her grandfather when the town was still growing and when people believed the future held nothing but promise. Now, with both her and her brother Tyson working with their parents, it looked set to continue. Her grandparents' original family property had passed to her uncle when they died, and he'd built it into a successful cattle operation over the years. Her father and uncle worked closely together, the store supplying feed and materials to the station at cost while the property provided them with a continuous supply of beef, a practical testing ground for new products and extra storage space when the store's sheds overflowed during busy seasons. It was a partnership built on blood and mutual benefit, the kind that worked between brothers who'd grown up in the same place and understood the land.

From the time she was a kid and into her teenage years, Ella had spent countless days working alongside her cousins during school holidays and weekends. She learned to muster cattle, mend fences, and to read the land and weather the way her uncle and father did. Most of her cousins eventually moved to larger towns chasing opportunities, but two had remained and built their own homes on different corners of the property, where they raised their own families on the same red soil that had shaped hers. Those years had given her moments that the city never could, creating an unbreakable bond with the land and the community

Her parents had been disappointed when she abandoned her career prospects. Sure, they tried to hide it behind supportive smiles and gentle questions about whether she was sure this was what she wanted. But they understood, eventually. City life and corporate ladders weren't for everyone.

She leaned on the broom handle and gazed through the large roller doors that opened onto the side yard. The building housed everything from horse feed to garden fertiliser, chicken wire to sheep drenches, work boots to water troughs. It was where everyone in town came for everything they needed for both their properties and animals. The building was also a gathering place as much as a business. A dust devil whirled across the empty block next door, the same block her father was hoping to purchase as an extension to the family business. It was roughly the same size as their current site and would be perfect for additional storage and, more importantly, her father's dream project, a men's shed.

'It could be our legacy to the town,' he'd told her countless times, usually while they were doing exactly this kind of work, side by side in the comfortable rhythm they'd developed. 'Mental health is a real problem out here. Men need somewhere to gather, work with their hands, and look out for each other.' Last year, he and her mother, Helen, had toured similar facilities across regional Victoria, gathering ideas and inspiration, coming back with notebooks full of drawings and possibilities. He'd even drawn up rough sketches of workshops, meeting areas, and a kitchen where blokes could share a cuppa and talk about what was bothering them instead of bottling it up until they snapped. All they needed now was to secure the block. It was the last vacant lot on the main street, perfectly positioned for what they had in mind. Close enough that the older men could walk there, but separate enough to feel like their own space. If the information Phil had given her was true, her father's dream could soon become reality.

The bell above the front door chimed, and she looked up to see Matt and Elsie entering with their blue cattle dog in tow. Both had recently returned to Matfield, and Ella had quickly reconnected with them, grateful for friends her own age who'd also chosen to come back. Matt was completing his final year of veterinary training with old Doc Harrison, learning the particular challenges of outback practice. Elsie had returned to her teaching position at the high school, the same one she'd left years ago to be with Matt while he studied. The couple had met in town years earlier, fallen in love, but then left for the coast so that Matt could pursue his studies. Now they were back. They'd just bought one of the weatherboard houses on Somme Street, the one with the big jacaranda tree in the front yard.

'How are you both?' Ella called out, emerging from behind the counter. She crouched down as the cattle dog bounded towards her, tail thrashing with excitement, tongue lolling in that goofy way that always made her smile.

'Hello, Bundy,' she laughed, accepting a thorough face washing from his enthusiastic tongue. He was still a puppy really, all paws and energy, nowhere near finished growing.

'Bundy, sit!' Elsie commanded sternly, her teacher voice in full effect. The dog eventually complied, though his tail continued to sweep dust across the concrete floor in wide arcs, and his whole body quivered with barely contained excitement.

'We're after some dog food and a new collar for this growing boy,' Matt explained, scratching behind Bundy's ears in that spot that made the dog's back leg thump against the floor. 'He's putting on size so fast we can barely keep up. The collar we bought a couple of months ago is already too tight.'

As Ella gathered their supplies from the aisle where

they kept all the pet products, she turned to Elsie. 'How's work going? I hope that nephew of mine is behaving himself in your classes.' Her older brother Tyson had married young and had been barely twenty when his wife, Evie, fell pregnant. Their son Liam was now in year eleven. From what she'd been hearing, the teenager was proving to be quite the handful for both his teachers and his parents, pushing boundaries in ways that had Tyson threatening everything from military school to immediate full-time employment at the store.

'He's actually fine with me,' Elsie replied diplomatically, though Ella caught the slight hesitation. 'Always polite, and I can usually get him to focus on his work. He's just at that difficult age where everything feels like a battle for independence.'

'That age,' Ella repeated knowingly, loading a twenty-kilogram bag of premium dog food onto the counter. 'Tyson's at his wit's end. He's half ready to pull Liam out of school and put him straight to work, though Mum keeps telling him that's exactly the wrong approach.'

Elsie's careful response confirmed what Ella suspected. Liam was pushing boundaries with most of his teachers, not just at home. The boy was smart enough and had always done well in primary school, but his attitude had shifted when he hit high school. Too much time on social media, according to Tyson. Not enough consequences, according to their father. Just normal teenage stuff, according to his mother. 'Teenagers can be challenging, but honestly, the kids here are pretty good overall compared to some schools I've worked at. I'm really enjoying being back, and the staff have been so welcoming.' Her face brightened, the genuine warmth breaking through the teacher diplomacy. 'Actually, they're organising a quiz night at the pub next Thursday. You should join our team!'

'Don't ask her,' Matt interrupted with a grin, passing his card over for the transaction. 'Tell her. Thursday, seven o'clock. You're on our team. Bring Cass too. We need four people, and I have it on good authority that the questions will be heavily weighted towards science and history this month.'

Ella laughed as they headed for the door, Bundy leading them eagerly towards the exit, probably already dreaming of the next interesting smell. 'That sounds brilliant. Cass'll be over the moon. She lives for social events.' As she watched them walk down the street, Bundy trotting obediently between them now that he was outside, she reflected on how well things were working out since her return to Matfield. She had her part-time research work with the Australian Space Agency, analysing satellite data from her home computer. It hadn't been in her original plan, but it kept her connected to her field without the soul-crushing office politics. The produce store kept her active and involved with the community while also giving her a sense of purpose and usefulness. Most importantly, she was surrounded by family and genuine friends who cared about her well-being.

Her gaze drifted towards the outskirts of town, where another block of land waited. Her thinking spot. Pazhvak Station. The property was about one thousand acres. Small by outback Queensland standards but big enough for what she wanted. Over the years, she had driven past it countless times and walked over most of it.

Since she'd been back, she walked out there most

weeks, imagining the small house she wanted to build on the gentle rise that commanded views across the valley. Nothing fancy, nothing that would cost a fortune or make a statement. Just a simple design where she could sit with her morning coffee and watch the stars fade into dawn, where she could finally feel like she'd found her place in the world. Her savings account was healthy, boosted by the inheritance from her grandfather's estate that had been divided among all the grandchildren. Now she had a solid plan, a future she could see and touch, not some vague dream that might never materialise. For the first time in years, she felt genuinely content with the direction her life was taking.

CHAPTER 5

*E*lla and Cass linked arms as they walked up the main street towards the pub, their boots clicking against the weathered concrete footpath that hadn't changed since Ella was a child. She had chosen her favourite dark jeans and a soft burgundy blouse that brought out the green in her eyes, while Cass wore a floral dress that swished around her knees, the kind of clothing that suited her friend perfectly. The main dining room had been almost completely booked for the monthly quiz night, organised as a fundraiser for the school. The turnout was always good for these events and was one of the few times when nearly everyone under sixty showed up.

Cass bumped her hip against Ella's playfully. 'I'm so glad you came back to town. I don't know what I'd do without you. Everyone else seems to be married with kids already. They talk about things like school zones and sleep schedules. It's brilliant to have someone who can get out any night of the week without having to arrange babysitters or check with their husband.'

'Like someone who has no other options,' Ella said with mock indignation. 'Are you saying I've got nothing better to do, so I'm an easy target for your social events?'

They laughed together, the easy laughter of friends who'd known each other since primary school. 'Pretty much,' Cass admitted. Then she sighed, and Ella heard the genuine longing beneath it. 'I'd love to meet someone I really connect with, though. I mean, I always go on about looks, I know I do, but right now I'm desperate to meet someone I could have a decent conversation with.'

'You mean someone interested in more than just footy scores and beer?'

'Exactly. All the good ones out here have been snapped up or moved away. There aren't many single blokes our age left, and the ones who are single...' She trailed off wistfully.

'The few single ones our age are boys we went to school with,' Ella finished. 'I feel like they're my brothers. Lovely fellas, great for a chat, but not exactly setting my world on fire romantically. I doubt I'll ever meet anyone who does.'

'Don't say that.' Cass squeezed her arm.

'I'm not worried about it. I don't mind being single. There's so much I want to do now that I'm back here and settled. The work with the Space Agency, helping Dad with the store and hopefully the men's shed. I don't need a man complicating all that.' Even as she said it, an image of a knowing smile flashed through her mind, and she pushed it away irritably.

Ella pushed open the heavy timber door of the pub,

releasing a wave of noisy chatter and music over the mouthwatering smell of dinner cooking that welcomed them inside like an embrace. The main dining room had been transformed with string lights draped across the exposed ceiling beams, casting a warm glow over the mismatched wooden tables and chairs that had been arranged for the evening's competition. About thirty people were already gathered, most clutching schooners of beer or glasses of wine, their voices creating a pleasant hum of anticipation. This was Matfield at its best, Ella thought, when everyone was together and competition brought out the fun rather than any real tension

'We've put two teams on each table,' Elsie announced, appearing beside them with a warm hug for both girls. 'We're over there. This is going to be good. I reckon we'll have the winning team tonight.'

They discussed the previous quiz champions with the kind of serious analysis usually reserved for grand final predictions. Last month it had been the library committee, surprisingly strong on pop culture. The month before, the cricket club had dominated with their knowledge of sports and Australian history.

'Ah yes, but they didn't have the learned Ella and quick-fire Cass on their team,' Matt declared as he joined their group, carrying a tray of drinks.

'I'm feeling very competitive tonight,' Ella admitted, scanning the room and waving to familiar faces. Rod from their earlier group, now at another table, and members of several families she'd known her whole life.

'Right then,' Matt said, noting the waitstaff hovering with laden trays of food. 'They're ready to serve the food. Time to get seated.' He guided them towards their designated table, weaving through the crowd. 'And here comes the other team.'

Ella settled into her chair and looked up to see Oscar approaching with his characteristic easy stride, wearing a crisp white shirt rolled up at the sleeves and dark jeans that suggested he'd come straight from the pub's kitchen after prepping for the evening. Behind him came Ernie, moving more slowly but with determined purpose, his weathered face creased into a smile above a neatly pressed button-down shirt that spoke of the effort he'd made for the evening. Ernie took these events seriously and always dressed his best. And behind him, making her stomach do an annoying flip, she recognised the two builders.

Dusty had traded his work clothes for jeans and a navy shirt that hugged his broad shoulders, while his dark hair looked like he'd run a comb through it for once. Eli wore similarly casual attire, his blonde hair still slightly damp from a shower. When he spotted Cass, his whole face lit up in a way that Ella would have thought sweet if she wasn't so busy panicking about Dusty.

Cass leant close, her voice barely containing her excitement. 'They're on our table. It's our lucky night.'

Ella rolled her eyes and smiled politely as Dusty pulled out the chair beside her. Of course he did. Of course the universe would seat him right next to her. 'Well. We meet again,' she commented.

'Fancy that,' he said, his voice dry with amusement. His gaze met hers and she saw the challenge in it, the memory of everything she'd said about him. 'Small town.'

Ernie patted her shoulder affectionately while Oscar flashed his trademark grin, completely oblivious to the undercurrent of tension. 'Bit of stiff competition here tonight. We'll have to lift our game, Ernie. Hopefully these two young fellas are as clever as they reckon they are.'

Everyone chuckled as they found their seats around the circular table draped with a checkered cloth. Cass positioned herself strategically where she could maintain eye contact with Eli, her cheeks slightly flushed with excitement, while Ella tried to ignore the way Dusty's presence seemed to fill the space beside her. She caught his scent again, pleasant and masculine. The room buzzed with conversation as platters of chicken wings, potato wedges, and spring rolls were distributed among the tables, along with bowls of chips and dipping sauces.

'Neither of us has been to one of these before,' Eli admitted, his attention clearly focused on Cass in a way that made her practically glow. 'We're counting on Ernie and Oscar to carry us through.'

The easy banter flowed as other patrons stopped by to greet the regulars and introduced themselves to the newcomers. Several of the town's single women found reasons to linger near their table, and Ella watched with barely concealed irritation as Jenny from the post office somehow found a reason to squeeze between Dusty's chair and the next table, her perfume creating a sickly scent as she laughed at his words. Sarah from the chemist kept finding opportunities to touch Eli's shoulder whenever she spoke, though at least Eli seemed genuinely interested in Cass and politely redirected his attention back to her each time.

'Like moths to a flame,' she murmured to Elsie, who'd ended up on her other side.

'Absolutely pathetic,' Elsie whispered back with a grin.

'Though I notice you're sitting very close to your own particular flame.'

'Don't start,' Ella warned, but she could feel heat creeping up her neck.

The evening's Master of Ceremonies, Braden from the hardware store who did this every month, rang a bell and called everyone to attention. 'Right then, folks. Time to separate the grain from the chaff. First round coming up!'

As the questions began, Ella forgot about her table companions and focused entirely on the competition. This was what she loved about these nights. The event should be a purely intellectual challenge, finding satisfaction in knowing obscure facts, and participating in a team effort.

The early rounds were straightforward. The questions related to Australian geography, basic maths, and recent news events. Most tables seemed evenly matched, with all teams getting most of the answers right. Cass and Elsie dominated in answering the pop culture questions for their team, rattling off celebrities and TV shows that Ella had barely heard of, while across the table, Ernie and Oscar handled the local history questions with casual authority, telling stories about many of the events they'd actually lived through.

The two builders had contributed only occasionally so far, and Ella wondered how they'd fare when the questions became more challenging. Probably useless, she told herself. All looks and no substance.

When Braden announced the next category, Ella's attention sharpened. This was her territory. 'Science and Nature, folks. This might separate those who know their stuff from those who reckon they do.'

'Which planet has the shortest day in our solar system?' came the first question.

'Jupiter,' Ella said immediately, reaching for the answer sheet before anyone else could speak.

'Jupiter,' Dusty said at the exact same moment, and she looked over to see him nodding in agreement.

She tried to ignore the flutter in her chest. Lucky guess.

'What causes the Northern and Southern Lights?'

This time Dusty beat her to it. 'Solar particles interacting with Earth's magnetic field.'

Ella felt a flicker of surprise. That was actually correct, and few would know the proper explanation. Maybe not such a lucky guess after all.

'At what distance is one astronomical unit measured?'

'The distance between Earth and the Sun,' they said almost simultaneously, then looked at each other with barely concealed irritation. His eyebrows raised slightly, and she saw the question in his eyes. How did a produce store worker know this?

'Approximately 150 million kilometres,' Dusty added, and Ella's eyebrows shot up. That was the kind of detail only someone with real knowledge would include.

The questions continued, shifting between various scientific disciplines, and suddenly it became clear that Dusty knew far more than she'd given him credit for. When Braden asked about the chemical composition of water, he answered. When asked the speed of light, he knew it in both metres per second and kilometres per hour. When asked what caused ocean tides, he gave a detailed answer about gravitational forces that was more complete than what she would have said.

When the questions moved to medical knowledge, Oscar and Matt leaned forward like racehorses at the starting gate. The story Oscar's wife Patricia always loved to tell seemed to be true. When Oscar was young he'd been offered a Rhodes Scholarship but hadn't taken it. It was clear that his brilliant mind certainly hadn't dulled. Combined with Matt's veterinary training, the two of them could hold their own in any medical discussion.

'What's the medical term for the kneecap?' Braden had barely finished reading the question before Oscar raised his hand.

'Patella,' he said confidently.

'Too easy,' Matt muttered. 'Give us a challenge.'

'Name the longest bone in the human body.'

'Femur,' they answered in unison, then glared at each other competitively, though there was warmth beneath it.

'Which organ produces insulin?'

'Pancreas,' Oscar said smugly, writing it down before Matt could respond.

'What's the gestation period of a horse?' Matt countered, though it wasn't actually a question yet, just him showing off.

'Eleven months,' Oscar replied without hesitation, and Matt's jaw dropped in genuine surprise.

'How the hell did you know that? You've never been within ten feet of a horse in your life.'

'Patricia's been researching getting into horses. I've been subjected to endless dinner conversations about breeding cycles, feed requirements, and stable designs. I could probably birth a foal at this point.'

The table erupted in laughter, and even Ella grinned. These were the moments that made Matfield special; the unexpected stories people revealed and the way every-one's knowledge contributed to the town's living history.

The science questions resumed, and Ella felt the competitive fire building. This was her subject, her field, and she wasn't about to be shown up by a builder from Melbourne, no matter how unexpectedly knowledgeable he seemed to be.

'What's the closest star system to Earth?'

'Alpha Centauri,' she said firmly.

But Dusty was shaking his head, and she felt her irritation spike. 'That's the closest star system, but Proxima Centauri is technically the closest individual star. The question could be interpreted either way.'

Ella's eyes narrowed. Was he seriously arguing semantics right now? 'The question said star system.'

'Which includes Proxima Centauri as part of the Alpha Centauri system, making it technically correct either way you answer.'

'Your point being?'

'Just that precision matters in science.' There was no malice in his voice, just that same amused tone that made her want to throttle him.

'How many moons does Saturn have?'

'Eighty-three confirmed,' Ella said quickly, confident in her knowledge. She'd literally just read an article about this last month.

'Eighty-four as of last year,' Dusty corrected. 'They discovered another one. Confirmed in May.'

'That hasn't been officially confirmed by the International Astronomical Union,' she shot back, but even as she said it, doubt crept in. Had she missed an update?

'Actually, it was confirmed in May. Pan-STARRS survey data. It's called S/2023 S1.' He said it gently, not gloating, just stating facts.

Ella stared at him. What kind of builder kept track of recent astronomical discoveries? What kind of builder knew survey names and moon designations? 'Fine. Eighty-four.' She changed her answer, feeling off-balance.

'What's the brightest star visible from Earth?'

'The Sun,' they both said flatly, then glared at each other for falling for the obvious answer.

'Apart from the Sun,' Braden clarified with a chuckle, and the whole room laughed.

'Sirius,' Ella said triumphantly, glad to have a straight-forward answer.

'In the constellation Canis Major,' Dusty added unnec-essarily, and she could hear the smile in his voice even without looking at him.

'I think we all know where Sirius is located.' She couldn't keep the irritation out of her voice.

'Do we? Because half the people here probably think it's that satellite radio service.' He kept his voice low enough that only she could hear, and despite herself, despite everything, Ella felt her mouth twitch. That was surprisingly funny, though she'd die before admitting it.

The questions moved through various categories, with each team member contributing their expertise. Cass nailed several questions about Australian flora that surprised everyone, and when asked how she knew so much, she shrugged and said she'd been obsessed with wildflowers as a kid. Eli surprised everyone with his knowledge of architectural history, correctly identifying the architect of the Sydney Opera House and explaining the controversy around the design. Matt and Elsie worked together on literature questions, finishing each other's sentences in that way that couples who knew each other well could do.

But as the evening progressed and the questions became increasingly obscure, it was clear that the competition was narrowing to just a few tables. Their table, the library committee table, and, surprisingly, the group from the cattle station, who apparently had someone with extensive knowledge of world geography.

'Final round, folks.' Braden's voice carried across the now-silent room. 'This is where we separate the true champions from the also-rans. These questions are worth double points, so everything's still on the table.'

The room fell silent with anticipation. Even the bar staff stopped moving, leaning against the wall to listen.

'This question is about World War Two. What was the code name for the German plan to invade the Soviet Union?'

Silence stretched across most tables. Ella racked her brain, trying to remember her high school history lessons, but came up blank. She looked around the table hopefully, but everyone else looked equally stumped. Then Ernie's weathered hand slowly rose, and when he spoke, his voice was quiet but certain.

'Operation Barbarossa.'

'Correct!' Braden called out, and their table erupted in quiet celebration. The library committee groaned audibly.

'Next question. Which Australian Prime Minister served the shortest term in office?'

Again, silence. Even Oscar, with all his knowledge, looked uncertain. But Ernie's hand went up again, and this time there was a sadness in his eyes that made Ella wonder what memory the question had triggered.

'Frank Forde. Eight days in 1945, after John Curtin died and before Ben Chifley was elected party leader. I was thirteen years old. My father cried when they announced Curtin's death on the radio. Only time I ever saw him cry.'

The room was utterly silent for a moment, the weight of that memory settling over everyone. Then Braden cleared his throat. 'That's correct. Final question. In 1932, what unusual war was fought in Western Australia, and what was the outcome?'

The room was dead quiet. Even the know-it-alls at the library committee table looked stumped. Ella had absolutely no idea, having never even heard of a war in Western Australia in 1932. She looked at Dusty, who shrugged, equally clueless. Matt and Elsie were whispering to each other but clearly had nothing. Oscar was frowning in concentration.

Then Ernie smiled slowly, his eyes twinkling with the satisfaction of someone who'd lived through the stories others only read about, who'd heard the tales firsthand from the people who'd been there.

'The Great Emu War,' he said, and several people laughed, thinking he was joking. But his face remained serious. 'After World War One, soldiers were given farmland as settlement. The military was called in to cull the emus that were destroying crops. The emus won. The soldiers gave up after a few weeks because the birds were too fast and too smart. Caused quite the embarrassment for the government at the time. My uncle was one of those soldiers. He came home with nothing but stories about trying to outsmart emus and losing.'

The room erupted in laughter and applause, not just from their table but from everyone. It was such a perfectly absurd piece of Australian history, such a wonderful reminder that sometimes the most unexpected things were true.

'Ladies and gentlemen, we have our winners!' Braden held up the small trophy, and their entire table stood, cheering and hugging.

As the congratulations flowed and Oscar accepted the trophy on behalf of their team, promising to put it behind the bar where everyone could admire Ernie's brilliance, Ella caught Dusty looking at her with an expression that might have been respect.

'Not bad for a country girl,' he said quietly, his voice pitched low enough that only she could hear.

'Not bad for a city boy who apparently knows more about astronomy than building,' she replied, and was surprised to find she meant it as a compliment rather than an insult.

Ella felt the mood shift between them. A subtle change that had nothing to do with competition and everything to do with the unsettling realisation that Dusty Camilleri might be more complicated than she'd given him credit for. Someone who knew about moon discoveries and astronomical units, who could discuss science with the same ease he apparently wielded a hammer, wasn't someone who fit neatly into the boxes she'd tried to put him in.

'Another drink?' Cass asked brightly, appearing beside them with Eli in tow, clearly oblivious to the undercurrent of tension at their end of the table. 'We're celebrating! Eli's never won anything in his life, have you?'

'First time for everything,' Eli agreed, grinning at Cass in a way that made her practically melt.

'Why not?' Ella said, still looking at Dusty. 'It seems like the night is full of surprises.'

After the quiz concluded, everyone began mingling and the room filled with the scraping of chairs and animated conversations as people moved between tables to congratulate winners and commiserate with the runners-up. The library committee were good sports about losing, admitting they'd never heard of the Emu War and demanding Ernie tell them the full story. Ella made a deliberate effort to steer clear of Dusty, though she found herself stealing glances in his direction more often than she cared to admit. Although she was intrigued and wanted to question him about his unexpected knowledge of astronomy, she refused to join the growing crowd of admirers surrounding both builders.

She watched Cass, who had positioned herself firmly in the group next to Eli, pushing her shoulders back and gazing up at him with the kind of rapt attention that suggested he held the answers to every question she'd ever wondered about. Eli, to his credit, seemed genuinely interested in her, asking her questions about her work at the kindergarten, and laughing at her stories about difficult parents. It was rather sweet, Ella had to admit, even if she was worried about her friend getting hurt when they inevitably left.

Taking a long sip of her wine, Ella glanced away, not wanting to be caught observing the social dynamics, particularly anything involving Dusty. The ambient lighting from the string lights overhead created intimate pockets of conversation throughout the room, while the old floorboards creaked pleasantly under the movement of the crowd. Someone had put music on low in the background, and a few people were already starting to dance near the bar.

'Penny for your thoughts,' Ernie appeared beside her, a schooner of beer held carefully in his weathered hand. His eyes twinkled with the satisfaction of their victory, and she noticed Oscar had pinned a makeshift medal made from bottle caps to his shirt collar. 'You certainly know your science, you and that young builder fella.'

'Never mind that,' Ella deflected, turning to face the elderly man properly. She gestured at the medal with a smile. 'What about you? Quite the history expert, aren't you? I loved the story about your uncle and the emus.'

Ernie chuckled, the sound warm and genuine, years of laughter contained in it. 'I've always been fascinated by history, and besides, I've lived through most of it at this point. When you get to my age, current events become historical events before you know it. Blink and suddenly something that happens is already in the past.'

'Oscar has quite a wealth of knowledge too. I know Patricia has talked lately about how he was awarded a Rhodes Scholarship but never took it. That medical expertise seemed to come out of nowhere.' She'd been genuinely surprised by the depth of Oscar's knowledge, the way he knew things that went well beyond general knowledge.

Ernie took another thoughtful sip of his beer, his expression growing more serious. He glanced across the room to where Oscar was holding court with a group of younger patrons, telling some story that had them all laughing. 'Oscar doesn't advertise it, but Patricia's story is spot on. He was offered a Rhodes Scholarship. Top of the list, he was. One of the brightest minds of his generation, from what I understand. Could have gone anywhere, done anything.'

Ella's eyebrows shot up in surprise. A Rhodes Scholarship was one of the most prestigious academic honours in the world, reserved for the absolute best and brightest. 'Really? What happened? Why didn't he take it?'

'That's the mystery, isn't it? He ended up here instead, met Patricia, and settled into small-town life like he'd been born to it. They became good friends with Todd's parents and they all ended up buying the pub together. These days it's Todd, Oscar and Patricia who own it. Penny is Oscar's niece, so I think she has a share also. He's a bit of a dark horse, our Oscar. Keeps his past tucked away where it can't bother him.'

Ella glanced across the room to where Oscar was engaged in an animated conversation with Matt about an idea that had them both gesturing enthusiastically. Probably another medical debate. 'You'd never know to look at him. He seems so content running the pub, so... settled. Like this is exactly where he was always meant to be.'

'Maybe that's exactly what he was looking for,' Ernie mused, his eyes distant with thought. 'Sometimes the brightest minds need the simplest lives to find peace. Not everyone wants to conquer the world, even when they're capable of it. Sometimes the real courage is in choosing a quiet life when everyone expects you to burn bright and fast.'

The words settled over Ella with unexpected weight.

She thought about her own choices, like coming back to Matfield when everyone had expected her to use her degree to start an impressive career. Maybe she and Oscar weren't so different after all. Maybe choosing peace over prestige wasn't giving up, but finding what really mattered.

'That's quite profound, Ernie.'

He winked at her. 'I have my moments. Now, are you going to talk to that young fella who keeps looking over here, or are you going to keep pretending you haven't noticed?'

Ella felt her cheeks flush. 'I have no idea what you're talking about.'

'Course you don't.' Ernie patted her shoulder and wandered off, leaving her standing alone with her wine and her thoughts, very carefully not looking in Dusty's direction.

CHAPTER 6

That night Ella tossed restlessly in her bed, her mind replaying fragments of the evening in an endless loop. Dusty's confident answers to the astronomy questions kept circling back, each one more puzzling than the last. Who was he really? Those weren't lucky guesses or casual knowledge picked up from documentaries late at night or brief Wikipedia searches. The precision of his responses, the way he'd corrected her on Saturn's moon count with such certainty, and knowing the survey name and the provisional designation, suggested someone with genuine expertise. Someone who'd studied it properly and who kept up with current research. She punched her pillow into a different shape, frustrated by her own curiosity and more frustrated that she cared so much.

The sweet fragrance of wattle blossoms drifted through her open window, carried on the night air. Somewhere in the distance, a barn owl called to its mate, that haunting sound that always reminded her of her grandmother's stories about night creatures. She could hear the occasional low murmur of cattle settling for the night in a distant paddock, and she listened to the noises of animals shifting and breathing in the darkness. The sounds were a world away from the constant hum of Melbourne traffic and sirens that had taken her months to tune out when she first moved to the city. The wail of ambulances at all hours, the rumble of trams, and the shouts of drunk people stumbling home from bars had been a foreign background noise. Now, lying in the familiar quiet of her bedroom, she felt her shoulders relax despite her racing thoughts.

Her gaze wandered around the small room with its faded floral wallpaper that her mother kept threatening to update but never did, and the bookshelf still crowded with her old astronomy textbooks alongside childhood favourites like the entire Narnia series and her grandfather's worn copy of Banjo Paterson's poems. Her telescope stood in the corner, the good one she'd saved for two years to buy when she was sixteen, still pointing towards the window even though light pollution from the town made serious observation difficult. Living in the cottage at the back of her parents' block of land was fine for now, practical even, and they'd been nothing but supportive since she'd returned. But it wasn't a permanent solution. At twenty-eight, she craved her own place. She needed somewhere she could make plans for in future years, areas where she could plant what she wanted and a property that she could walk for miles over, putting her feet into the dusty soil that she owned.

Pazhvak Station beckoned once more, pulling at her with an almost physical force. She mentally sketched the simple house she wanted to build there, complete with a wide verandah perfect for late-night stargazing. There was no light pollution out that far and nothing between her and the vast expanse of sky. She'd have a proper observation deck on the roof, maybe with space for a bigger telescope. There'd be solar panels to keep her independent and a vegetable garden because the soil out there was good. There'd be room for a dog and some hens to keep her in eggs.

But even as she tried to focus on her future plans, trying to imagine the details of door frames and kitchen layouts, her thoughts kept drifting back to dark eyes and an infuriating smile. She recalled the way Dusty looked at her when he said precision mattered. The intensity in his gaze when he'd talked about Proxima Centauri, and his determined manner, showed he genuinely cared about astronomical accuracy rather than just trying to show off. What was a builder from Melbourne doing with that kind of scientific knowledge? And why did she care so much about finding out? Why couldn't she just write him off and move on with her life, as she had always intended?

She rolled over, staring at the ceiling where she had stuck glow-in-the-dark stars when she was twelve. It used to be a cottage where family or friends stayed, where excess produce was sometimes stored or when they were teenagers, where they'd come to hang out and play loud music. Now the faint green lights of the stars were barely visible. Her thoughts returned to Dusty. Maybe she kept thinking about him because she was wrong about him. She had judged him entirely on appearance, had dismissed him as shallow and temporary, but he'd turned out to be something else entirely. She hadn't expected that and didn't quite know how to categorise him. That bothered her more than she wanted to admit.

She thought about the way he smiled when she grew flustered over the moon count, not mocking but almost fond, as though her competitive streak amused rather than annoyed him. He had appreciated Ernie's knowledge about history, showing respect for the older man's experience, but then he talked about recycled timber with Oscar, showing a genuine appreciation for old materials rather than the builder's typical preference for new and easy.

Ella groaned and pulled the pillow over her face. This was exactly what she'd been trying to avoid. Getting interested in someone temporary who'd be gone in a few months, leaving her with nothing but memories and regrets in a town where everyone would know her business. She'd been through this before and she wasn't going to make the same mistake again. She knew how it would end.

Except Dusty wasn't Trent. Wasn't even close. Trent had been controlling from the start. She could see that now with the clarity of passing time. Dusty had corrected her factually but without any attempt to make her feel small. He had competed with her as an equal rather than trying to dominate or intimidate and looked at her with interest rather than possession.

She sat up abruptly, threw off the covers, and padded over to the window. The night sky spread above Matfield, brilliant and clear in the way it never was in cities. The Milky Way blazed across the darkness, a river of glittering light that always made her breath catch. Somewhere up there, Proxima Centauri burned with its small red light, four point two light years away, and she smiled despite herself. Of course he'd known the closest star. Of course he had.

Tomorrow she'd see him again at the campdraft everyone was talking about. The whole town would be there, which meant she couldn't avoid him even if she wanted to. And the troubling truth, the one she was finally admitting to herself as she stood at her window watching the stars, was that she didn't want to avoid him at all.

* * *

DUSTY WOKE with a dry mouth and the lingering taste of too many beers, though the fuzzy feeling in his head had more to do with satisfaction than alcohol. Last night had been unexpectedly enjoyable, not just for the company but for the chance to dust off knowledge he rarely had occasion to use these days. Everything he'd absorbed over the years was still there, filed away and ready when needed, and he'd felt a familiar spark of pride in his ability to recall precise details about astronomical phenomena. That moment when Ella's eyes had widened as he corrected her about Saturn's moons and the flash of surprise followed by grudging respect, had been worth every tedious lecture he'd sat through at university.

When he first left school, he'd thrown himself into science studies with the enthusiasm of someone who had found his calling. The stars and planets had fascinated him since he was a kid lying in the backyard with his father pointing out constellations, and the mathematics of orbital mechanics and stellar evolution had clicked into place with an ease that had surprised his teachers. Astronomy had felt like the perfect blend of physics, mathematics, and pure wonder. His family was thrilled when he had been accepted into the program at Melbourne University.

The reality of university life, however, had been less appealing than he had anticipated. Endless lectures where professors droned on about concepts he'd already grasped from reading. Theoretical assessments that felt removed from actual observation and discovery. The prospect of years more study before he could actually do anything meaningful had left him restless and frustrated. He'd wanted to be outside looking at the stars, not trapped in lecture halls discussing them. After twelve months of feeling like he was slowly suffocating behind a desk, watching other students thrive in an environment that made him miserable, he walked away from his degree and never looked back.

His family was devastated. His mother had been quietly disappointed, while his father tried to reason with him and to explain that feeling restless was normal. Everyone struggled in the first year. His siblings offered to tutor him, assuming he was failing rather than simply choosing to leave. None of them could understand that he wasn't escaping failure but pursuing a different pathway, a career that felt more authentically him.

Carpentry had been a revelation, discovered almost by accident when he helped a friend's father with a renovation project. He revelled in working with his hands, creating tangible and useful structures and spending his days outdoors rather than in lecture halls. It felt like he'd come home to himself in a way university never had. The skills came naturally, or at least more naturally than sitting still for hours, and within months he discovered not just competence but a genuine passion for the craft. There was satisfaction in seeing a structure take shape under his hands and using his intellect to solve practical problems with immediate solutions. He went on to earn his builder's licence and never regretted the choice, even when his family struggled to understand it or others asked pointed questions about when he'd go back and finish his degree.

His decision made him an anomaly in his family. He was the black sheep who rejected the path everyone else had followed without question. His mother, Isabella, had arrived from São Paulo in her early twenties with nothing but determination and a fierce curiosity about the world beyond Brazil. She left behind a comfortable middle-class family, turning down her father's plans for her to marry a suitable Brazilian man and settle into the life of a doctor's wife. Instead, she'd wanted to be the doctor herself. She met Dusty's father, David, at a backpackers' hostel in Byron Bay during her first week in Australia, and their romance had unfolded across two continents before they settled in Melbourne to pursue their medical degrees together. It had been hard for both of them, David working night shifts to support them while Isabella struggled with English medical terminology. But they'd done it together and went on to build a strong family life after that.

David became a cardiac surgeon, Isabella a specialist in midwifery, and both had devoted themselves entirely to their careers and raising their five children. Their house in Toorak was elegant without being flashy and filled with

Brazilian art and relics from places they had travelled to. They worked brutal hours when Dusty was growing up, but somehow they made it work, showing up for every school event, having family dinners and always being present, even when exhausted.

Dusty's four siblings had followed the family template with impressive steadiness. His sister Carmen was an ophthalmologist, while another sister Sofia, was a dentist. Both had thriving practices in South Yarra in Melbourne. His brother, Miguel, had become a GP and the other brother Paulo was a paediatrician. Miguel worked in community health and Paulo worked at a children's hospital. They were all married, all with children, and all living the kind of structured professional lives their parents had modelled. Sunday dinners were competitions of achievement, everyone sharing stories of difficult cases solved, patients helped, and lives saved or improved.

As the youngest, Dusty grew up surrounded by academic achievement and medical conversations. He was doted on by siblings who still treated him like their baby brother despite his thirty-two years. They had all been protective when he left university, although worried that he was throwing away his potential. They offered him money, connections, and opportunities to get back on track. None of them could understand that he wasn't off track but heading down his own path.

Sunday dinners at his parents' Toorak home were lively affairs conducted in a mixture of Portuguese and English. They were filled with updates on grandchildren's achievements and gentle but persistent questions about when Dusty might settle down and start a family. His mother still introduced him to suitable women at every opportunity. There had been dates with daughters of her friends from the Brazilian community, and work colleagues who were young doctors or nurses.

He understood his family's concern. They loved him and wanted him to have stability, success, and a family of his own like they had. But the truth was, he'd found contentment in a life that looked nothing like theirs. The work satisfied him in ways that sitting in an office never could. The freedom to choose his projects and locations had led him here to Matfield, where morning light was already streaming through the thin curtains of his rented cottage. Today would bring more demolition work at the pub, more progress on Oscar's renovation dreams, and quite possibly another encounter with a certain green-eyed woman who'd looked at him last night as though he was a puzzle she couldn't quite solve.

He smiled at the memory of her face when he'd known about the new moon. That flash of surprise. The way her competitive streak had come out was intriguing, and the intelligence in her eyes when she fired back with her own knowledge had impressed him. Ella Patterson was nothing like the women his mother kept introducing him to. Nothing like Tanya, who had wanted him to be someone he wasn't, who'd kept her thoughts from him while sharing them with everyone else behind his back. Ella was sharp and stubborn and didn't hide either quality. She'd judged him harshly, true, but at least she was honest about it. And last night, for the first time, he'd seen that judgment waver.

He rolled out of bed, already looking forward to the weekend and the campdraft Todd had mentioned. It would be a chance to see Ella again, away from the pub and the town's watchful eyes. Maybe it would even be a chance to prove that he wasn't what she assumed. The thought shouldn't have excited him as much as it did, but he was done pretending he wasn't interested. Life was too short for that kind of deception.

CHAPTER 7

*E*li and Dusty were deep in concentration, dismantling the old framework piece by piece, when Oscar and Todd entered the room. The morning sun streamed through the windows they'd uncovered yesterday, highlighting the dust specks that continuously danced in the air. Both men moved with the easy confidence of business owners who genuinely enjoyed their work, and Dusty had come to respect the partnership they'd built over the weeks of working together. The pub ran with the efficiency of a well-oiled machine, from the kitchen that turned out delicious meals, to the front bar that served as the unofficial town meeting place where conversations ranged from weather patterns to cattle prices, along with the ever-fluctuating return on beef.

They both stopped working as the owners approached, and Dusty straightened up, feeling his back protest slightly from the morning's labour. He set down the crowbar he'd been using to carefully extract the old timber framing, wiping his hands on his work shorts.

Todd ran his weathered hand along one of the vertical posts they'd managed to preserve, his fingers tracing the grain with obvious appreciation. 'Beautiful old timber. I'm glad to see you're stacking it all for us rather than binning it. We'll hopefully find a good use for it somewhere.'

'We'll use it alright,' Eli agreed, wiping sweat from his forehead with the back of his sleeve. Even this early in the day, the temperature was climbing. 'It's far too good to waste. The craftsmanship in these old buildings puts modern stuff to shame.'

'Recycled timber like this is gold,' Dusty added, examining the rich grain of a beam they'd just removed. The wood was dense and heavy, old-growth timber that you couldn't get anymore. 'I reckon I could make some fantastic shelving for that back wall. Look at this grain pattern. You don't find material like this anymore, not unless you're willing to pay a fortune for imported stuff.'

The four men had hit it off immediately when they'd first met, spending hours poring over plans and discussing design possibilities before any actual work had begun. Although Todd and Oscar had clear ideas about what they wanted, they were open to suggestions, the kind of clients every builder dreamed of working with. Todd, who could also turn his hand to carpentry work when he had time, had organised a small weatherboard cottage for them to rent at a fraction of the usual rate. It was situated just two streets back from the main drag and was basic but comfortable. The price meant they could save most of what they earned. The renovation was expected to take months, possibly longer if they kept finding hidden problems behind walls, and it was clear Todd wanted to keep them in town for as long as possible.

Good builders were hard to find, and those willing to work in remote locations even harder.

The arrangement had worked out perfectly for everyone involved, thanks to a connection between Dusty's father and Oscar. Most builders Oscar and Todd contacted had quoted ridiculous prices, as they simply weren't interested in leaving the city for months at a time.

'Great to see you both getting involved in the social events around here,' Oscar said, his eyes twinkling with amusement. He leant against one of the support posts they'd left intact. 'Last night was quite the evening of surprises for everyone.'

They laughed, and Todd shook his head in amazement. 'I heard about the quiz night from Penny this morning. Sounds like you lads more than held your own. She was disappointed to have missed it, but the baby's been keeping her up at night and she needed the sleep.'

'Those girls were sharp as tacks,' Oscar continued, clearly impressed by the evening's competition. 'You should have seen Ella and that friend of hers, Cass, going hard answering the questions. They were absolutely firing on all cylinders. Haven't seen Ella that animated in a long time. Usually, she's more reserved.'

Dusty felt his interest sharpen at the mention of Ella's name, though he tried to keep his expression neutral. Oscar seemed to notice anyway, a knowing smile playing at the corners of his mouth.

'I'll have to bring Penny to the next one,' Todd said, oblivious to the undercurrent. 'She'd love that sort of intellectual competition.'

'I think I met your wife this morning at the bakery,' Dusty said, grateful for the opportunity to change the subject. 'She knew who I was and introduced herself. You have a little one and then a new baby. Looks like you both have your hands full. She has an English accent?'

'That's her. Came out here on what was supposed to be a holiday and to visit Oscar and Patricia.' Todd's face softened with the expression of a man still amazed by his good fortune. 'It's a long story, but she's Oscar's niece. Took us both a while to work out we were meant to be together. There was some miscommunication and stubborn pride on both sides, but we're happier than either of us thought possible. Mind you, this second baby was a big surprise. But we're loving family life.'

'That must have been a huge adjustment for her, moving from England to somewhere like this,' Eli observed. He'd been to London once and couldn't imagine anyone voluntarily leaving it for outback Queensland.

'It was a massive change, bigger than either of us anticipated,' Todd admitted. 'She missed England at first. Little things like being able to pop to a bookshop or see a show. But she's taken to living in Matfield like she was born here. Turns out she's got a real knack for country life and loves the space and the community. Her family visits when they can, and having Oscar and Patricia nearby means she's got some family support. Makes all the difference when you're so far from home.'

'What about you two?' Oscar asked, his tone casual but curious. He pulled out a measuring tape and made a note on his clipboard. 'Anyone special back in Melbourne?'

Both men shook their heads. 'Not for me,' Dusty said firmly, thinking of Tanya and the relief he felt when that relationship finally ended. 'I've been burnt a couple of times in the past. Happy with the single life for now.'

Eli nodded in agreement. 'Same here. Bit of a relief not having to worry about anyone else's plans or expectations. We can go where the work takes us without having to justify it.'

But even as he said it, Dusty felt the words ring slightly hollow. Last night had reminded him of what it felt like to connect with someone, to have that spark of mutual interest and challenge. The memory of Ella's face when she'd been arguing with him about astronomical units, the intelligence and passion in her eyes, made the idea of staying single feel less like contentment and more like avoidance.

Dusty quickly shifted the conversation back to the renovation, outlining his ideas for repurposing the salvaged timber. He explained how they could use the old beams as feature pieces, how the patina and character of aged wood would add warmth to the renovated space. The men talked for another twenty minutes, discussing techniques and timelines, Oscar making detailed notes while Todd occasionally interjected with questions or suggestions. Before they left, Todd had another question.

'What are you two doing this weekend? Make sure you give yourselves a proper break. There's a campdraft on Saturday and Sunday.' He tucked his clipboard under his arm. 'It's mainly for the kids during the day. They'll be learning basic riding skills and cattle work, but there's some serious adult competition in the afternoon. Then there's a big barbecue Saturday night. You should both come along. Plenty of food, cold drinks, and entertainment. The local band plays, plus there's the school choir and drum ensemble performing. There'll be a few stalls selling bits and pieces, crafts and preserves mostly. Bring a chair and your hat. You'll love it.'

Dusty pushed his sleeves up, feeling the warmth building despite the early morning hour. For a winter month, August was heating up quickly, and the physical work was becoming more demanding. The temperature was supposed to hit thirty-two by midafternoon. 'I reckon we should definitely take the weekend off. That sounds like exactly what we need. I've never been to a campdraft before. What do you think, Eli?'

'Absolutely. Food and drink?' Eli grinned, his face brightening at the prospect. 'I'll go anywhere for that combination. Count me in. Will there be many people there?'

'The whole town basically,' Oscar said with a laugh. 'It's one of the big events of the year. Everyone comes out. It's more about the community gathering than the actual competition. Though the competition can get pretty fierce. Some of these riders take it very seriously.'

After Oscar and Todd left, Eli turned to Dusty with a knowing smile. 'So, Ella's going to be there.'

'Probably,' Dusty said, trying for casual and failing completely.

'Definitely,' Eli corrected. 'Oscar said the whole town. That includes stubborn astronomy-obsessed produce store workers who think you're a misogynistic dickhead.'

Dusty threw a piece of old timber at him, which Eli dodged easily. 'She doesn't think that anymore.'

'You sure about that? Because from where I was sitting last night, she looked pretty confused about what to think.'

'That's an improvement on hostile,' Dusty pointed out.

He grabbed his crowbar and attacked the next section of wall. 'Besides, I'm not interested.'

'Right. And I'm not completely smitten with Cass.' Eli picked up his own tools. 'We're both liars, mate. Might as well admit it.'

Dusty didn't respond, but as he worked through the morning, he found himself thinking about the weekend ahead. A campdraft. The whole town. Which meant Ella would be there, and this time he'd have a chance to talk to her properly, away from the intensity of competition and the watchful eyes of the quiz night crowd. The prospect shouldn't have excited him as much as it did. Matfield was proving to be far more interesting than he'd ever anticipated.

The sun beat down on the showgrounds with the kind of intensity that made everyone grateful for the massive eucalyptus trees scattered around the perimeter, their shade providing relief from the climbing temperature. Ella wiped perspiration from her forehead as she wrestled with a couple of wooden staging boards that refused to cooperate with her plans to fix a small section of a performance area. The timber was old and warped, probably salvaged from some previous event, and no matter how she positioned the pieces, they refused to sit flush against each other. Children's voices carried across the dusty grounds as they helped their parents set up gazebos, arrange hay bales for seating, and string bunting between fence posts. The brightly coloured triangular flags fluttered in the hot breeze, red and yellow and blue against the washed-out sky. The annual campdraft was shaping up to be one of the biggest community events of the year, with families from properties scattered across the area making the journey to Matfield for the weekend competition.

Cass appeared beside her, carrying a box of sound equipment, her usually immaculate hair already showing signs of the heat and dust. Wisps had escaped from her ponytail and stuck to her damp forehead and there was a smudge of red dirt across her cheek. 'This is going to be brilliant once it's all set up. The weather's perfect for it.' She gestured towards the main arena where several riders were putting their horses through practice runs, stirring up clouds of dirt that caught the morning light and turned the air hazy. 'Matt's over there helping check the horses before the competitions start. He's in his element. You'd think it was Christmas morning the way he's been excited about this all week.'

Ella nodded towards the far end of the grounds where Elsie had marshalled a group of primary school children into an efficient assembly line, organising craft stalls and face-painting stations with the kind of military precision that came from years of classroom management. Even from this distance, Ella could hear her friend's voice carrying across the space, firm but encouraging, exactly the tone that made students want to please her. 'Elsie's got those kids working. She'll have the entire children's area set up before lunch at this rate.'

The distinctive rumble of a diesel engine drew their attention to the car park, where a dusty white ute was pulling up in a cloud of dust. Ella recognised the vehicle immediately, though she tried to appear disinterested as Dusty and Eli climbed out, each grabbing folding chairs from the tray before making their way towards the main setup area. Both men wore broad-brimmed hats and long-sleeved shirts despite the heat, clearly taking Todd's advice about sun protection seriously. The hats were new, she noticed, probably bought specially for today. Dusty carried a small esky while Eli had what looked like a tool bag slung over his shoulder, and they moved with the easy confidence of people who were starting to feel comfortable in unfamiliar surroundings.

'Well, well,' Cass murmured with barely concealed delight, her eyes tracking Eli's progress across the showground. 'The Melbourne boys have made an appearance. This day just got a lot more interesting.'

Ella returned her attention to the staging with renewed determination, trying to push the same two boards to align properly so she could secure them with the brackets she'd borrowed from her father's store. The timber was old and warped, probably from being stored outside for years. Every time she thought she had it right, one end would spring free, leaving her with a wobbly, unsafe section. It was only a small area but she'd been at this for nearly an hour, her frustration building with each failed attempt. Everyone else seemed to be busy with other setting up work and this had seemed like a simple job for her to do.

'Having some trouble there?' Dusty's voice came from directly behind her, and she turned to find him studying the staging setup with a practised eye. Up close, she could see that his navy work shirt was already darkened with sweat across the shoulders, and his dark hair was damp where it escaped from under his hat. He'd pushed his sleeves up to his elbows, revealing those forearms she'd noticed before, tanned and marked with the evidence of physical work.

'Nothing I can't handle,' she replied, though even as she spoke, the board she'd been trying to secure slipped again and clattered to the ground with a sound that made several nearby people turn to look.

'Right.' His tone was dry but not unkind, and she saw amusement dancing in his eyes. 'Looks like the brackets are bent and the timber's warped from being stored outside. You're fighting a losing battle trying to make those pieces work together.' He turned towards Eli, who was setting up their chairs in the shade of a large gum tree. 'Mate, can you pass me the tool bag? I think we can sort this out pretty quickly.'

'You don't need to do that,' Ella protested. 'I'm sure I can work it out.'

'I'm sure you could, but this'll be faster and safer. Besides, it's what I do for a living.' He accepted the tool bag from Eli with a nod of thanks, then knelt down to examine the damaged brackets more closely. 'These are completely shot. Look at this.' He held one up, showing her where the metal had bent and twisted. 'Lucky I've got some spares in the ute from a previous job that'll do the trick.'

Within minutes he returned with replacement hardware and efficiently dismantled her attempted construction. Ella watched the way his hands moved as he worked.

'You don't have to stand there supervising,' he said without looking up, though she could hear the smile in his voice. 'I promise I know what I'm doing.'

'I wasn't supervising. I was observing.' She crossed her arms defensively, feeling foolish for being caught staring. 'There's a difference.'

'Is there now?' He glanced up with that infuriating

half-smile she was beginning to recognise. 'And what conclusions have your observations led you to?'

'That you're annoyingly competent at fixing a problem that should be simple but apparently isn't.' The words came out impatiently, frustration at her own failure mixing with irritation at how easily he'd solved the problem.

'I'll take that as a compliment.' He returned to his work, quickly aligning the boards and securing them with the properly fitted brackets. His movements were sure and precise, no wasted motion, and within minutes, he accomplished what she'd been struggling with. 'There. That should hold.'

Ella tested the section of staging by stepping onto it and bouncing slightly. It was completely solid, professionally finished, and exactly what she'd been trying to achieve. 'Thank you,' she said, the words coming out a little more grudgingly than she intended.

'You're welcome. Though you might want to work on your gracious acceptance of help. It needs a bit of polish.' He was grinning now, clearly enjoying her discomfort.

Before she could formulate a suitably cutting response, he packed up his tools and wandered off to rejoin Eli, leaving her standing on the stage feeling both grateful and irritated. She watched him walk away, noting the easy way he moved and how several women in the vicinity found excuses to call out greetings or wave. He was becoming part of the community, she realised with an uncomfortable jolt. People liked him. And that made it much harder to maintain her careful distance.

* * *

THE DAY PROGRESSED with the kind of easy community spirit that made Matfield feel like a scene from a different era. It was like a day from her grandparents' time when everyone knew everyone and neighbours helped each other without question. Children raced between activities with faces painted as tigers and butterflies, their laughter high and bright in the warm air, while adults gathered in shifting groups to catch up on news, discuss the unseasonably warm weather, and debate the merits of various horses and riders. The aroma of sausages and onions from the barbecue area mixed with the dust and eucalyptus to create a distinctly Australian collective bouquet that spoke of country gatherings and shared traditions. Someone had set up a speaker playing classic country music, Slim Dusty and John Williamson music, creating the perfect soundtrack for the day.

Ella crossed paths with Dusty several more times throughout the day, each encounter brief but somehow charged with an undercurrent she couldn't quite identify. When she was helping serve coffee from the CWA stall, balancing paper cups and making change, he appeared in the queue with Eli. Both men were clearly popular with the local women who found excuses to linger and chat. Mrs Henderson from the bakery practically simpered at them, and even stern Mrs Walsh from the library was smiling. When Ella was judging the children's art competition, she carefully examined crayon drawings of horses, families, and the Queensland countryside. She noticed him watching from a distance, his expression unreadable. Each time, she felt that same flutter of awareness that annoyed her precisely because she couldn't control it. Her body was betraying her carefully maintained indifference, and that was unacceptable.

'You're doing a lot of looking for someone who claims not to be interested,' Cass observed as they restocked the coffee supplies behind the stall, pulling fresh cups from a cardboard box.

'I'm keeping an eye on things. Community vigilance.' Ella busied herself with arranging the cups, avoiding her friend's knowing gaze.

'Is that what we're calling it?' Cass's voice was full of amusement. 'Because from where I'm standing, it looks a lot like you can't stop staring at him. And he keeps looking over here too, in case you haven't noticed.'

'I haven't noticed anything.' The lie was unconvincing even to her own ears.

The afternoon competition began with junior riders, but Ella's attention was focused on preparing for her own event. She'd been riding since childhood, first on her family's property and later at various competitions around the region, but she hadn't participated in a camp-draft for over two years. Life had been too busy, first with university and then with settling back into Matfield, and she missed these events more than she realised. Her horse, a chestnut gelding named Bandit, belonged to her uncle and was known for his intelligence and quick reflexes, essential qualities for the precise teamwork required to separate a single beast from the herd and guide it through a designated course.

She changed into her competition clothes behind her father's truck. Moleskin pants, a long-sleeved shirt in pale blue, and the leather boots she'd worn to countless similar events during her teenage years were comforting, even as her nerves tightened with anticipation. This was who she'd been before going to Melbourne, before Trent and before everything had got so complicated. This was a part of herself she had almost forgotten.

Bandit stood patiently as she adjusted his tack, his ears pricked forward with the kind of alertness that suggested he was as eager for the competition as she was. He was a beautiful animal, all lean muscle and nervous energy, and she ran her hand down his neck feeling the power beneath the warm coat. 'You ready for this, boy?' she murmured, and he tossed his head as if in agreement.

The women's open campdraft attracted eight competitors, a good field that included several riders from neighbouring properties with reputations for skill and determination. Ella watched the first few runs carefully, noting how the cattle were behaving and which strategies seemed most effective. The steers were fresh and skittish, which would make things interesting. When her turn came, she guided Bandit into the camp with the calm confidence that came from years of experience, her focus narrowing to the job at hand. Everything else fell away; the crowd, the heat and Dusty's presence somewhere in the stands. There was only the horse beneath her and the work ahead.

The steer she selected was a solid Angus that looked calm but moved with the kind of intelligence that suggested he wouldn't be easily fooled. She'd learned to read cattle over years of working with her uncle, to see which ones would bolt and which would try to outsmart you. Working in perfect partnership with Bandit, she separated the steer from the herd with minimal fuss, reading the subtle shifts in his body language. She responded to the steer's movements before he could act on them, then began the delicate process of guiding him towards the gate at the far end of the arena. The crowd fell silent as horse and rider demonstrated the kind of seamless communication that made the difficult look effortless. Bandit responded to the slightest shift in her weight while keeping the steer moving in the right direction at exactly the right pace.

They completed the course in a time that had the announcer reaching for superlatives and the crowd erupting in appreciative applause. Ella dismounted with a grin that she couldn't suppress, her earlier nerves replaced by the satisfied exhaustion that came from a job well done. Her hands were shaking slightly from the adrenaline and sweat soaked her shirt. Several competitors congratulated her as she led Bandit back towards the holding area. Sarah Jenkins clapped her on the shoulder and said, 'That was bloody brilliant!' Coming from Sarah who was a seasoned competitor, that meant a lot.

'That was seriously impressive.' Dusty's voice came from beside the rail where he'd been watching, and she turned to find him looking at her with an expression of unmistakable admiration. His eyes were bright with genuine appreciation. 'I've never seen anything like that before. The way you and that horse worked together was incredible. Like you were reading each other's minds.'

'It's just practice and a good partnership,' she replied, though she couldn't help feeling pleased by his obvious respect. 'Bandit does most of the work. I just try not to get in his way.'

'Don't sell yourself short. That took real skill.' He studied Bandit with the appreciation of someone who recognised quality when he saw it, reaching out carefully to let the horse sniff his hand before gently stroking his neck. Bandit allowed it, which surprised Ella. The gelding was usually wary of strangers. 'How long have you been riding competitively?'

'On and off since I was about twelve. My father's family have a property outside town and I spent a lot of time there when I was growing up. Horses were just part of life. I still ride whenever I can. Not as much as I'd like these days.'

Todd appeared beside them, beaming with the pride of someone whose town had just produced a winner. 'Ella's being modest. Her grandparents and now her uncle's property is one of the biggest in the district. She grew up in the saddle, practically. That win wasn't luck, it was pure class.'

'I can see that,' Dusty said. His gaze returned to Ella with a new level of interest. Suddenly she felt self-conscious. Sweat trickled down her back and no doubt her face was red from exertion and heat. She wished she'd taken a moment to at least splash water on her face. 'Seems like there's a lot more to this town than meets the eye. And a lot more to you.'

Before she could process his words and formulate a response, Cass appeared with Eli in tow, a panicked expression in her eyes. 'Ella, we need you over at the children's area. One of the kids you sometimes babysit has taken a tumble and his mum's not here. The medic is checking him over, but they want someone he knows to keep him calm while they work out if he needs to go to the hospital.'

'Of course.' Ella turned back to Dusty, already handing

Bandit off to her uncle who was standing nearby. 'Thanks again for the compliment. I should go help.'

As she hurried away with Cass towards the commotion near the face-painting station, her boots kicking up dust, she missed seeing Elsie approaching the two builders with the kind of determined expression that suggested she was on a mission. Her auburn hair was escaping from its ponytail and her blouse was dusty, but her eyes sparkled with the enthusiasm of someone who'd just had a brilliant idea and was about to rope unsuspecting victims into it.

* * *

'Perfect timing, you two. I've been looking for you gentlemen all afternoon.' Elsie beamed at Dusty and Eli with the kind of smile that should have immediately made them suspicious. 'I have a proposition that I think you'll find very appealing.'

Eli looked immediately suspicious, taking a step backwards. 'That sounds ominous. What kind of proposition? Because the last time someone said that to me, I ended up volunteering to coach under-tens footy for an entire season.'

'The school's running a Shave for a Cure fundraiser next month, and we're looking for some special volunteers to help us raise money for cancer research. The idea is to have surprise guests who'll shave their heads at the event, and I think you two would be absolutely perfect.' She said it all in a rush, as though getting the words out quickly would make it harder for them to refuse.

Dusty and Eli exchanged glances, both wavering

between amusement and alarm. 'You want us to shave our heads?' Dusty asked slowly, making sure he heard correctly.

'Completely bald. In the school hall, in front of the whole school and probably most of the community. For charity.' Elsie's smile widened, but there was steel beneath the sweetness. This was a woman who knew how to get what she wanted. 'Think of the fundraising potential. Two handsome newcomers sacrificing their hair for a good cause. We could raise thousands. The novelty factor alone would bring people out.'

'I don't know,' Eli said, running a hand through his blonde hair as if checking it was still there, assessing how much he'd be losing. 'This is thinning anyway. I'm not sure how long it will be around. My dad was bald by the time he was forty, so I'm probably on borrowed time.'

Dusty took his hat off and patted the top of his head, his dark hair thick and wavy, falling across his forehead. 'I've been growing this for a while. It sort of needs a cut anyway. It's getting long.'

'That's exactly why it would be so effective,' Elsie pressed, sensing an approaching win. 'There's plenty there to cut and then shave. We'd keep it a secret until the day of the event. You'd be the surprise entrants. Plus, hair grows back, but the money we raise could help fund research that saves lives. Real lives, real people.'

Dusty was quiet for a moment, and when he spoke, his voice was more serious than usual. 'My maternal grandmother died of breast cancer when I was fifteen. She fought it for three years before it finally beat her. She was from Brazil and my mum had only just brought her out here before she was diagnosed. She was the toughest person I knew, and it still wasn't enough.'

'My dad suffers from skin cancer,' Eli added quietly, his usual jovial expression evaporating. 'Had another melanoma removed last year. They got it early, but it's always there in the back of our minds, wondering if the next one will be the one they catch too late.' He looked down at the ground. 'We lost a close friend to the same thing a couple of years ago. He was only forty.'

The mood shifted as the personal stakes became clear, and Elsie's expression softened with understanding and genuine sympathy. 'I'm sorry. I didn't know. I wouldn't have been so flippant about it if I'd realised.'

'No reason you should've known,' Dusty replied, putting his hat back on. 'But it does make the cause pretty hard to refuse. When's the event?'

'Three weeks from today. Saturday afternoon at the school. We'll have other activities too, bake sales and raffles, but the head-shaving will be the main attraction.' Elsie looked between them hopefully, hardly daring to breathe. 'You'd really be helping the whole community get behind a fantastic cause. We've never raised more than a couple of thousand before, but with you two involved, I think we could double or even triple that.'

Eli sighed dramatically, but there was real emotion beneath the performance. 'Well, I suppose if we're doing this for cancer research, I can sacrifice my magnificent locks. When you put it like that, vanity seems pretty shallow. Besides, it's only hair.'

'Count me in too,' Dusty agreed, though he looked slightly ill at the prospect. 'But I reserve the right to wear a hat for the next few months while it grows back. And

I'm not doing this again, so don't even think about making it an annual thing.'

Elsie clapped her hands together with delight, her whole face lighting up. 'This is fantastic! Remember, it's our secret until the day. The surprise element is crucial for maximum impact. Don't tell anyone, not even your new friends here in town. Can you both promise me that? We'll fundraise for "special guests". That'll keep everyone guessing.'

'Our lips are sealed,' Eli promised, making a zipping motion across his mouth. 'I might need to start mentally preparing myself for the shock, though. Maybe take some photos now for posterity.'

As Elsie hurried away to continue her organisational duties, practically skipping with excitement, Todd shook his head with amusement. 'You two have just been expertly managed by a professional. Elsie could probably convince people to volunteer for anything. She once talked the entire town council into a charity swim in the dam in the middle of winter.'

'Seems like a good cause,' Dusty said, watching Elsie disappear into the crowd, already pulling out her phone to make notes. 'And it's not like we've got anyone here to impress with our hair anyway. Might as well make ourselves useful.'

* * *

THE AFTERNOON CONTINUED with various competitions and activities, the community gathering momentum as more families arrived and the barbecue area filled with the sounds of sizzling meat and lively conversation. Dusty found himself drawn into conversations with locals, answering questions about his work and his impressions of country life. He was gradually feeling less like an outsider and more like a temporary resident with a place in the community's social fabric. By the time the sun began its descent towards the horizon, painting the sky in shades of orange and pink, Dusty realised he felt more at home in Matfield than he had in Melbourne in years.

CHAPTER 9

The next few weeks crawled by with the predictable rhythm of work and sleep that defined life in a small town. Dusty sat on the narrow verandah of the weatherboard cottage he and Eli were renting, nursing a beer and watching the night settle over Matfield's quiet streets. The beer was cold against his palm, condensation running down the bottle in the warm evening air. A flickering streetlight cast erratic shadows across the footpath, and he watched a large possum scurry boldly across the road before scrambling up a power pole with the confidence of a creature that owned the place. The possum paused at the top, its eyes catching the light and glowing red for a moment before it disappeared into the foliage. Apart from the occasional distant bark of a dog or the rumble of a late truck on the highway, the town settled into the kind of silence that city dwellers paid therapists to help them find.

Eli had turned in early, exhausted from another twelve-hour day dismantling walls and salvaging timber.

Their evenings had fallen into a comfortable routine. Every night they would clean up and grab dinner at the pub where Patricia always gave them generous portions. They'd exchange pleasantries with whichever locals were propping up the bar, then head home to collapse in front of whatever football match was playing on their tiny television. It was a simple existence, and Dusty found he didn't mind it as much as he expected. The work was satisfying in a way office work never could be, the pace unhurried compared to Melbourne's relentless pressure, and he was sleeping better than he had in months. There were no stressful dreams and no waking up at three in the morning worrying about things he couldn't control.

He'd only encountered Ella and Cass once during those two weeks, a brief exchange outside the post office that reinforced his growing irritation. Ella's attitude frustrated him. Cass had been her usual friendly self, chatting about the weather and asking after their progress at the pub, genuinely interested in the details of the renovation. But Ella stood beside her friend with the kind of polite smile that didn't reach her eyes, her body language screaming discomfort. She was hot and cold, impossible to read. At the campdraft she'd seemed friendly enough. But now she answered his questions with the bare minimum of civility, as if fulfilling some social obligation rather than engaging in genuine conversation. What was her bloody problem? They'd had enough interaction by now for her to realise that neither he nor Eli matched whatever preconceived notions she'd formed about city builders. Her loss, he decided. They could have had interesting conversations about astronomy, maybe even become friends, but he wasn't about to grovel for anyone's approval. If she wanted to maintain her frosty distance, that was her choice. He had better things to do than chase after someone who'd already made up her mind about him.

* * *

THE NEXT MORNING, Dusty emerged from his bedroom to find Eli already dressed and pacing around their small kitchen, an untouched cup of coffee growing cold on the counter. The house Todd had found for them was basic but comfortable, consisting of two bedrooms, a functional bathroom with temperamental water pressure, and a kitchen that opened onto a lounge room. Mismatched furniture somehow worked together. The furniture kept them comfortable. There was a sagging couch that was surprisingly soft, two armchairs that didn't match each other or the couch, and a coffee table scarred with water rings from years of use. The back verandah looked out onto a small garden that was slowly recovering from years of neglect, and the whole place had the kind of worn charm that spoke of a never-ending cycle of tenants who'd cared just enough to keep it liveable.

'You're up early, mate,' Dusty observed, pouring himself coffee from the pot Eli had made. The coffee was strong and bitter, the way Eli always made it. 'Everything alright?'

Eli stopped pacing and turned to face him, his expression grim, his usual easy smile completely absent. 'Gran's in hospital. Mum rang about an hour ago. She's not good, Dusty. They reckon she's only got weeks, maybe a month or two if she's lucky. The cancer's spread and they've stopped treatment.'

Dusty set down his mug, immediately understanding the weight of what Eli was telling him. He'd met Eli's gran a few times, a tiny Italian woman with a fierce love of family and a tendency to pinch cheeks and force-feed anyone who came within reach. 'What do you need to do?'

'I can leave as soon as I pack up, drive south and be back down south with the family in a couple of days. I know the timing's terrible with the pub renovation, and I hate leaving you in the lurch, but I need to say goodbye to her properly.' His voice cracked slightly. 'She had the flu when I left, so I didn't get to see her before we came here. I just gave her a wave through the window because she was contagious. That can't be the last time I see her.'

'Don't even think about the job,' Dusty said firmly, moving around the counter to grip Eli's shoulder. 'Oscar and Todd will understand completely. Family comes first, always. I can keep things ticking over here until you get back. The work will wait.'

'I'm really not sure how long I'll be gone. We're a close family, and everyone's coming home to spend time with her while we can. My cousins are flying in from Perth and my aunt's driving over from Adelaide.'

'Take a month, take two if you need it. Take however long it takes.' Dusty looked his friend in the eye, making sure he understood. 'I mean it, Eli. Don't cut your time short because of work. This is your gran. You only get one chance to spend time with her and say goodbye properly.'

Eli nodded gratefully, already reaching for his phone to call Oscar and explain the situation. Within two hours, he'd packed a bag and loaded his ute with supplies for the long drive south. Dusty stood in the driveway watching his friend disappear down the main street, dust kicking up behind the ute. He felt the weight of solitude settle around him for the first time since they'd arrived in Matfield. The cottage suddenly felt too big and too quiet.

Three days later, he found himself driving alone to the high school for the Shave for a Cure event, wishing Eli were there for moral support. The school building looked exactly like every regional high school he'd ever seen, its red brick weathering to orange and metal roofing that would be deafening in the rain. It had that particular institutional smell of floor polish and teenage hormones that hit him the moment he walked through the front doors. Memories of his own school days flooded back, not all of them pleasant.

The principal, a woman in her fifties with dark hair and kind eyes, greeted him warmly and led him through corridors lined with student artwork and motivational posters that also brought back uncomfortable memories. Posters about being your best self, about persistence and growth mindsets. He took a deep breath. The posters were a reminder of all the things teachers believed would make a difference.

'Thank you so much for doing this,' she said as they walked towards the main hall, her heels clicking on the polished floors. 'When Elsie told us you'd volunteered, we were thrilled. It's wonderful to have someone from outside the community supporting our fundraising efforts. It's a shame your offsider couldn't make it also but we completely understand.'

The hall was already buzzing with activity when they arrived. Students were filing into rows of plastic chairs, their voices echoing off the high ceiling while teachers tried to maintain some semblance of order. Parents with cameras clustered near the front, clearly prepared to document every moment of their children's sacrifice. Dusty could also see a couple of professional-looking cameras that suggested the local paper was covering the event. A stage had been set up at the far end, complete with chairs arranged in a line and electrical outlets for the clippers that would soon be put to enthusiastic use.

Elsie spotted him immediately and hurried over with the kind of bright smile that suggested she was running on pure adrenaline and caffeine. Her eyes were slightly manic, and she clutched a clipboard like a lifeline. 'Dusty! You made it. I was worried you might have changed your mind. Poor Eli. He rang me and let me know. I hope he gets there before his Granny passes. Now, are you ready for this?'

'Ready as anyone can be for public humiliation,' he replied, earning a laugh from several nearby parents who had overheard.

'It's for a good cause,' she reminded him, guiding him purposefully towards the stage, her hand firmly on his elbow. 'Besides, you'll be in excellent company. We've got five students brave enough to sacrifice their hair today. They've been fundraising for weeks.'

As he climbed the steps to the stage, the full reality of what he'd agreed to hit him. The hall was packed with what seemed like half the town's population. There were easily three hundred people, all of them looking expectantly at the row of chairs where the volunteers would soon be shorn like sheep. He recognised some of the faces in the audience. Oscar and Patricia from the pub were sitting in the front row with matching proud expressions, while Todd with his wife Penny, were seated next to them. Familiar faces of those whose names he was still learning and countless others who had made him feel welcome over the past few weeks nodded or waved to him.

'Ladies and gentlemen, boys and girls,' Elsie announced into the microphone, her voice echoing slightly through the hall's sound system, causing a shrill noise that made several people wince. There was some laughter and chatter from the audience as they waited for one of the teachers to fix the problem, then silence as Elsie held her hand up. 'Thank you all for coming to support our Shave for a Cure fundraiser. Today we're raising money for cancer research, and we have some incredibly brave volunteers who've agreed to sacrifice their hair for this important cause.'

A cheer went up from the students, punctuated by wolf whistles and someone yelling, 'Go Macca!' at one of the teenage boys sitting beside Dusty. The boy grinned and waved, clearly loving the attention.

'Let me introduce our volunteers,' Elsie continued, consulting her clipboard. 'We have Year Twelve students Sarah Mitchell and Emma Thompson, Year Eleven boys Connor McCarthy, Jamie Singh, and Dylan Parker.' Each student stood as their name was called, and the applause was genuine and warm. 'And our very special surprise guest, Dusty Camilleri, who's travelled all the way from Melbourne to help renovate our pub and has kindly agreed to support our fundraiser today. His offsider, Eli, had also agreed to be here today but he has been called back south for a family health issue. He has, however, raised over one thousand dollars while in Melbourne for this amazing cause.'

The applause that greeted his introduction was surprisingly enthusiastic, and Dusty found himself grinning and waving at the crowd like some sort of minor celebrity. Maybe he wasn't as much of an outsider as he thought. He caught Oscar's eye and the older man gave him a thumbs up.

'Now, our wonderful parent volunteers are going to take care of shaving our students' heads,' Elsie announced as several mothers appeared behind the chairs, armed with electric clippers and looking slightly nervous about the task ahead. They were all wearing aprons and had towels draped over their arms, smiling at appearing professional in their preparation. 'But we had a special arrangement for Dusty. Tina from Hair Expressions was going to handle his shave, but...' She paused dramatically, her timing perfect. 'She went into labour about an hour ago!'

The crowd erupted in laughter and cheers, someone shouting, 'Good on ya, Tina!' and another voice calling out, 'Boy or girl?'

'Too early to tell, but mother and baby are doing well according to her husband,' Elsie added with a grin. 'So I had to make some emergency phone calls to find a replacement. The best alternative I could find is someone who's well known in our community for her expertise with clippers and her steady hand with grooming. She's our district champion in livestock presentation, an award-winning dog groomer, and apparently the only person in town brave enough to take on this challenge at short notice. Please welcome Ella Patterson!'

Dusty's head snapped towards the side curtains as applause filled the hall, and he held his breath as Ella emerged from behind the fabric, clutching a professional-looking set of clippers and wearing an expression of barely concealed panic. Her eyes found his across the stage, and for a moment they simply stared at each other in mutual horror, both clearly wishing they were anywhere else on earth.

She was dressed in dark jeans and a simple white shirt, her hair pulled back in a practical ponytail, and she looked about as thrilled to be there as he felt. The irony struck him. The woman who'd been avoiding him for weeks was now going to run her hands through his hair with a pair of electric clippers. The universe clearly had a twisted sense of humour.

'Well,' he said as she approached his chair with obvious reluctance, moving like someone walking to their own execution, 'this should be interesting.'

'I'm going to try very hard not to take your ear off,' she replied quietly, her voice barely audible above the crowd noise. 'But I make no promises.'

'That's comforting. How exactly did you get roped into this?' He watched as she fumbled slightly with the power cord, her hands not quite steady.

She plugged in the clippers, her jaw tight with tension. 'Elsie called me twenty minutes ago in a complete panic. Apparently, my reputation for grooming horses and dogs qualifies me as a hair professional. She caught me at the store and wouldn't take no for an answer.'

'And you agreed because...?'

'Because I'm an idiot who can't say no when it's for charity.' She held up the clippers and tested them briefly, the buzzing sound causing several students to cheer in anticipation. The vibration was loud and aggressive, and Dusty felt his resolve waver slightly. 'Plus she mentioned you'd be sitting here looking smug, and I thought someone should take you down a peg or two.'

'Ah, there's the Ella I remember. For a minute I thought you might actually be nice to me.'

'Don't get used to it. This is a temporary ceasefire for the good of cancer research.' But he caught the faintest hint of a smile at the corners of her mouth.

Elsie's voice came over the microphone again. 'Are we ready, everyone? On the count of three, let's begin this transformation! One... two... three!'

The hall erupted in cheers as the clippers came to life across the stage. Dusty felt the vibration against his scalp as Ella made the first pass, her touch surprisingly gentle despite her obvious discomfort with the situation. He'd expected her to be rough, almost vindictive, but instead her movements were careful and precise.

'You know,' he said, pitching his voice low enough that only she could hear over the noise of multiple clippers and the crowd's excitement, 'this is probably the longest conversation we've had since that night at the quiz.'

'I was hoping to keep it that way,' she replied.

He caught a slight note of levity in her voice, the tension easing fractionally. 'Why? What exactly is it about me that bothers you so much?' He genuinely wanted to know. The question had been eating at him for weeks.

She paused in her clipping, and he could feel her considering her answer, the silence stretching between them. 'You really want to know?'

'I really want to know.'

'You're not what I expected, and that annoys me more than it should.' The admission seemed to surprise her as much as it did him, the words coming out reluctantly, as though she hadn't meant to say them aloud.

'What did you expect?'

Another pass with the clippers, more hair falling to the stage floor in dark waves. He watched it accumulate around the chair legs, his hair mixing with the students' various colours. 'Someone shallow. Someone who'd be gone in a few weeks after making a quick dollar and leaving chaos behind. Someone like...' She stopped herself.

'Someone like who?'

'Someone I used to know. Someone who taught me to be more careful about judging people too quickly, except I seem to have learnt the wrong lesson.' She was talking more to herself now than to him.

'And instead you got...?'

'Someone who knows more about Saturn's moons than most people know about their own postcode. Someone who volunteers to get their head shaved for charity. Someone who fixes staging for school choirs and doesn't make a big deal about it. Someone who...' She trailed off, clearly regretting how much she'd revealed and how the words had poured out.

'Someone who what?' He kept his voice gentle, not wanting to spook her when she was finally opening up.

'Someone who makes me question my usually excellent judgment about people.' The words came out quietly, almost reluctantly, and his chest tightened.

She worked in silence for a few minutes while the crowd cheered and took photos around them. Parents were filming on their phones, and students were laughing and shouting encouragement to their friends. Dusty found himself oddly relaxed despite the surreal circumstances, perhaps because this was the most honest conversation they'd had. No barriers, no audience they were performing for, just the two of them caught in an uncomfortable situation and finally being real with each other.

'For what it's worth,' he said eventually, as she worked on the back of his head with careful precision, 'I had you figured wrong too.'

'How's that?' Her fingers brushed against his neck and he suppressed a shiver that had nothing to do with the temperature.

'I thought you were just another small-town girl who'd made up her mind about outsiders and wasn't interested in changing it. Someone stuck in their ways, unable to see past their own prejudices. Turns out you're more complicated than that.'

'Complicated. Is that supposed to be a compliment?' There was amusement in her voice now, the tension that had been there at the start dissolving.

'In my experience, the most interesting people usually are. Simple people are boring. You can figure them out in five minutes and then there's nothing left to discover.'

She made another careful pass with the clippers, her movements becoming more confident as she worked, finding a rhythm. 'Don't think this means we're friends now.'

'Wouldn't dream of it. Though I have to say, for someone who claims to hate me, you're being remarkably careful not to scalp me.' He tilted his head slightly as she worked around his ear, trusting her not to hurt him.

'The day is young.' But there was warmth in her voice

that hadn't been there before, a softness that suggested her walls were cracking.

Despite her threat, she continued working with professional precision, and Dusty found himself enjoying the unexpected intimacy of the moment. Her hands in his hair were oddly soothing, the gentle pressure of her fingers as she guided the clippers and the concentration he could sense in her movements creating a rhythm that relaxed him despite the situation. She smelled faintly of flowers, probably shampoo, and he found himself hyper-aware of every time she leaned closer or her arm brushed against his shoulder.

'There,' she said finally, stepping back and surveying her work with a critical eye. She tilted her head, checking for any spots she'd missed. 'You're officially bald.'

He reached up to run his hand over his newly smooth scalp, surprised by how different it felt. The skin was warm and unfamiliar, and he could feel every slight breeze. 'How do I look?'

'Like a criminal.' But her eyes were soft, and her expression suggested she wasn't entirely displeased with the result.

'Thanks for the confidence boost.'

'You asked.' Actually, it's not terrible. You've got the head shape for it. Some people look weird bald, but you... It suits you.'

The compliment, grudging as it was, made him smile. 'Was that a nice thing you just said to me?'

'Don't let it go to your head. Your newly bald head.' She was fighting a smile now, and he could see the battle between her determination to maintain distance and her natural inclination towards honesty.

The crowd cheered again as all six volunteers stood to display their new looks, arms around each other's shoulders, and Dusty found himself swept up in the enthusiasm despite his initial reluctance. Parents were taking photos, students were cheering, and there was a genuine feeling of community spirit that made the sacrifice feel worthwhile. The principal presented each of them with a certificate and asked for a round of applause, and he was surprised by how good it felt to be part of an event that mattered to the community, to have contributed in some small way.

As the formal part of the event concluded and people began mingling around the hall, students rushed the stage to take selfies with the newly bald volunteers. Dusty caught Ella's arm before she could disappear into the crowd. Her skin was warm under his fingers, and he felt her tense slightly at the contact before relaxing.

'Thank you,' he said seriously, holding her gaze. 'I know this wasn't exactly how you planned to spend your day. And I know you could have made this much more painful than you did.'

She looked down at his hand on her arm, then back up at his face, something unreadable in her eyes. 'You're welcome. Try not to scare any small children on your way home. Though I have to admit, it really does suit you. The whole tough guy look.'

'I'll do my best. Maybe I'll invest in some good hats. A beanie collection.'

'That would be wise.' She started to turn away, then paused, seeming to wrestle with her thoughts internally. 'Dusty?'

'Yeah?'

'For someone I'd decided to dislike, you're not completely terrible.' The words came out quickly, like she needed to say them before she lost her nerve.

Before he could respond or process what that admission meant, she slipped away into the crowd, leaving him standing there with a newly bald head and the unsettling realisation that Ella Patterson was definitely more complicated than he gave her credit for. And therefore, more interesting. And possibly, just possibly, she was starting to see him as someone other than the enemy.

He watched her disappear through the crowd, noting the way people greeted her warmly, the way she smiled at the students and how she congratulated them on their bravery. This was her community, her home, and he was still the outsider. But maybe, just maybe, that was starting to change.

CHAPTER 10

*E*lla swept the scattered hair into neat piles, trying not to think about how the dark strands had felt between her fingers or the way Dusty's scalp had been surprisingly warm to touch. The stage looked like a shearing shed after a busy day, with clumps of hair in various shades scattered across the wooden boards like strange confetti. She focused on the methodical work of cleaning up, grateful for the distraction from thoughts that had no business occupying her mind. Sweep, collect, dump in the bin bag. Repeat. The rhythm was soothing, mindless.

'That went better than I expected,' Elsie said, appearing beside her with a dustpan and brush, her earlier manic energy settling into satisfied exhaustion. 'You did a fantastic job on Dusty. Very professional. Tina couldn't have done better herself, and she's been cutting hair for twenty years.'

'It's not exactly rocket science. Clippers work the same way whether you're grooming a horse or a human.' Ella kept her tone deliberately casual, though she could feel heat creeping up her neck. The truth was, she'd been acutely aware of every moment during that haircut, from the way he'd sat perfectly still despite her obvious reluctance to the surprising gentleness in his voice when he thanked her. His shoulders had relaxed under her hands in a way that felt oddly intimate, and she admired his implicit trust in letting someone hold a buzzing blade that close to his head.

'He looked rather striking with the shaved head, didn't he?' Elsie's tone was innocent, but Ella recognised the speculative gleam in her friend's eyes and the way she was watching for a reaction.

Ella paused in her sweeping, considering her response carefully. Striking was definitely one word for it. Without the dark hair to soften his features, the strong lines of his jaw and cheekbones had become more pronounced, giving him an unexpectedly commanding presence. The olive tone of his skin had made the newly exposed scalp look healthy rather than pale, and his eyes seemed even more intense, framed by the stark simplicity of his bald head. He'd looked older somehow, more serious, and undeniably masculine in a way that caught her completely off guard. 'I suppose it suits him well enough,' she said finally, dumping another pile of hair into the bin bag. 'Better than I thought it would, anyway.'

'Better than you thought it would?' Elsie repeated with obvious amusement, a laugh bubbling just beneath the surface. 'That's high praise coming from you. I seem to remember Cass telling me you said he was a misogynistic dickhead.'

'Don't read too much into it. I just meant he doesn't

look ridiculous, which was my main concern. The last thing we needed was for our guest volunteer to look like he'd been attacked by a lawn mower.' Ella moved to the next section of stage, but she could feel Elsie's knowing smile even without looking at her and could sense her friend's delight at catching her off guard.

'Of course. Purely professional concern for the fundraiser's success.'

'Exactly.' Ella straightened up and fixed her friend with a warning look. 'Don't start getting ideas, Elsie. Just because I didn't accidentally scalp the man doesn't mean anything's changed.'

'I wouldn't dream of suggesting such a thing.' Elsie's voice was perfectly innocent, but her eyes were dancing with mischief. 'Though I did notice you two seemed to be having quite the conversation while you worked. Very intense. Very focused on each other.'

'We were being polite. For charity.' The words came out defensively, and she could see Elsie filing that information away for future reference, adding it to whatever mental dossier she was keeping about Ella's interactions with Dusty.

They worked in silence for a few minutes, collecting certificates and folding chairs while the hall gradually emptied around them. Students were still buzzing with excitement, parents were congratulating the volunteers, and there was a general atmosphere of goodwill and accomplishment. Ella found her thoughts drifting back to the moment when Dusty had run his hand over his newly smooth head, the gesture unconsciously confident despite his altered appearance. He'd looked almost vulnerable without the dark hair that usually fell across his forehead.

She'd glimpsed a different version of him, the real man beneath the easy charm and the builder's confidence.

'You know,' Elsie said eventually, breaking into her thoughts, 'I think today went better than anyone expected. The fundraising total was fantastic. We raised over eight thousand dollars, which is three times what we managed last year. The local businesses really went all out with their donations and everyone seemed to enjoy themselves.'

'It was a good turnout,' Ella agreed, grateful for the change of subject. 'The kids were brilliant.'

'And Dusty was a real sport about the whole thing. Not everyone would volunteer to have their head shaved by someone they barely know, especially in front of half the town. Particularly when that someone made it clear they didn't like them very much.'

Ella's hands stilled on the folding table she was dismantling. The comment hit closer to home than she cared to admit. The experience had felt oddly intimate, the simple act of cutting his hair creating a connection between them that hadn't existed before. 'He seemed to handle the attention well enough,' she said carefully, resuming her work on the table. 'I'm sure he's used to people looking at him.'

'What do you mean by that?' Elsie had stopped pretending to work and was watching her with open curiosity now.

Ella shrugged, though she could feel her cheeks warming again. 'Nothing specific. Just that he's the type of person who probably gets noticed wherever he goes. You know, confident, good-looking with the kind of presence that makes people turn their heads.'

'Interesting,' Elsie said slowly, and Ella could practically hear the gears turning in her friend's head. 'Very interesting indeed.'

'Don't,' Ella warned, pointing the folded table leg at her. 'Whatever you're thinking, just don't.'

'I'm not thinking anything.' But Elsie's smile was pure satisfaction, and Ella knew she'd revealed far more than she'd intended. The problem with having friends who knew you well was that they could read you like a book and see through every defence you tried to construct.

As they finished cleaning up and locked the hall behind them, Ella tried to convince herself that the burning sensation on her face had nothing to do with Dusty Camilleri and everything to do with the stifling heat of the afternoon. But the lie sat uncomfortably in her chest, and she knew that sleep would be difficult tonight, her mind replaying the feel of his hair between her fingers and the warmth in his eyes when he thanked her.

It was another couple of weeks before Ella saw Dusty again. She'd purposely avoided the pub and any other community events where she might risk running into him, turning down invitations with flimsy excuses that probably fooled no one. The surprising intimacy of the shaving moment had been far too unsettling for comfort.

Instead, she threw herself into work and managing her finances, meticulously reviewing her budget and savings to ensure everything was perfectly aligned for purchasing her dream property. She created spreadsheets, calculated deposit amounts, researched loan options, and generally did everything possible to prepare for the moment when the properties might become available. Phil, the real estate agent, had finally returned from his extended holiday in Thailand, sporting an impressive sunburn and a collection of stories about late night parties that no one wanted to hear. She gave him exactly two days to settle back into work mode before she started pestering him about the possibility of making private offers on both blocks before they hit the market. The anticipation was killing her, a constant low-level anxiety that made her restless and short-tempered. She knew patience was essential when dealing with property transactions in small towns though, so she held her breath and waited.

* * *

IT WAS the Friday before a long weekend, and the temperature climbed to thirty-six degrees by midday, turning the back area of Matfield Produce into a furnace. The corrugated iron roof radiated heat like a giant element, and even the industrial fans did little more than push hot air around. Ella was determinedly sorting through a delivery that had arrived that morning. There were bags of fertiliser that left her hands gritty and chemical-smelling, rolls of wire mesh that caught on everything, and assorted hardware that needed to be organised and stored before the heat made the work unbearable. Sweat ran down her back, soaking her shirt, and she'd already gone through two litres of water. Her parents had left for a long-awaited overseas holiday, leaving her and Tyson in charge of the store. It wasn't the first time she'd managed the business single-handedly, but with her brother concentrating on dealing with a broken water pump on his own property and some other work commitments, she had only her nephew, Liam, helping out after school and on weekends.

The sound of a vehicle pulling up on the grassy verge next door caught her attention, and she glanced up to see a familiar white ute parking on the vacant block adjacent to their property. A high timber fence separated the produce store from the empty lot, its boards weathered grey by years of sun and rain. Gaps between the boards provided clear sight lines for anyone curious enough to look. Ella recognised both the vehicle and the man who climbed out. He leaned back in to grab a baseball cap and pulled it down over his freshly shaved head as he looked around. The hair has started growing back, dark stubble covering his scalp.

That cap's going to be useless out there, she thought. He needs a proper wide-brimmed hat if he's planning to spend time in the sun. The practical concern was quickly pushed aside by a more pressing question. What the hell was he doing on that block?

His position meant he couldn't see her behind the fence, giving her a perfect vantage point to observe his movements without detection. She wasn't used to worrying about anyone being on the block. Occasionally a maintenance person would come and do some work, but there was often not much for them to do as her father kept it tidy. Now she watched with growing unease as Dusty began what could only be described as a systematic survey of the property.

He walked slowly around the entire perimeter first, his hands on his hips as he studied the boundaries and natural features. Then he paced from corner to corner, his steps measured and deliberate. He paused frequently to examine the gentle slope that rose towards the back of the lot, the established shade trees that marked the fence line, and the proximity to both the main street and her family's business. His movements were methodical and purposeful, like someone conducting a professional assessment rather than a casual exploration. He pulled out his phone at one point and seemed to be taking photos. He zoomed in on particular features, like the angle of the slope and the position of the trees.

Ella felt a growing sense of dread, her mouth going dry despite the water she'd been drinking all morning. Surely he couldn't be considering buying it. How could he possibly have learned that it might soon be available? The owners lived down south somewhere and rarely visited Matfield. They communicated only through their solicitor and the occasional phone call to Phil at the real estate office. The possibility of the land coming up for sale was still just speculation. It was insider knowledge based on Phil's discussions with some of his contacts. How would Dusty even know about it?

She crept closer to the fence, abandoning all pretence of working. Positioning herself behind a stack of hay bales she observed his movements through a wider gap in the boards. Dusty walked to the centre of the block and stood with his arms crossed, slowly turning in a complete circle as though visualising a scene she couldn't see. A building, maybe. A house. The way he studied the land suggested intimate familiarity with assessing sites for development. The realisation hit her hard, stealing her breath. Of course he would know how to evaluate property. He was a builder. This was probably second nature to him and an assessment he did automatically whenever he saw a vacant block.

The unfairness of it made her want to scream, to storm around the fence and demand to know what he was doing and what he was planning. Someone like him, from Melbourne, would have access to capital she could never dream of matching. Property prices in Matfield were laughably cheap compared to city standards, which meant he or his developer friends could probably buy multiple blocks without even needing a mortgage. They probably had savings from years of city investments, maybe family money, and connections to banks that would approve loans based on Melbourne assets. Meanwhile, she'd been scrimping and saving for years, calculating down to the last dollar to make her dream financially viable, sacrificing holidays, new clothes and anything that wasn't absolutely essential.

After spending nearly forty minutes walking every inch of the property, examining corners and testing the ground with his boot, Dusty returned to his ute and climbed into the driver's seat. Instead of leaving however, he pulled out his phone and began what appeared to be an intense conversation. Ella watched him gesture towards the block while speaking, his free hand moving expressively as he occasionally reached for a notepad to jot down information. The call lasted another thirty minutes, and she grew increasingly agitated with each passing moment, her fingernails digging into her palms.

By the time he finally drove away, leaving a cloud of red dust swirling in his wake, Ella was consumed with anxiety about what his interest in the property might mean for her own plans. Her heart was racing and her thoughts spiralled into worst-case scenarios. She tried to tell herself she was overreacting, that there could be dozens of innocent explanations for his presence on the block. Maybe he was just curious about the neighbourhood. Maybe he was considering recommending the site to someone else. Maybe he was simply enjoying the view from the elevated back section. Maybe this had nothing to do with buying the land at all.

But the systematic nature of his survey, together with the lengthy phone call suggested a motive far more serious than casual interest. The possibility that Dusty Camilleri might be working for someone who planned to buy her father's dream property was almost too devastating to contemplate, yet she couldn't dismiss it as paranoia. The timing was too coincidental, and his behaviour too purposeful for her fears to be entirely groundless. He'd been thorough, professional, exactly the way someone would act if they were seriously considering a purchase.

As she returned to sorting the morning's delivery, her movements were mechanical and distracted, her hands moving on autopilot while her mind raced. Every few minutes she glanced towards the vacant block, half expecting to see the white ute returning for another inspection. The afternoon stretched ahead under the weight of uncertainty, the heat pressing down on her like a physical force, and she knew that sleep would be elusive until she could find some way to discover the truth about Dusty's intentions.

The long weekend suddenly felt less like a break and more like an eternity of waiting for answers she might not want to hear.

CHAPTER 12

$\mathcal{E}$lla decided not to waste any more time, and the next morning she walked towards the real estate office at the far end of the main street. She strolled along the footpath, her wide-brimmed hat providing blessed relief from the sun that was already scorching at nine in the morning. The temperature gauge outside the bank read thirty-five degrees, and the forecast was for forty by midafternoon. It was going to be one of those killer days that made people question why anyone lived out here. She'd left Liam in charge of the store with strict instructions about handling the morning deliveries.

'I'll only be half an hour. Just ring me if you need anything.'

'I'm sure I can manage,' he replied sarcastically, throwing her an annoyed look that reminded her uncomfortably of herself at seventeen. The same stubborn set to his jaw, the same restless energy that came from feeling like life was happening somewhere else. She gave his arm a playful punch in response.

'Come on, don't be cranky. You should be happy it's a long weekend.'

'Yeah, something's got to be good about this place. No school for three days. That's reason enough to celebrate.' His voice carried that particular teenage bitterness that suggested he wasn't joking.

At seventeen, Liam was all elbows and attitude, his lanky frame stretched into the kind of height that suggested he'd inherited the Patterson genes for tallness and stubbornness. His sandy hair stuck up in multiple directions despite obvious attempts to tame it with gel, and his shirt was already rumpled even though the day had barely started. He had the kind of restless energy that came from feeling trapped in a town too small for his ambitions. Ella recognised the signs because she'd been exactly the same at his age, feeling the desperate need to escape, to prove herself somewhere that mattered, somewhere bigger and more important than Matfield.

'Speaking of school,' she said, unable to resist poking at the ongoing family drama that had her brother at his wits' end, 'your dad mentioned you've been talking about leaving again.'

His jaw tightened defensively, his whole body going rigid. 'Why shouldn't I? I'm seventeen. I could get a job. Start earning money instead of wasting time learning about books from a hundred years ago and algebra I'll never use. What's the point of any of it?'

'And do what? Stack shelves? Drive trucks? You're smart enough for university, Liam. Don't throw that away because you're bored.' She kept her voice gentle, remembering how defensive she'd been at his age when adults had tried to give her advice.

'University's just more school. More years of sitting in classrooms learning stuff that doesn't matter while everyone else gets on with real life.' His frustration was palpable, his hands clenching into fists at his sides. 'Besides, Dad left school at sixteen and he's done alright. He's got the property and his work here. He's got his life sorted.'

'Your dad also spent the next ten years wishing he'd finished school. Ask him sometime about the jobs he couldn't get and the courses he couldn't do, because he didn't have Year Twelve. Ask him about the opportunities he missed.' Ella fixed him with her most serious expression, the one that said she wasn't just lecturing but speaking from experience. 'You've got one year left. Stick it out. You can always decide what to do after that. But if you leave now, getting back on track is so much harder than you think.'

He shrugged with the kind of casual indifference that teenagers had perfected, but she'd caught the flicker of uncertainty in his eyes, the momentary crack in his defensive armour. The conversation was far from over, but she left it there for the morning, knowing that pushing too hard would only make him dig in deeper.

Thinking about his restlessness, she stopped to chat with Ernie and the other men who occupied their usual perch on the timber bench seat outside the pub. The morning ritual of the local patriarchs gathering to discuss weather, politics, and whoever happened to be passing by, was as reliable as the sunrise in Matfield. They'd been doing this for decades, this same group of men in this same spot, watching the town change around them.

'Morning, love,' Ernie greeted her, tipping his worn

Akubra hat with old-fashioned courtesy. 'You're up and about early for a Saturday.'

'Business to attend to,' she replied, settling into the comfortable rhythm of small-town pleasantries. These conversations followed a pattern, a dance everyone knew the steps to. 'How are you all bearing up in this heat?'

Another regular at the pub, Philly, replied, 'Could be worse.' His face had weathered to leather from a lifetime of sun damage that no amount of sunscreen could have prevented. 'At least there's a breeze today. Not much of one, but better than nothing.'

'Your mate Dusty's working in the back there this morning,' Ernie added, gesturing towards the pub with his coffee cup. Steam rose from it despite the heat, because Ernie drank his coffee hot, no matter the weather. 'Not sure why he's putting in hours on a Saturday when most sensible folk are taking it easy. I reckon his partner's due back next week though, so maybe that's it. Nice to see young blokes with such a solid work ethic.'

'Hmph.' The sound escaped before Ella could stop it, and she saw Ernie's eyebrows rise with interest. She should have left then, given her excuses and continued to the real estate office, but something kept her rooted to the spot. Curiosity, maybe, or the stubborn part of her that refused to be driven away by Dusty's presence. The part that had always resented being told what to do or where to go.

They talked for another ten minutes about the weather forecast, which predicted no relief for at least another week, and the upcoming harvest season, which would be terrible if they didn't get rain soon. But Ella found her attention drifting towards the pub's interior, wondering what kind of work was keeping him there on a weekend. What was so urgent that it couldn't wait until Monday? When the front door opened and Dusty emerged, she felt her breath catch. This happened despite her best efforts to remain indifferent, despite telling herself she didn't care what he looked like, or what he was doing.

He was covered in fine sawdust that clung to the dark fabric of his work shirt, turning it grey in patches, and his face gleamed with perspiration in the morning light. She noticed with grudging approval that the baseball cap he'd worn yesterday had been replaced by a proper wide-brimmed hat.

She nodded curtly in his direction, keeping her expression neutral. 'Morning.'

'Morning, Ella.' He approached their group with the easy smile that seemed to come naturally to him, though she caught the way his eyes lingered on her face a moment longer than strictly necessary. His expression held a question she couldn't quite read. An invitation, maybe, or just curiosity. He turned away for a moment and wiped his face with a cloth he took from his back pocket. When he turned back to her, his face carried a wide smile that made her chest tighten. 'Not working this morning?'

'Just taking a morning walk,' she replied, though the excuse sounded weak even to her own ears. No one took morning walks in this heat unless they had somewhere specific to go.

'Business or pleasure?'

'A bit of both. I need to sort out some family matters.' The words came out clipped but she couldn't quite bring herself to be friendlier. Not when the memory of him systematically surveying the block next door was still fresh in her mind.

He studied her for a moment, his look thoughtful, and she had the uncomfortable feeling he could read more in her expression than she wanted to reveal. 'Speaking of family business, do you stock galvanised bolts at the produce store? Eight mil diameter and about fifty mil long?'

The question caught her off guard with its practicality, pulling her out of her spiralling thoughts. 'We might. What do you need them for?'

'Securing some framework in the pub renovation. The hardware store has run out of that size, and I need them before we can continue with the next stage. Otherwise I'm looking at a trip to the nearest hardware, and in this heat I'd rather avoid the drive if possible.'

'We've got a decent selection of bolts and screws. Different gauges and lengths.' She responded automatically to the professional inquiry despite her determination to keep things cool between them. This was business, she told herself. Nothing personal about selling hardware. 'You'd have to come in and see what we've got.'

'I might do that later this morning, if that's alright. Save me a trip if you've got what I need.'

'The store's open until four today.' The words were polite but distant, her tone deliberately cool, and she saw him register the change. There was a flicker in his expression that might have been disappointment or confusion.

'Right then. I'll see you later, if you're around.'

She nodded without committing to anything, then excused herself to the gathered men before continuing on her way to the real estate office. As she walked away, she could feel Dusty's eyes on her back. She sensed his confusion at her coolness after what had felt like progress at the charity event, but she refused to turn around or alter her pace. Whatever game he was playing concerning the vacant block, she wasn't going to make it easy for him by being friendly or accommodating. The real estate office couldn't give her the answers she needed fast enough.

CHAPTER 13

She returned less than half an hour later, deflated and feeling like she'd taken twenty giant steps backwards. The walk back to the store seemed twice as long as it had taken that morning, her feet dragging against the footpath, the weight of disappointment physically pulling her down. Phil had been apologetic but devastatingly blunt, delivering news that shattered every carefully constructed plan she'd been nurturing forever.

'They're not selling,' Phil said, spreading his hands in a gesture of helpless finality. 'I couldn't speak to the owners directly, so I went through another mate in the business who's got connections with their solicitor down south. He's certain that neither property, that is the one next to your produce store or Pazhvak Station, is coming onto the market anytime soon. Believe me, if anyone could coerce owners into selling, it would be him. He's got a reputation for talking people into deals they never thought they'd make. This is a definite no, regardless of what you might offer them.'

'What?' The word had escaped as barely more than a whisper, her voice strangled by shock and disbelief. 'The block next to us and Pazhvak Station have sat there for decades without anyone paying them the slightest bit of attention. What's the point of that? Surely they'd want to get some return on their investment after all this time. I thought you indicated they were going to put them on the market and Dad and I would have a good chance of purchasing both of them.'

'Well, things have changed. You can't force someone to sell their land, Ella. My contact said the properties are held in a family trust, and the trustees are well aware that the blocks have been sitting empty for years. That doesn't mean they're ready to part with them.' Phil glanced at his watch with the kind of subtle impatience that suggested he had other appointments, but Ella was too stunned to take the hint.

She'd studied his expression carefully, her instincts telling her there was more to the story than his careful words were revealing. Phil Maloney had been handling real estate transactions in the district for over fifteen years, and she'd known him since primary school. She could tell when he was holding back information, and right now his reluctance to share what he knew was fairly obvious to her.

'There's more to this, isn't there, Phil? I know you, and you're not telling me everything.'

He shifted uncomfortably in his chair, avoiding her direct gaze. 'Well, there might be some movement on both those properties in the future. I thought that what I was seeing indicated their wish to sell, but it appears otherwise, or they may sell privately rather than going to the market. Apparently there have been enquiries made through the council offices. Whoever it is isn't from around here. The block next to your family's store is zoned commercial, so there are development possibilities that might interest certain parties. I'm not sure what the plans are for Pazhvak Station. I'll be honest, though, it appears there are plans for both of them. I haven't got any further information. I've pushed to find out more but I'd say it's being kept hushed up.'

The words hit her like a slap, and her anger bubbled. 'Are you trying to tell me that someone's planning to build some hideous commercial building on the block that my father has been maintaining for years without anyone asking him to? Why else would they try and keep the details quiet? And what would they want with the property out of town?'

'Look, I'm not saying anything definitive. I'm just telling you there's been some activity, some interest from parties who might have development plans. They usually keep it under wraps so that the locals don't jump up and down. They'll get their ducks in a row before they go public with whatever it is they have planned. I know that for certain.'

Ella straightened in her chair, her mind racing to connect dots she desperately hoped wouldn't form the pattern she was beginning to suspect. 'Would that interest happen to involve one of those builders from Melbourne? The ones working on the pub renovation?'

Phil's hesitation was answer enough, even before he cleared his throat and mumbled words about client confidentiality and not being able to discuss specific inquiries.

'I saw one of them walking over the block next to us

yesterday,' she pressed on, her voice growing sharper with each word. 'He was obviously assessing it for development. Someone's got plans for that land, and they've managed to get the owners interested when a local buyer couldn't.'

***

She walked out of his office fighting to maintain her composure, but inside she was seething with a mixture of anger and devastation, her hands shaking as she pushed open the glass door. How could this be happening? Just when she was ready to purchase the property out of town, after saving every spare dollar and planning every detail of the house she wanted to build, someone else had simply walked in and claimed her future.

The unfairness of it was staggering. Not only had her dream just been destroyed but also her father's. The block next to the produce store had been part of their daily landscape for as long as she could remember. In between the irregular maintenance visits from an outside contractor, her father had mowed it and kept it presentable out of nothing but neighbourly consideration. He had never asked for anything in return and had always let it be known that, if it ever came on the market, he wanted to know. Now some outsider was going to swoop in and build God knows what commercial monstrosity, probably some ugly shed or cheap shopfront that would destroy the character of the main street.

And what was going to happen to Pazhvak Station? The place where she'd planned to build her dream house with the verandah and views across the valley? That was apparently also out of reach, obviously destined for some other purpose.

As she approached the produce store, she could see Liam through the front windows, leaning against the counter with his phone in his hands, probably texting friends about weekend plans. The sight of his casual indifference to the family business that had been her refuge and her anchor suddenly irritated her beyond measure. Here she was, fighting to secure a future in this town, while he couldn't wait to escape it. The irony was bitter enough to taste.

She pushed through the front door, causing the old bell to clang against the doorframe. Liam looked up from his phone with mild curiosity, clearly unprepared for the storm clouds gathering on his aunt's face.

'How did it go?' he asked, though his attention was already drifting back to his screen.

'It didn't,' she replied curtly, not trusting herself to elaborate without unleashing a tirade that would accomplish nothing except frightening her nephew and confirming her reputation as the family member with the shortest temper.

She moved through the store towards the back office, needing space to process what she'd learned and decide what, if anything, she could do about it. The dream of owning her own piece of Matfield seemed to be slipping away, just as surely as her revised assumptions about Dusty Camilleri and his reasons for being in town. If he were indeed involved in whatever development plans were brewing for the commercial block, then every interaction they'd had took on a different meaning. His presence at community events, his easy charm with the locals, even his willingness to shave his head for charity, suddenly looked different. Less like genuine community spirit and more like a calculated campaign to win over potential critics of whatever project he and his developer mates were planning.

CHAPTER 14

*S*itting in his ute in the customer car park had given Dusty a clear view of the vacant block next door to Ella's family store, and he found himself mentally cataloguing details he'd noticed during his previous inspection. There was a gentle slope that would be perfect for drainage, established shade trees along the back boundary, and proximity to the town centre that would make any construction project highly visible to the community.

Running his hand over his newly smooth scalp, he wiped his face with a clean rag and adjusted his wide-brimmed hat. At least he could try to look presentable when he encountered Ella. She continued to intrigue him. It was a feeling that went beyond the obvious physical attraction, or even their shared interest in astronomy. She was defensive and frequently short with him, but when she thought he wasn't paying attention, he caught glimpses of something more. Sharp intelligence and genuine passion for her community suggested there were depths behind the guarded front she maintained.

The bell above the front door chimed as he entered the store, but instead of Ella behind the counter, a tall, sandy-haired young man looked up from a stock list he'd been checking. The teenager straightened up with the kind of eager professionalism that suggested he was trying to make a good impression.

'G'day. I'm Liam,' he said, extending his hand across the counter with a firm grip that spoke well of his upbringing. 'What can I do for you?'

Confident for someone his age, Dusty thought. 'I'm Dusty. Good to meet you, mate.' He was genuinely impressed by the youngster's manners and direct approach. 'I'm working on the pub renovation. and after some galvanised bolts. I spoke to Ella about them this morning.'

'She's my aunt,' Liam said with obvious pride. 'Dad's her brother.'

'Right. She thought you might be able to help me out.'

Dusty pulled a folded piece of paper from his pocket, containing a handwritten list of the hardware specifications he needed. 'The local hardware store is all out of these sizes, but Ella suggested you might stock them.'

' Ella's out doing deliveries. Yeah, we try to cover what the hardware store usually runs short on. Too far to travel if we don't have what people need.' Liam studied the list with the kind of focused attention that suggested he knew his way around the inventory. 'I reckon I've got everything on here. Follow me. I saw you get your head shaved at the school. Great cause.'

As they moved through the store, Dusty's eyes roamed

over the impressive range of stock crammed into the available space. Rows of animal feed in various formulations lined one wall, while agricultural supplies, farming implements, and hardware filled every available corner. Despite the sheer volume of merchandise, everything was organised and clearly labelled, suggesting someone with an eye for efficiency was managing the operation.

'Fantastic setup you've got here,' he observed, genuinely impressed by the scope of the inventory. 'You certainly cover all the bases for rural supplies. I love the old frontage that's been kept. I felt like I was walking back in time when I came in.'

'Yeah, it's been in the family for generations. Lot of history to this place. We try and keep everything the townspeople and farmers need, as well as some hardware and building supplies. Have to out here. Too far to go anywhere else if we don't stock what people need.' Liam began pulling items from various shelves, checking each against the written specifications. 'We carry a massive amount of stock for a town this size. Ella does all the ordering and bookwork, as well as working the floor. Thank goodness she came back when she did, because Grandpa and Nan are getting on and need the help.'

'And you work here full-time as well?'

'No, just when I can or when I'm needed. I'm still at school, but I want to leave.' The words came out with the kind of frustrated intensity that suggested this was a recurring source of conflict. 'I hate school. I'd rather work here, or if I could manage it, I'd leave town and get an apprenticeship. I want to do what you do. Carpentry and building.'

Dusty's attention sharpened immediately. 'That's how I

started out. Carpentry at first, then I moved into broader building work once I got my licence. You can't go wrong with those skills, mate. There's so much demand, you'll always be busy.' He paused, considering the obvious problem. 'I'm guessing there's no chance of a local builder taking you on here?'

'None. There aren't any builders in Matfield at the moment, and the nearest towns don't have much either. All our tradies come from the larger regional centres or the city. There's nothing here for someone like me.'

The disappointment was written clearly across Liam's face, and Dusty recognised the expression from his own teenage years when university had felt like a prison sentence and practical work had seemed impossibly out of reach. The kid was obviously ready to learn tangible skills that would challenge his hands as well as his mind.

He paid for the supplies and accepted the cardboard box Liam had packed with his order. As he prepared to leave, an idea struck him.

'Tell you what, mate. Why don't we work out some kind of arrangement while Eli and I are here? Some work experience, maybe even paid work if you prove yourself. I reckon we'll be on the pub job for at least six months, and Oscar's already talking about other renovations for his house and the upstairs section of the pub.

Liam's eyes lit up, and he straightened to his full height with barely contained excitement. 'Are you serious? I'd work any hours you want. I'll do anything you need. Lifting, carrying, stacking, labouring. Whatever you want me to do.'

'Look, I can't guarantee a formal apprenticeship because we're just not sure how long we'll be in town, but we could certainly give you some real experience while we're here. See if you actually like the work as much as you think you will.'

The enthusiasm radiating from the teenager was infectious, and Dusty found himself genuinely excited about the prospect of having an eager student to work with. Eli would probably appreciate the extra pair of hands as well, once he returned.

'I could ring Dad right now and ask him,' Liam said, already reaching for his mobile phone. 'There's not much happening at school anyway. All my assessments are finished for the term.'

'Might be worth checking what the school situation is first,' Dusty suggested. 'Make sure you're not going to get yourself into trouble for non-attendance.'

Liam was already ringing, his face flushed with excitement. When his father answered, he put the phone on speaker and launched into an explanation that tumbled out in a rush of barely controlled enthusiasm.

'Dad, it's me. You know that builder I mentioned, the one working on the pub? He's here at the store, and he's offered me some work experience. Maybe even paid work if I can prove myself. Can I do it? Please?'

'Slow down, son.' Tyson's voice came through the phone speaker with the patient tone of a father accustomed to his teenager's enthusiasms. 'Let me talk to this builder first.'

Dusty introduced himself and explained the situation more succinctly than Liam had managed, outlining his background, the scope of work they were doing in Matfield, and his impression of Liam's suitability for learning basic construction skills.

'I appreciate the offer,' Tyson said thoughtfully. 'Liam's been talking about leaving school and getting into a trade for months now. His mother and I have been trying to convince him to finish Year Twelve first, but maybe some real work experience would help him understand what he's really signing up for.'

'That's exactly what I was thinking,' Dusty agreed. 'Better to find out now whether he's got the temperament and physical capacity for this kind of work, rather than starting a formal apprenticeship and discovering it's not what he expected.'

'How would this work practically? He's still got school until the term ends.'

'We could start with two weeks while school's still on, working around his class schedule. Then he'd have the two-week holidays to really get stuck into it full-time. After that, we'd reassess based on how he's handled the work and whether the school's willing to arrange some kind of work placement program. We may have other work here in town after the pub. Not one hundred percent sure yet but it's looking that way.'

There was a pause while Tyson considered the proposal. 'And you'd be willing to pay him?'

'If he proves he's worth it, absolutely. I'm not looking for free labour, but I also need to know he's serious about learning rather than just trying to get out of school.'

'Fair enough. Liam, what do you think about starting slowly while you're still at school?'

'I think it's perfect, Dad. I can handle both. I promise I won't miss any classes, even though there's not much happening now that assessments are finished.'

Another pause, then Tyson's voice came through with

the tone of a father making a decision he hoped he wouldn't regret. 'Alright then. Let's give it a try. I'll contact the school on Monday and see what we can arrange.. Two weeks to start with, then we'll see how the holidays go.'

'Thanks, Dad!' Liam's grin was wide enough to split his face. 'You won't regret this.'

'I hope not, son. Dusty, I appreciate you taking an interest in Liam. He's a good kid, but he needs some direction that school doesn't seem to be providing.'

'No worries at all. I think he's got real potential, and we can certainly use the extra hands on the project.'

After they ended the call, Liam was practically vibrating with excitement, already asking questions about what kind of work they'd start him on and what tools he'd need to bring. Dusty found himself caught up in the young man's enthusiasm, remembering his own relief when he'd finally found work that engaged both his mind and his body.

As he put the box of supplies on the back seat of his ute, he reflected on the unexpected turn the day had taken. He'd come to the store looking for hardware and ended up giving a young fella a career to aim for. It felt good to be in a position to offer real opportunities, especially to someone who clearly had the motivation to make the most of them.

CHAPTER 15

$\mathcal{E}$lla noted that the car park outside the store was empty when she returned from her deliveries, the gravel spaces vacant except for the usual scatter of eucalyptus leaves blown down by the afternoon breeze. As much as she told herself she had no desire to encounter Dusty again, there was an irritating flutter of disappointment at the absence of his white ute. She gave herself a sharp mental shake, annoyed by her own contradictory impulses. The man was trouble. He was too charming, too helpful, and apparently about to become part of whatever development scheme was planned for the block that should have been her family's opportunity to expand their business and contribute a meaningful addition to the community. He was probably employed by some large development conglomerate who were only interested in exploiting the town to make a profit. Surely there were plenty of other places they could have found. Why Matfield?

She knew about the ridiculous cost of property in the

cities and how developers were looking further afield to capitalise on the significantly lower prices in regional places. 'Bloody city opportunists,' she muttered under her breath, hauling her delivery receipts from the passenger seat. The afternoon heat was becoming oppressive, and she was looking forward to the cooler relief of the store's interior when Liam's face appeared at the driver's side window, wearing a wide grin.

He rapped on the glass with his knuckles, then practically launched himself into the air, clicking his heels together. The display of enthusiasm made her wonder if someone had slipped caffeine into the town's water supply.

'What's gotten into you?' she asked, stepping out into the furnace-like heat. 'Did the Education Department declare an unexpected holiday or something?'

Standing beside him in the shade cast by the ute, she was struck again by how much he resembled her brother Tyson at that age. He was all gangly limbs, restless energy, and desperate to shed the constraints of adolescence and join the adult world. The resemblance was so strong it sometimes took her breath away.

'I haven't seen you this excited since that girl from Rockhampton smiled at you at the agricultural show,' she observed.

'Guess what,' he said, batting his eyelashes at her with theatrical enthusiasm. 'Just guess what happened while you were out.'

'I don't know. Did that same girl finally agree to go out with you?'

'Nope.'

'You won a million dollars in the lottery?'

'Nope.'

She shook her head, already feeling perspiration gathering at her hairline despite the vehicle's shade. 'I give up. What's happened that's got you acting like you've won the Melbourne Cup? Tell me before we both melt into puddles out here.'

He grabbed her arm and tugged her towards the shade, his excitement practically radiating off him in waves. 'You'll never believe it. Remember that builder, Dusty? The one you told to come in for those bolts?'

'Yes. So, what's up?'

'Well, we got talking after I found everything he needed, and he's offered me paid work experience. Real construction work, Ella. Maybe even the chance for a permanent job if I prove myself capable.'

'What?' The word escaped before she could moderate her tone. 'But what about your education? Your father will have an absolute fit about this.'

'Actually, I think Dad's finally accepted how serious I am about leaving school and getting into a trade. Dusty spoke to him directly over the phone, and they seemed to get along really well. Dad's agreed to let me try it, as long as the school approves the arrangement, which they should since all my assessments are finished for the term.'

She pulled a face that clearly communicated her scepticism, and watched Liam's expression deflate like a punctured football. 'I thought you of all people would understand what this means to me.' He paused, his excitement dimming. 'Why have you got that look on your face like this is a bad idea. This is an opportunity I never imagined would be possible here in Matfield.'

'And what happens when they pack up and head back

to Melbourne? They're city people, Liam. I imagine they're only here to extract what profit they can before returning to whatever comfortable urban lifestyle they're accustomed to. Do you honestly think they plan to stay long enough for you to learn anything much?'

'Crikey, Ella. I had no idea you were so quick to judge people.' His tone carried a note of hurt and her chest tightened with guilt. 'How can you be so certain about their characters when you barely know them? Dusty seems like a genuinely decent bloke, and look at everything he's already contributed to the community. He was telling me about a playground project he's planning to donate his time to once Eli returns. For the kindergarten. Completely free labour. And he hinted they might have more work on the go after the pub work is done. A new construction project, not reno work. A bigger build than what they're doing now.'

'Really. How interesting.' What Phil had said this morning about them getting their ducks in a row, came to mind. 'Do you really believe he's that selfless and doing all this other work out of goodwill?' She crossed her arms defensively. 'I'd wager there's an ulterior motive behind all this community spirit. I saw him surveying the vacant block next door recently, and the real estate agent confirmed there's development interest in the property. He's obviously involved in whatever commercial project is planned for that site, and it will probably be some hideous industrial building that completely destroys the character of our main street. There'll be a big development company behind it all for sure. Poor Dad has been hoping to purchase that block for years to create the men's shed project. Now there's no possibility of that happening because city developers with deep pockets will be swooping in to capitalise on our cheap land prices.'

Liam shook his head and turned away, walking back towards the store entrance with slumped shoulders. 'You can think whatever you want about his motives. I'm sorry I bothered sharing this news with you.'

She caught up to him in a few quick strides, guilt overriding her suspicion. 'Look, Liam, I do think it's a valuable opportunity for you, and I'm genuinely pleased you've found a career path that interests you this much. But please don't sacrifice your education based on promises that might not materialise. This arrangement will eventually end, and then what will your options be?'

'Who knows? But at least I'll have gained practical experience and learned whether I actually enjoy this kind of work. And if they do return to Melbourne, maybe I'll consider going with them.' His voice carried a challenging edge. 'Just because city life and university didn't work out for you doesn't mean I'm doomed to the same fate. You chose to leave your degree program. How is me leaving school any different from your decision to abandon your career?'

The comparison stung because it contained enough truth to be uncomfortable. She reached out and gently squeezed his arm, feeling the wiry strength that came from years of farm work and weekend labour around the store. 'Alright. I'm going to try to be happy for you and supportive of this opportunity. Make the most of it and learn everything you can. I just think this Dusty character is presenting himself as too perfect to be true. Don't trust either of them completely. Keep your instincts sharp and your guard up.'

He leaned down and enveloped her in a hug that smelled of hay dust and teenage optimism. 'Thanks, Ella. Your support means a lot to me, even if it's only given grudgingly.'

She watched him practically dance towards the back of the building, calling out that he was going to reorganise the hay bale storage area in celebration. As she observed his enthusiastic progress, she couldn't completely suppress a surge of happiness for him. His excitement was infectious, and she genuinely hoped it would be a good opportunity for him, despite her reservations. But there was definitely something suspicious about these two builders and their apparently selfless involvement in community projects. The timing was too convenient, their generosity too comprehensive, and their integration into local life too seamless for her comfort.

The whole situation felt calculated rather than spontaneous, and she planned to monitor every aspect of their activities, with particular attention to Dusty's movements. If he was planning to help some big developer transform their main street into a commercial nightmare, she was going to gather enough evidence to rally community opposition before any irreversible damage was done.

Her instincts told her that Dusty Camilleri was not the unselfish community benefactor he appeared to be, and she trusted her instincts more than his charming smile and apparent generosity. Time would reveal his true intentions, and she planned to be watching when it did.

CHAPTER 16

Another month passed, and Ella mastered the art of avoiding Dusty. The moment she spotted his white ute in the car park, she'd vanish into the back office, or suddenly remember urgent stock that needed checking in the shed. She'd send Tyson out to serve him while she found other important work to do elsewhere. Eli still wasn't back from Melbourne, and word around town was that family issues were keeping Eli away longer than expected. What really got under her skin was how relaxed Oscar seemed about the whole thing when she asked him about the delays.

'Your nephew's doing a bloody good job though,' Oscar had said, leaning against the counter while she packed his weekly order. 'Only been at it four weeks and Dusty reckons Liam's one of the best workers he's ever had. He's talking about making it official. An apprenticeship.'

Ella stopped shoving things into the bag. 'What? Liam never said anything to me about that. I saw him on the weekend. How's that going to work when they pack up and go back to the city?'

'Apparently they'll work it out. Dusty's hinting they might be sticking around a lot longer than expected. Some other work. A big project. Sounds like they could be here for quite a while.'

She made a sound somewhere between a grunt and a sigh. 'There's definitely movement with that block next door. Dad'll be furious because we've been eyeing it off for years and I was finally getting somewhere with trying to buy it for the men's shed. Now some city developer has got other plans. You hear anything about what they want to build?'

'Nah, nothing specific. But it was bound to happen eventually. Council's very hush-hush about it at the moment. Block's been sitting there doing nothing for decades.'

The way Oscar brushed off her family's disappointment left a sour taste in her mouth, but she tried to push her feelings aside and kept packing his supplies. The second his ute disappeared, she let her smile drop. Trouble was brewing, and every instinct told her Dusty was right in the middle of it.

* * *

MEANWHILE, Dusty was discovering that training Liam Patterson was one of the most rewarding parts of his job. The kid soaked up everything like a sponge, asked smart questions, and attacked every task like his life depended on it. Liam's years of hauling stock at the family store had made him strong, and his frustration with school left him hungry to learn skills that actually mattered to him.

'You're picking this up faster than blokes I've seen with six months under their belts,' Dusty told him as they cleaned up at the end of another solid day's work. 'I'm impressed, mate.'

Liam tried to play it cool, but his grin gave him away. 'Doesn't feel like work when you want to be there. Thanks for taking a chance on me, Dusty. You didn't have to.'

'It's working out for both of us. And speaking of working out, all your apprenticeship paperwork came through today. You're officially a first-year carpentry apprentice now.' He pulled the papers from his toolbox and handed them over. 'Congratulations. This is the real deal now.'

Getting through all the government forms and bureaucratic rubbish had taken weeks, but seeing Liam's face when he held those official documents made every phone call worth it. The kid deserved this chance, and it felt good to be able to give it to him.

'What happens when you and Eli head back to Melbourne?' Liam asked as he read through his apprenticeship papers.

'That's the thing. We might not be heading back anytime soon. There're a couple of small jobs and then another big job lined up right here in Matfield. Between that and finishing everything Oscar wants done, we could be looking at a year and a half, maybe more.'

He didn't go into details about the second job. Partly because the contracts weren't signed yet, and partly because he didn't want the community to know what was planned until it was official.

After Liam headed home with his papers, Dusty climbed into his ute and drove out of town. This afternoon he was going to have another look at a second property. The block of about one thousand acres was five kilometres out and on a rise with views towards the hills to the west. It was big enough for a decent house and workshop and far enough out for some privacy.

The idea of staying in Matfield permanently had been growing stronger every week. Every time Eli called from Melbourne and talked about the traffic, the noise, the people rushing around like ants, Dusty felt his chest tighten. The city that used to energise him now felt like a cage. Out here, everything moved at a pace that made sense. People had time to talk. Work felt like it mattered.

But settling down out here meant more than just a change of address. It meant becoming part of a community where everyone knew everyone, along with your business. It meant dealing with people like Ella Patterson on a permanent basis instead of just until the job was finished.

Ella. She was still a puzzle he couldn't solve. The woman seemed convinced he was some sort of con artist who'd come to fleece the locals and disappear. Never mind that he'd been nothing but helpful since the day he arrived. Never mind that he was training her nephew and giving him opportunities that wouldn't exist otherwise. She'd made up her mind about him, and nothing he did seemed to change it.

Maybe she'd have even more reason to dislike him when the plans for the block next to her store became public. The development was exactly what Matfield needed. But change always upset someone, and he was aware her family had been planning to buy that land for their own purposes.

He turned off the sealed road onto the gravel track that led to the property he was visiting. The sun was starting to move towards the horizon, throwing long shadows across the empty paddock. In the distance, he could see the rusty old windmill and the fence where the property started. Beyond that, the paddocks were painted a golden rusty colour. A line of bushes marked what would become a small creek in rainy times. Low hills on the horizon were tinged with the darkening late afternoon light and he walked more quickly, making sure he could get to where he wanted and back before the sun set.

Parking beside a fence post, he got out to walk across the paddocks nearby. The land felt right under his feet. Solid. Permanent. The kind of place where a man could build a structure that would last. The question was whether he had the guts to burn his bridges in Melbourne and bet everything on a future in a town that was miles from anywhere and the complete opposite of where he had always lived.

CHAPTER 17

The sun was sliding down the western sky when Ella stopped beneath the eucalyptus trees that bordered the area where she'd parked her ute. The pale green leaves hung limp and dusty, pointing towards the parched ground with the defeated look of vegetation enduring another rainless week. A few white blossoms drifted down. She held out her palm to catch them before they hit the dirt, their delicate petals already browning at the edges from the heat. Everything was dry and rain was desperately needed. The weather bureau kept promising it, showing rain projection patterns on their maps, but the sky offered only clouds that darkened, hung teasingly, but then disappeared with no relief.

Behind the tall trees lay the remains of a dwelling that had once housed the owners. That had been over fifty years ago now. Sometimes the old-timers would talk about how the family had simply packed up and vanished without saying goodbye or leaving word of where they had gone. The stories about their sudden departure varied wildly depending on who was telling them and how much they'd had to drink. Some claimed that although the family's first child was a boy, their second child, a girl, had died from neglect because foreigners like them only valued sons over daughters. Others whispered that the woman was one of them camel-people, not Christian, not white, and nothing good comes of that sort of thing. The ugly prejudice of the past, she thought, still lingered in some people's memories.

After a long walk on Pazhvak Station about six months ago, Ella had questioned her father about what he remembered. He told her he only vaguely recalled the family from his own childhood but his recollection was different to the gossipy stories she had heard. 'I only remember because the man occasionally called into the store for supplies, and he always had a boy with him. Same age as me probably, maybe a bit younger. But he didn't go to school. My dad said they taught him at home.'

She had pressed him for more details once, curious about the mystery. 'Some of the older residents said there was a young boy and a girl who died when she was only a baby.'

'I never saw a baby and I never saw the mother. The father looked European, and the boy was dark-skinned. He always smiled at me though. I remember that smile. He was shy but friendly. Dad gave us both a lolly once. We just stood there sucking on them, staring at each other like kids do. The boy's father sort of prompted him to say thank you in English, which he did. He was very polite and seemed happy, probably because he'd just got a lolly.'

'So why did they move away? And why has that property stayed unused all these years?'

'Not sure. Different times back then. There were quite a few European families who tried to make a go of those smaller properties after the war. Would've been tough unless you were used to the conditions out here. The heat, the isolation, the way the land fights you at every step.'

'And probably no one ever helped them either? Not like all the established families who'd been here for generations and looked after each other?' Ella had felt anger rising in her chest, thinking about how hard it must have been.

Her father had looked thoughtful, his face settling into the serious expression he got when confronting uncomfortable truths. 'You're right. It was pretty racist back then, I guess. You have to remember it was only about twenty years after the war. Locals were suspicious of anyone who looked foreign, or spoke with an accent. It wasn't right, but that's how it was.'

'They wouldn't have wanted to live in Melbourne then. Multiculturalism personified. Every nationality you could think of. It's what I loved about the place, especially after growing up here where everyone's the same.' She meant it too. The diversity of Melbourne had been one of the best parts of moving away. She had loved the way you could walk down one street and hear five different languages, or smell the cooking aromas from a dozen different cultures.

'Now Ella, don't get on your high horse. We only knew what we were taught and what we grew up with. And not everyone thought like that. Plenty of people in town hired the man for work, and I know Elaine at the bakery said she always wrapped up an extra loaf of bread and a sweet slice for the family.' He paused to think. 'Being from a different place was tough, I guess. It's an issue we've never had to deal with. Thank God for the food all these different nationalities brought with them though. We don't really have much to offer except the old basic meat pie and lamingtons to claim as our heritage.'

She smiled. 'That reminds me of all the amazing places to eat in the cities. My last night in Melbourne, my friends took me to an incredible Italian restaurant near where I was living. The old Nonna was in the kitchen and the grandad out the back, pouring drinks.' She stopped talking and thought back to those moments. 'It was a real family operation, three generations working together.'

Her father interrupted. 'Oh, I can almost smell the food cooking. It's a long time since your mother and I went to places like that.'

'You'll have to take Mum to an Italian restaurant when you go overseas. Not long to go now Dad. You and mum really deserve a break, and you haven't been overseas in years. It's great to travel to different places. Although I wouldn't like to live back in Melbourne, my memories are precious. Just like that night. We had so much fun. The Nonna got talking to us and said when she arrived in the fifties everyone called them dagos and made jokes about their spaghetti. Now she reckons everyone loves spaghetti and half the country wishes they were Italian.'

He laughed, the sound warm and genuine. 'How true. The food, the wine, their passion for life. So many Europeans came out after the war. Part of our history now. I reckon that's where this man might have come from, the father of that boy. He looked Italian or maybe Greek. That's what people said after they left. He was a European immigrant who arrived after World War Two, but never truly understood how to manage Australian conditions.

When the drought hit and stretched on for months, they simply lacked the knowledge and resilience to weather it.'

Ella tended to believe the story she'd heard from her grandmother before she passed, that there had been a child's death, and the family couldn't bear to remain in the place they blamed for their loss. That made more sense to her and felt more human than stories about not understanding the land. Whatever the truth, they'd never returned or tried to sell. No one was sent to properly check the property and the place had been left to decay, only occasionally maintained and forgotten by everyone except the locals, who occasionally wondered what would become of it.

Dry grass stretched across paddocks where cattle had once grazed, now nothing but brittle stalks that crackled underfoot and created perfect fuel for bushfires. Heat shimmers rose from the baked earth, distorting the view of distant hills into wavering mirages. The fence posts were grey and weathered, connected by wire that sagged between them like the remainder of abandoned spiderwebs.

Despite the desolation, she loved this place. She often parked under these same trees and imagined where she would build her dream home. Nothing grand or pretentious, just a solid timber house with large windows to let in the morning light. A kitchen where she could see out across the valley while she cooked. A verandah where she could sit with her coffee at dawn and watch the valley wake up below, the mist rising from the gullies, the kangaroos moving through the paddocks. A place that would be entirely hers.

Today she wore her heavy walking boots because the

warmer weather meant snakes would be active and seeking out whatever moisture they could find. Toting her small backpack, she wanted to explore further down towards what was usually a creek, though it would certainly be dry now. If this property was also going to be developed or remain forever locked away by absent owners, she needed one last proper look at it and a chance to say goodbye to a dream that was slipping away. A heavy feeling settled in her chest at the thought. If she couldn't build her home out here, she'd have to start over with completely different plans.

Her boots scuffed through the brittle grass as she walked, stirring up dust that caught in her throat and made her cough. Above her, a wedge-tailed eagle circled lazily on thermal currents, scanning for unwary rabbits or lizards foolish enough to move in the heat. Two kangaroos watched her approach their shady resting spot behind a cluster of mallee scrub. Their ears swivelled to track her movement, before they bounded away with fluid leaps that carried them over a collapsed fence and a pile of rotting timber that had been there since she was a child. Such a waste, she thought, anger mixing with sadness. What was the point of owning property if you just abandoned it to rot? What was the point of holding onto land you'd never use, never visit, or care for?

She walked for nearly an hour, stopping occasionally to peer out from under her wide-brimmed hat and survey the landscape. It really was remarkable country, with gentle hills rolling north towards another road that formed the property's side boundary. In the distance she saw the top of the old windmill that was on the fenceline, its blades still and rusted from decades of no use. Even though everything was rotting, rusty or fallen down, the bones of a good property were still there, waiting for someone to recognise them.

She hadn't ventured this far in years, and she shielded her eyes against the glare to study the terrain more carefully. She was grateful for her heavy boots, denim shorts, and the long-sleeved pink shirt that protected her arms from the sun. The heat was still fierce, that dry furnace heat that sucked moisture from everything, and she paused to drink from her water bottle. The water was warm, almost hot, but she drained half of it anyway.

Movement in the bushes that lined the dry creek bed caught her attention, making her freeze mid-sip. Someone was walking along the gully, their progress barely visible through the scrub and fallen branches. She froze, suddenly aware that she was completely alone and a long way from help. She'd never encountered another person out here in all the years she'd been coming, and her mind immediately went to stories of transients camping wherever they could find isolation and of men hiding from the law, or running from debts. Before she could decide whether to retreat or call out, the figure emerged from the vegetation, ducking under low branches before straightening up on the creek bank and readjusting his backpack.

When he removed his hat and looked directly at her, she felt her stomach drop. It was Dusty.

For a moment they simply stared at each other across the dry paddock, both clearly as surprised by the encounter as the other. He was dressed for serious bush-walking in sturdy boots, long pants despite the heat, and a shirt with the sleeves rolled up to reveal his tanned forearms. A wide-brimmed hat dangled from his hand, and his face was flushed from exertion and heat, his short hair damp with sweat. Without his usual cap or the distraction of work, she could see the strong lines of his jaw more clearly and the hair that had grown since his head had been shaved. He stared at her with such intensity that she wanted to look away, but somehow couldn't. The sight of him in this place, her private sanctuary where she came to dream about her future, felt like an intrusion she couldn't quite put into words. Like he'd violated sacred ground.

'Ella.' He said her name like a statement rather than a greeting.

'What are you doing here?' The words came out sharper than she'd intended, but she was too rattled to moderate her tone.

He started walking towards her, his movements careful on the uneven ground, testing each step before committing his weight. 'Same thing you are, I'd guess. Walking. Having a look around. Appreciating the country.'

'This is private property. You're trespassing.' She stood her ground, refusing to step back even though every instinct told her to put more distance between them.

'So are you.' His response was mild, but she caught the slight smile that accompanied it, that infuriating amusement that suggested he found her defensive anger entertaining.

She felt heat rise in her cheeks that had nothing to do with the sun beating down on them. 'I've been coming here for years. Everyone knows this place is abandoned. It's practically public land at this point.' She stood up taller, squaring her shoulders. 'I had thought that one day it might be up for sale and there could be the possibility of buying it and turning it into what it should be. What it deserves to be.'

'That doesn't make it any the less private property.' He'd closed half the distance between them now, and she could see the perspiration on his forehead, the dust on his clothes and the way his shirt clung to his shoulders and chest. 'Though I'm not here to cause trouble for anyone. Not here to report you to anyone for trespassing.'

'Then why are you here?' She crossed her arms defensively. 'Doing a bit more surveying for your friends' development plans? Taking measurements? Making notes about how you can carve this place up into residential lots?'

His eyebrows rose slightly. 'Development plans?'

'Don't play innocent with me. I know you've been looking at property around here. I saw you on the block next to our store? Measuring and photographing, then talking on your phone for ages. Obviously, you're working for some big city developer. And now you're out here wandering around like you own the place. I'm not stupid. What's the next project you and your mates have lined up? Another commercial building? Maybe a housing estate that'll ruin the character of the whole area? Turn Matfield into just another sprawling mess?'

For a long moment he just looked at her, and she had the uncomfortable feeling he was seeing more than she wanted to reveal, almost like he was seeing past her anger to the fear and disappointment underneath. The way his gaze held hers caused a flutter in her chest that she immediately tried to ignore. 'You really think I'm some sort of property developer, don't you? Some vulture come to pick over the bones of your town.'

'Aren't you?'

'I'm a builder, Ella. Sometimes that involves looking at land, but not always for the reasons you seem to think.' He adjusted his hat against the glare, his movements deliberate and careful. 'What if I told you I was looking at this place for the same reason you are?'

'What's that supposed to mean?' Her voice was sharp with suspicion, refusing to be charmed or manipulated.

'It means maybe we both see the potential in a piece of country that's been sitting empty for over fifty years.' His voice was quieter now, more serious, and he took another step closer. 'Maybe we both understand what it could become in the right hands. '

His suggestions were so unexpected that she was left momentarily speechless. She studied his face, looking for signs of deception or manipulation, for that calculating expression men got when they were working an angle. But she found only the same appreciation for the landscape that she felt herself, the same understanding of what this place could be. It unsettled her more than his presence already had, again loosening her carefully constructed assumptions about who he was and what he wanted.

'You don't know anything about this place, and you'd have to buy it first,' she said finally, though with less conviction than before. The words sounded weak even to her own ears and she added the last statement with more conviction. 'Besides, the owners aren't selling.'

'Is that right? Maybe I know more than you think. It's been sitting abandoned for decades. Some of the best grazing country in the district, with permanent water and good access to town. I know the soil quality is excellent and the elevation provides natural drainage.' He paused, his gaze sweeping across the hills before returning to her face. 'And I know it's beautiful enough to make someone stand out here in forty-degree heat just to look at it. Just to imagine what it could be.'

Despite herself, Ella felt her hostility wavering, cracking like dried earth after too long without rain. The way he spoke about the land suggested genuine connection rather than cold commercial calculation. He sounded like someone who understood, even maybe who felt what she felt when she looked at this place. 'How do you know all that? About the permanent water and the soil quality?'

'I just know.' He took another step closer, close enough that she had to tilt her head back slightly to maintain eye contact. 'You know Ella, it's a shame you've never given me a chance. Right from when I arrived, you've been anything but friendly, and I'm not sure why. What did I do to make you dislike me on sight?'

She screwed up her mouth, caught off guard by the directness, by the way he just said what he was thinking without games or manipulation. 'I'm not a gushy person.'

'I didn't expect gushy. I just thought newcomers might get a bit more of a welcome from you country folk, although you're probably the only person I've encountered who's held back on that front. Everyone else has been great, really welcoming and friendly.' His voice was calm, conversational, but there was genuine hurt in his eyes. 'I just wonder why. What did I do wrong, or what could I have done differently?'

She pulled her hat down lower. The truth was complicated and messy, tangled up with past mistakes and protective instincts she didn't want to examine too closely. With an attraction she didn't want to feel and dreams that were slipping away. She was standing here in the middle of nowhere with a man who made her aware of herself in ways she'd been trying to avoid. A man who threw her off balance in ways that had nothing to do with the uneven ground.

'Look, we're both standing here in the heat,' she said finally, making a decision that surprised her even as the words left her mouth. An olive branch she hadn't planned to extend. 'I'm about to have a cuppa and a bite to eat. There's a shady area just over here.' She took a deep breath and tried not to notice how the genuine hurt in his eyes was already fading, replaced by a look that might have been cautious hope. 'Join me? It's too hot to be walking around arguing.'

His smile transformed his face and she noticed not for the first time how straight and white his teeth were. Too perfect to be real, ran through her mind, and then she stopped herself. Maybe he was right. Maybe she had been unfriendly without real cause. Maybe she'd been projecting Trent onto someone who was nothing like him at all.

He stretched a bit, rolling his shoulders in a way that drew her attention to the breadth of them, the play of chest muscles under his damp shirt, before she forced her gaze away. 'Sounds good. I've got my own tea and sweet biscuits in my pack. My Nanna's recipe. Might even be enough to share.'

'How good are they?' She started walking towards the shade, and he fell into step beside her.

'Best biscuits this side of the range, according to family legend. Nanna made them for every special occasion. I made these from her own recipe, handwritten and everything.'

She laughed despite herself, the sound surprising her. 'What range?'

'Who knows? But in my family, these biscuits are the undisputed champion. She'd make them and we'd eat them all in one sitting.' His grin widened, boyish and genuine, and she felt a shift in the air between them. The emotion felt slightly dangerous and one that she should probably resist, but instead, she found herself leaning into the moment.

As they walked together towards the shady stand of trees, neither spoke. Ella kept her gaze fixed on the path ahead, careful not to trip on the uneven ground, aware of the grasshoppers launching themselves out of their way. He'd shortened his stride to match hers, she noticed, maintaining a respectful distance between them. She told herself this was just a civil conversation over tea, nothing more. Two people who happened to be in the same place at the same time. That was all. At least she could be polite and 'not unfriendly' as he had stated. That didn't mean anything had changed. That didn't mean she was letting her guard down, or forgetting all the reasons she needed to be careful.

A small clearing in the shade made the perfect spot to rest. The heat that pounded down from above was broken up by the canopy of trees shading them, their leaves creating a shifting pattern of light and shadow that moved with the faint breeze. A group of galahs hung and played in the branches, squawking and peering down at the unexpected visitors from time to time, their pink and grey feathers brilliant against the blue sky. Apart from the birds and the occasional rustle of a lizard in the dry grass, there was no one else for kilometres. Ella dumped her pack on the ground and pulled out her travel mug of tea, then placed a few biscuits on a brown paper bag that she positioned on one of the other rocks.

Dusty did the same, setting his biscuit container on the rock next to hers with careful precision. 'A feast,' he said before taking a long drink from his travel mug. His gaze swept across the landscape, taking in the way the light fell across the valley, the distant shimmer of heat rising from the plains. It really was a stunning spot, and from where they sat, they had a broad view across the flat ground that Ella had obviously crossed to reach this location.

It was as if she'd read his mind. 'You must have come from the other direction,' she said. 'From the northern boundary. Not the easiest way to see the property.' She took a sip of her tea, watching him over the rim of her mug.

'There are interesting paths through there. Well, sort of paths. I think they're either cattle tracks or made by smaller animals. Either way, it was the scenic route. Got a few scratches from the scrub for my trouble.' He held out the biscuit container.. 'Try one.'

She chose one and took a bite. 'This is really good,' she murmured, genuine surprise in her voice. She finished it and accepted another when he offered. 'Light and tasty but sweet at the same time. I love them. I will say, however, that they taste pretty similar to my mother's rumball recipe. I can taste the cocoa, sultanas and dates. No rum though. What's the secret?'

He chuckled, the sound warm and unguarded. 'I can give you the recipe if you like. I've made them so often, I hardly needed the recipe to make these. Practical and simple, so my kind of cooking. I think over the years though, she substituted the traditional ingredients more for what was available to her. I'm not sure that Weet-Bix would have been in the original biscuits.'

'Yummy anyway,' she said as she took another one and sipped her tea.

He watched her, noting the way she'd let her guard drop, even if just slightly. She was a walking contradiction. Usually prickly, distant and barely communicative, but in this environment she seemed to soften, revealing glimpses of what her personality might really be like underneath all that defensiveness. The way she looked at the landscape, the appreciation in her eyes, told him more than her words did.

'I wonder why the people who own this have never returned,' she said, her voice thoughtful. 'Apparently the rates are always paid on time, and weed control notices are dealt with promptly. Apart from that, no one ever comes near the place. It's as if they want to keep it but can't bear to see it. And now it seems like they're making deals to sell it.' She frowned and looked down at the ground.

'How long have you been coming out here?' he asked.

'Since I was a teenager. It was somewhere I could ride to from our family property, which is now my uncle's place. I can't explain it, but this place has always drawn me back.' She paused, staring out across the valley. 'Like it's been waiting all these years. For someone to see it properly.'

She stopped talking suddenly and took another sip of her drink. He could tell she'd let her guard down and revealed more than she intended. After a pause, she continued, her voice more careful now. 'Anyway, it's a project for me. I'm going to keep working on contacting the owners and finding out if they'd consider selling it to me. It's probably a long shot, but I have to try.'

He looked down at his boots, then glanced up at her. Her face had lost its earlier openness, suspicion creeping back in like fog. 'That is, unless someone like your developer friends have already beaten me to it?'

He stretched out his legs in front of him, his dusty

boots and jeans resting in the dirt. For a long while he watched the shimmering heat dancing across the plains, a single hawk circling above before gliding off into the haze. He was well outside his familiar territory, but this place affected him profoundly in ways that went beyond investment potential. 'I understand what you mean. This place has a quality you can feel. Look at how these large rocks are positioned. Obviously someone well before us sat here in the same way.' They both looked around at the rocks, imagining the people who might have rested here over the decades. But she remained silent, her expression closing off.

'You've gone quiet,' he observed, noting the shift in her posture.

She packed her mug and paper bag back into her backpack and zipped it closed. Standing up, she stretched and then bent down to retie one of her shoelaces, perhaps buying herself time to think. He tried not to notice her toned legs, or the way her muscles moved as she did up the laces on her well-worn hiking boots. Her denim shorts were covered in dust, and her long-sleeved cotton shirt, though loose and buttoned down the front, suggested a neat figure beneath. He forced his gaze away, focusing on the horizon.

'I've got nothing to say,' she replied with a guarded expression, all the softness from moments before completely gone. 'I could say plenty, but I have a strong feeling you're not being honest with me. Why on earth would you just happen to be out here on this exact property in the middle of nowhere, having a look around? Just a random spot you picked?' Her voice was sharp now, accusatory.

He stood as well, packing his belongings and swinging his backpack onto his shoulders. 'Someone I know has asked me to have a thorough look over this block. It's not for the reasons you're thinking though. I'm happy to discuss it when you're feeling more open to actually listening properly and fairly about what I could tell you.'

'Oh really,' she replied flatly, crossing her arms. 'So I'm right. You are here for a specific purpose. Not just out for a pleasant walk like you claimed.'

'Yes. And I have a feeling you could be the right person to help me.' The words hung in the air between them.

'Help you with what? Help you and your mates purchase and destroy a property that's always been my dream? I think not.' Her laugh was bitter.

'If you'd just give me a chance to explain my situation instead of being so hostile, I think you'd have a better understanding of me and why I'm here today. It's not what you think. It's a plan you might want to be involved in.'

'I doubt it,' she said as she turned away, already dismissing him. 'See you around.'

He stood staring at her back as she walked the way she'd come, her stride angry and determined. Why was he even bothering to try and win her over? Really, why did he care what she thought? He could do what he needed to without her involvement. Her blonde ponytail swung nearly down to her waist, bouncing as she marched across the rocky ground with the kind of furious energy that made him want to both shake and kiss her in equal measure.

Once he stepped out of the shade, the sun was brutal, and he took a long drink of water, letting the warm liquid ease his dry throat. He considered his options for a while, watching her figure grow smaller in the distance, then started walking as well, heading back the way he'd come. She was impossible. Absolutely impossible.

CHAPTER 19

The walk back to her ute gave Ella plenty of time to think, her boots crunching on the dry grass with each angry stride. She mulled over the conversation with Dusty and tried to work out what he was actually up to. Maybe if she talked to him properly, really listened instead of assuming, she could discover who owned the place. With that knowledge, perhaps she'd have a better chance at purchasing the property. There was still a glimmer of hope, wasn't there? Maybe his contacts in the industry and his obvious knowledge of the block could be her ticket to buying it. She needed to meet with him and talk. Change her tactics from suspicious to cooperative. Stop letting pride and fear get in the way of what she wanted.

* * *

SHE LET some time pass before attempting to contact him again, telling herself she needed to think things through, plan her approach. He hadn't been into the store much, which annoyed her. That would have given her the perfect opportunity without making it look like she was chasing him down. She didn't want to appear too keen, or reveal how much she'd been thinking about their conversation. Instead, he sent Liam when he needed supplies, and the few times he did appear himself, he barely made eye contact and was in and out as if the building was on fire.

'I don't want to miss any time working with him,' Liam explained when she questioned the arrangement, his face eager and earnest. 'You should see what I've learned in just a few weeks. He's really skilled and patient, and yesterday he showed me how to...'

Ella had cut him off mid-sentence, immediately feeling guilty but too frustrated to listen. 'You've told me about twenty times already, Liam. Yes, yes, off you go. We'll catch up another time.' It was the same with everyone else in the community. She was getting thoroughly sick of hearing about Dusty's various contributions to local life and the constant stream of praise. Was she the only person in Matfield who could see what was really happening?

Another month had passed since their encounter on the property, and word around town was that Eli would be returning within the week. 'I'm really going to go after him this time,' Cass told her over coffee at the bakery one afternoon, her eyes bright with determination. 'No more mucking around. He's the one for me, and I'll let him know exactly how I feel. I think I'll just ask him on a proper date. If I don't, someone else is going to get in before me. Jenny's been circling like a shark.'

Ella listened, making appropriate noises while her mind wandered. Her head was full of things she needed to do. There were orders to be delivered, goods to be catalogued and priced, and an entire back shed that desperately needed sorting out. Her brother Tyson was working with her most days, but there seemed to be a sudden surge of both orders and customers to process. At least business was thriving while her parents were away. Colin and Helen had worked hard for decades, and the whole family had encouraged them to go, confident that Ella and Tyson could manage the business.

Ella had also been to the real estate office a few times to try and make some more progress by finding out what was going on with the properties. That was to no avail though, and Phil seemed to be less and less interested in her queries. He'd tried showing her some other places that were going to go up for sale. 'Forget those ones,' he said. 'There are bigger players involved and the more I ask the more closed up the information becomes.'

* * *

Elsie stopped by that afternoon to put flyers up in the front window of the store, her energy as boundless as ever. 'It's going to be massive. A proper country fete with a bush dance and fireworks. The students are organising most of it, and the senior home economics class is running stalls and a café as part of their assessment.' She sticky-taped a poster to the wall as well, standing on tiptoe to reach the top corner. 'Plus there's a bake-off competition. That builder, Dusty, is making a special display table and judging platform for it. All donated labour, of course.'

'Of course he is,' Ella mumbled under her breath, unable to keep the sarcasm out of her voice. 'And no doubt he'll enter some amazing creations as well. Is there anything that man isn't involved in?'

'Not much, now that I think about it. And yes, he is in the baking competition. Oh, and I've put your name down to judge that and another cooking category. Figured you wouldn't be entering either yourself.' Elsie gave her a knowing look.

'Thanks for the vote of confidence. But you're right. Me and baking don't really go together, unless you count burning cakes or making scones that could be used as building materials.'

Elsie turned to face her properly. Her expression was more serious, and she looked as if she was about to state an important point. 'You know, Ella, you've been missing out on heaps of social events lately. Over the last couple of months, we've had so many functions, and I've noticed you're not showing up. Cass says she's tried to get you there, but you won't come. Is everything alright? Because if there's a problem, or you're going through a tricky time, you can talk to me.'

She gave a nervous laugh that sounded unconvincing even to her own ears. 'Of course everything's fine. I've just been busy with the store.' Trying to placate Elsie's concerns, she added, 'Mum and Dad are overseas, and with Liam working for Dusty instead of being here to help, I'm swamped. I'm completely fine.'

'Good. Then you can come for dinner at our place tomorrow night. Just a barbecue, nothing fancy. If you could bring a bottle of wine and a chair, that would be brilliant.' She stepped down from the small ladder she was standing on and passed the tape and scissors back to Ella, who was already thinking of plausible reasons to decline.

'No excuses, thanks,' Elsie said, holding her hand up in front of Ella's face before she could speak, her teacher voice in full effect. 'See you at six sharp. Matt's doing his famous marinated sausages, and I've already told him you're coming. He's bought extra just for you.'

After Elsie left, Ella stood behind the counter feeling cornered and slightly panicked. The truth was, she had been avoiding social gatherings, and for good reason. Every single event seemed to feature Dusty Camilleri front and centre. He was either contributing something, helping someone, or generally being the kind of community-minded citizen that made her look petty and antisocial in comparison. It was exhausting watching everyone fall over themselves to praise him, and even more tiring pretending she didn't care. It was also exhausting fighting this pull she felt towards him, despite every instinct telling her to keep her distance.

The bell above the door chimed, and she looked up to see Oscar wandering in with his usual easy gait, his weathered face breaking into a smile. 'Afternoon, Ella. How's business?'

'Busy. Which is good, I suppose.' She tried to inject some enthusiasm into her voice, but failed.

'That's the spirit,' he said, with a grin that suggested he saw right through her. 'I need a couple of bags of that premium cat food Patricia likes. The stuff with the kangaroo meat in it. She swears Bertie's coat has never looked better.'

As she fetched his order from the back shelf, he leaned against the counter with the casual confidence of someone who'd known her all her life. 'You coming to Elsie's barbecue tomorrow night?'

'Apparently, I don't have a choice.' She set the bags down.

'She does have a way of making things non-negotiable, doesn't she?' He chuckled, the sound warm and knowing. 'Should be good though. Dusty and Eli will be there. Eli just got back this morning. Liam's been a great offsider but Dusty must be exhausted. You'd never know it to look at him though.'

'He seems to be managing just fine,' she replied sharply, unable to keep the edge out of her voice.

Oscar gave her a thoughtful look. It was like he was seeing more than she wanted to reveal. 'You know, I've been meaning to ask you a question. What's your issue with Dusty? I've noticed you give him the cold shoulder whenever you cross paths. It's pretty obvious, Ella.'

Ella busied herself scanning his items, avoiding eye contact as the barcode reader beeped. 'I don't have an issue with him.'

'Right.' He waited until she had to look at him, his gaze steady and patient. 'Come on, Ella. I've known you since you were knee-high to a grasshopper. That young bloke is bothering you, and I'm curious to know why you feel like that. He's been nothing but helpful since he arrived. Practically a model citizen.'

'That's exactly the problem,' she blurted out before she could stop herself, the words escaping in a rush. 'He's too helpful. Too perfect. Too involved in everything. And he's looking at properties around here like he's planning to develop half the district. Really, he has no connection to the area, so why now is he suddenly involved and interested in everything Matfield? It doesn't make sense, unless he or the developers he's probably in business with have an agenda.'

'Ah.' Oscar nodded slowly, understanding dawning on his face. 'So that's what this is about. You think he's some sort of property developer who's going to ruin the town. Or maybe you're worried about an entirely different matter.'

'Isn't he? A developer, I mean.'

'Not that I'm aware of. He's doing a commercial job for someone, yes, but that's just building work. As for the rest, maybe he's just a bloke who likes being part of a community. Some people are like that, you know. They find a place that feels like home, and they build a life.' He picked up his bags. 'Might be worth trying to really talk to him instead of avoiding him at every turn. You might be surprised at what you learn.'

After he left, Ella stood in the empty store feeling thoroughly unsettled, Oscar's words echoing in her mind. Maybe Oscar was right. Maybe she was being unfair, letting past experiences taint her judgment of someone who'd done nothing to deserve it. Or maybe everyone else was being naive, and she was the only one who could see through Dusty's carefully constructed image. Either way, she was going to have to face him at that barbecue tomorrow night. The thought made her head spin with a reaction that wasn't entirely annoyance. A feeling of frustration filled her, but there was also an uncomfortable anticipation at the prospect of being in the same space again.

CHAPTER 20

Thank goodness Eli was back. Although he wasn't starting work until tomorrow, just knowing his partner had returned took a load off Dusty's mind. The cottage felt less empty, less like a temporary stop and more like a home with his mate's belongings scattered around again. Liam had proved his worth ten times over during Eli's absence, and Dusty was already working out how to keep the kid on with them long-term, maybe even after the Matfield jobs were finished. But there was a benefit to having a trusted mate who knew your work style inside and out, and who could anticipate what you needed before you asked for it. He and Eli had been working together for years, and now they'd be able to tackle the second phase of the pub renovation properly.

He looked in the mirror as he pulled a brush through his thick dark hair, which had finally grown back enough to style after the charity head shave. Three months had already passed since he'd arrived in Matfield, and it never ceased to surprise him that, apart from his family and a handful of mates, there was absolutely nothing about life in Melbourne that he missed. Not the restaurants, not the culture, not the convenience. Nothing.

Even Eli had been eager to get back from Melbourne. 'Who'd have thought I'd miss this little town,' he told Dusty. They both peered into the one small mirror hanging on their bathroom wall, jostling for space. 'Crikey, Dusty, we scrub up alright. I'm really getting into these boots and hats that everyone wears out here. Feel like a proper country bloke now.'

Dusty laughed, noting his friend's enthusiasm. 'Are you trying to impress someone in particular?'

'Not really. I don't mind Cass though. Hard to tell what she's thinking. One minute she's keen to talk, and then she won't come near me. That was before I left. Maybe she'll be at the barbecue tonight.' His voice was casual, but Dusty caught the hope in his tone.

'Maybe. From what I saw when you were around before, she backed right off whenever that fan club of yours appeared.' He grinned. 'There are quite a few single women in this town interested in you. Jenny practically follows you around like a shadow.'

'There are. What about you? Any progress with anyone while I was away?' Eli looked at him in the mirror.

'All I've done is work, and you know I'm not chasing after anything like that.' Dusty adjusted his collar, avoiding the question he knew was coming.

'So what? You're planning to stay single forever? Live like a monk in the outback?'

'Maybe one day I'll meet the right person. There's no point trying to force it. I believe it has to happen naturally.' Dusty adjusted his collar in the mirror again, suddenly finding it very interesting.

'What about Ella? I noticed something between you two. Like a spark or tension. The air practically crackled when you were in the same room.'

'You have to be joking. A spark, sure. A fiery one that's likely to burn the whole town down. She can't stand me, and it's even worse now that she's seen me on the block next to their store. Then the other day I ran into her when I went to look at that other property out of town. She reckons she's had her eye on both places for years. Apparently, she's trying to contact the owners to buy that one and the one next to their produce store.'

Eli pulled a face, wincing sympathetically. 'Really? Well, she won't be happy then, will she? When she finds out the truth.'

'Nope.'

'Have you told her what's going on with those blocks? The real story?'

'No. She won't give me the chance. I asked her to let me explain, but she refused and walked away. I haven't heard from her or seen her since, and in a place this small, that takes effort. She's been actively avoiding me. I reckon she crosses the street when she sees me coming. She genuinely dislikes me, mate.'

'Or maybe she's trying really hard not to like you, which is different.' Eli grinned. 'Trust me on this.'

'You've been reading too many romance novels.'

'I don't read romance novels. I watch rom-coms, thank you very much. There's a difference.' Eli checked the time on his phone, his expression amused. 'Come on, let's go. At least we don't have to walk far. Another thing I like about this place. Nothing's more than five minutes away. No parking hassles, no traffic lights.'

They locked up the cottage and started walking the three blocks to Elsie and Matt's house. The evening air was finally cooling down after another scorching day, that magical time when the heat finally breaks and you can breathe properly again. The distinctive smell of gum trees mixed with quite a few barbecues firing up drifted around them on the breeze. Locals out in their yards called out greetings as they passed, and Dusty realised he had relaxed into the rhythm of this small-town life that had become surprisingly comfortable. It felt right in a way Melbourne never had.

'So, what's the latest with those properties then?' Eli asked as they turned onto the street where Elsie and Matt's barbecue was being held, lowering his voice even though no one was nearby. 'You've been pretty tight-lipped since I've been back.'

'Because it's complicated, and I didn't want to talk about it before everything's finalised. Having said that, as you know, the block next to the produce store is a straightforward development that the town actually needs. Nothing controversial, though Ella seems to think it'll be some hideous monstrosity that'll destroy the main street's character.'

'And the other one? The property out of town?'

Dusty was quiet for a moment, choosing his words carefully. 'That one's become personal. I'm now looking at it for myself. Somewhere to build a proper house if I decide to stay here permanently. Somewhere with space and views and room to breathe.'

Eli stopped walking and stared at him, genuine shock

on his face. 'Wait, you're thinking about staying? Like, actually moving here? Leaving Melbourne for good?'

'I'm considering it. Don't make a big deal about it.'

'Mate, that's a massive decision. What about Melbourne? Your family? The business we've built up there over the years?' Eli's voice was urgent now, concerned.

'My family will understand. They always knew I was different from the rest of them, that I was never going to follow the same path. As for the business, we've got enough work here to keep us busy for at least two years, maybe more if other projects come through. You could go back and forth, or we could take on someone local to help. Liam, for instance. There are options.' Dusty started walking again, not wanting to dwell on the enormity of what he was considering. 'It's just an idea at this stage. Nothing's decided.'

'Does this have anything to do with a certain blonde woman who can't stand you?' The question was direct, challenging.

'No. It has to do with me enjoying my life for the first time in years. I love waking up without having to think about fighting traffic or dealing with difficult clients. Working on projects that matter to real people instead of just adding another cookie-cutter development to some suburb where no one knows their neighbours is exhilarating. And I find being somewhere I can walk to a barbecue instead of sitting in my car for an hour each way breathing exhaust fumes, refreshing.' He paused, acknowledging the truth he'd been avoiding. 'Though I wouldn't mind if that certain blonde woman stopped treating me like I'm personally responsible for ruining her life. That would be a nice bonus.'

They could see Elsie and Matt's house now, with a few cars already lining the street and the sound of voices and laughter floating through the evening air. Twinkling fairy lights, visible through the side gate, were strung across the backyard, and the smell of barbecuing meat made Dusty's stomach rumble with anticipation.

'Well, mate,' Eli said, clapping him on the shoulder with genuine affection, 'if she's going to be here tonight, you'll have your chance to either clear the air or make things even worse. My money's on worse, knowing your track record with her.'

'Thanks for the vote of confidence.'

'That's what mates are for.' Eli grinned, that easy smile that had charmed half of Matfield already. 'Now let's go eat some food and see if Cass actually talks to me this time, or if she does that weird thing where she pretends I don't exist while staring at me from across the room.'

'Maybe I should be more open about my feelings, you know, towards Ella?'

'This should be interesting,' Eli chuckled and then murmured beside him. 'Try not to get a beer thrown in your face. I'd like to enjoy this party without having to defend your honour.'

'No promises,' Dusty replied, although he was already wondering if maybe, just maybe, tonight would be the night Ella let him explain himself. Or at the very least, stop looking at him like he was some sort of villain in her personal story. Either way, it was going to be an interesting evening.

As they walked through the gate into the backyard, Dusty scanned the crowd automatically. He was looking for a blonde ponytail and a face that would probably glare at him the moment she spotted him. He told himself he was just preparing for the inevitable confrontation, but even so, he felt disappointed when Ella was nowhere to be seen. He looked around the crowd more closely, but she didn't appear to be here. Perhaps she wouldn't turn up tonight?

CHAPTER 21

Elsie had been right. It had been too long since Ella had properly participated in any social events. Work was exhausting, and the long hours in the produce shed, despite the massive industrial fans working overtime, became increasingly unbearable during these relentless hot months. The heat built throughout the day until even standing still felt like hard labour, sweat soaking through her shirt before lunchtime. By the time she got home each evening, made herself dinner and cleaned up the kitchen, she was usually ready to collapse on the lounge with a book or whatever movie she could find streaming. Her online astronomy work had thankfully paused for a while, which at least gave her the luxury of properly relaxing once she got home instead of staring at satellite data until midnight, her eyes burning from screen fatigue.

Home was the small worker's cottage on the rear portion of her parents' block of land. Their modest low-set weatherboard house faced Gallipoli Street. A stand of thick bottle brush trees formed a dense hedge between the two dwellings, providing privacy and shade. The colourful divider, with a mixture of red and pink flowers created a living wall that rustled pleasantly in any breeze and gave a welcome respite of brightness especially during these dry times. The block had frontages on two streets, and Ella's cottage faced in the opposite direction to her parents', onto Fromelles Lane.

The streets in this part of town were all named after different battles of World War One, a naming convention that had seemed unremarkable when she was growing up but now felt weighted with history. Gallipoli, Fromelles, Somme, Ypres, Passchendaele. Each name a reminder of Australian blood spilt on foreign soil. The monument and cenotaph that bore the names of local soldiers who had died in various wars stood at the end of her lane, visible from her kitchen window. On Anzac Day and other significant dates, the lane and surrounding streets would be packed with locals and visitors who gathered to pay tribute to those who had fallen and given their lives for their country.

Thank goodness last year the council had finally erected an equally sized cenotaph honouring the Indigenous men who had also served and sacrificed in World Wars One and Two. Fancy leaving them off purely because of the colour of their skin, she thought, still angry about the decades of exclusion, the casual racism that had written these brave men out of history. The people of Matfield and the surrounding areas had eventually come together to show their recognition of the twenty-one men who had been excluded from the original lists because they were Indigenous or considered foreigners. Now, as she walked past the two cenotaphs, she stopped to rearrange the flowers someone had left that had blown over in the afternoon breeze. Last week had been November 11th, Remembrance Day, and she'd told her brother, Tyson, that he could attend the ceremony while she looked after the shop. Only one person had come in during that hour, which gave her some time to clean up and rearrange. Everyone else would have been at the memorial service.

The sun was lowering in the western sky, and she paused to appreciate the colours that formed a dramatic backdrop to the cenotaphs. Shades of pink and orange were starting to paint the horizon, deepening as she watched, and with not a cloud visible in any direction, she figured they were in for another sweltering night with no prospect of rain. The eucalyptus trees lining the footpath were suffering, their leaves wilting and browning before covering the ground in a crispy carpet that crunched underfoot. The town desperately needed rain. Although they always sold more feed than ever during extended dry spells, she, along with everyone else in the district, hoped that the dry would break soon. Local farmers were getting desperate, and desperation always led to difficult conversations and tighter budgets.

Clasping her bottle of wine in one hand and with her fold-up chair under her other arm, she walked briskly up Fromelles Lane, turning onto Somme Street where Elsie and Matt lived. The houses along this stretch were typical Queensland workers' cottages, built decades ago with an understanding of how to survive the brutal heat. Each sat on short stumps to allow air circulation beneath, with wide verandahs wrapping around at least two sides to provide shade throughout the day. Most were weatherboard construction, painted in faded colours like cream, pale blue or soft green. The tin roofs, once bright, had dulled to a muted silver that reflected the setting sun with a warm glow. The yards were generous, although most showed signs of the prolonged drought. A few determined residents maintained small gardens where struggling roses and native plants clung to life.

As she walked, she mentally rehearsed her strategy for the evening. Everything was so close in Matfield that she rarely needed to drive anywhere, which tonight meant she could enjoy a few drinks without worrying about getting home safely. She would just have to remember her plan to be pleasant to Dusty, draw out information about the property owners, and use whatever she learned to help with her purchase negotiations. Surely she could manage to be nice for one evening? It was just a few hours. How hard could it be? She'd be charming, strategic, and leave with the information she needed.

The sound of music and laughter drifted down the street as she approached Elsie and Matt's place, carried on the evening breeze along with the smell of barbecuing meat. She could see the glow of fairy lights strung across their backyard, twinkling against the darkening sky. Several utes and cars lined the street, confirming that a decent crowd had already gathered. She recognised most of the vehicles; Oscar's distinctive red ute with the bumper stickers advertising the pub, the Hendersons' ancient Land Cruiser that was more rust than metal, and Cass's little hatchback that she'd covered in environmental bumper stickers. Voices sounded from the backyard, mingled with laughter. She instantly recognised the tone. Dusty. There was no mistaking it.

Her nerves jangled despite her resolve. This was fine. She was an adult and could handle a simple social gathering without making a scene, or saying words she'd regret. 'Charming, pleasant, and strategic,' she muttered under her breath. Get the information she needed about those properties and do it without letting him see that he'd gotten under her skin.

Taking a deep breath and adjusting her grips on the wine bottle and chair, she pushed open the gate and stepped into Elsie and Matt's front yard. The grass was brown and patchy, crunching under her boots, but someone had made an effort with potted plants on the verandah and solar lights lining the path to the side gate where voices and laughter beckoned. She could smell barbecued meat and the distinctive scent of Matt's marinade that he was famous for, a secret recipe involving lemon, garlic, and about fifteen other ingredients he refused to reveal. Her stomach rumbled, reminding her that she'd skipped lunch in her rush to get everything sorted at the store before leaving Tyson in charge to clean and close up.

As she rounded the corner into the backyard, she took in the scene. Fairy lights were strung between the trees and across the patio, creating a warm glow. A proper crowd of at least thirty people clustered in groups. Matt presided at the barbecue with a beer in one hand and tongs in the other, his face flushed from the heat. Elsie flitted between guests, ensuring everyone had drinks and food, her laughter carrying across the yard. The setup was casual and welcoming, exactly the kind of gathering that used to make her feel at home before she'd started isolating herself.

And there, standing near the drinks table, talking to Eli and Oscar, was Dusty. He looked relaxed in jeans and a casual shirt, his dark hair now grown back enough to fall across his forehead. He was laughing with Oscar, the sound carrying across the yard, genuine and unguarded. Even from across the yard, she could see the easy confidence in his posture and the way people naturally gravitated toward him.

She looked away before he caught her staring, but it was too late. As if sensing her presence, his head turned, and their eyes met across the crowded backyard. For a moment, neither of them moved. The noise of the party seemed to fade, the conversations around them becoming distant. Then Ella lifted her chin slightly, squared her shoulders, and walked toward the drinks table with all the determination she could muster. If she was going to do this, she was going to do it properly. Even if it killed her.

Cass pounced on her the moment she stepped into the backyard, materialising out of the crowd as if she'd been lying in wait. 'Thank goodness you came! Finally. And you look fantastic.' She held her arms out and looked Ella up and down with exaggerated appreciation, her movements slightly loose. 'You look hot, lovey. Hot and sexy.'

Ella could feel her face burning. Cass's voice carried across the entire backyard, and several heads turned in their direction, curious eyes taking in the scene. 'Shh, Cass. How many drinks have you had already?'

'Three glasses of champagne and nothing to eat. I'm going all out tonight. It's all or nothing.' She grabbed Ella's arm with slightly unsteady hands, her grip tighter than necessary. 'He's here.'

Ella dumped her chair on the lawn and sat her wine bottle on it before grabbing Cass by the arm.

'I presume you're talking about Eli. Come with me right now.' She dragged her friend over to the food table and started loading a plate with sausages, potato salad, coleslaw, and bread. A couple of other friends joined them, greeting Ella with genuine warmth and asking where she'd been hiding. Since Ella was hungry, she piled her own plate high, the food looking and smelling far better than anything she'd managed to cook for herself lately. Matt was busy at the barbecue, flipping meat with that focused expression he got when he was in his element. Elsie waved from where she was talking to Todd and his wife, Penny, her face lighting up when she saw Ella had shown up. Ella returned the wave, then nodded a greeting to Todd and Penny as well. It had been far too long since she'd seen anyone socially, and she had to admit it felt good to be surrounded by familiar faces and friendly conversation. It was a reminder of why she'd chosen to come back to Matfield in the first place.

Penny cradled a newborn in her arms, the baby making small snuffling sounds, while Todd wrestled with their toddler, who was determined to escape his father's grip and investigate the barbecue with its dangerous flames and hot metal. The yard was filled with laughter and the comfortable hum of people who'd known each other for years, sharing history and community ties. As the sun slid below the horizon and the air cooled just a fraction, still warm but bearable now, Ella took a deep breath and let herself relax slightly.

Cass was seated and attacking her meal like she hadn't eaten in a week, sauce dripping down her chin. Ella had made sure to put a large glass of water in her hand and hoped some food and hydration would calm her down before she embarrassed herself. If she genuinely wanted to make an impression on Eli, being drunk probably wasn't the best strategy, although knowing Cass, it might work anyway. As wary as Ella was of both builders, if Cass had maintained this infatuation for months since meeting Eli, maybe she should actually go for it instead of just pining from a distance and making herself miserable.

A flock of corellas passed overhead, their raucous calls announcing their journey to roost for the night, their white bodies catching the last of the sun's light. A road train sounded its horn from the highway in the distance, the deep note carrying across the evening air, a reminder of the world beyond this small gathering. These were the usual sounds of the outback, and as orange and red hues filled the enormous sky, Ella looked up, marvelling at the sunset. No two were ever the same, and the sheer scope of the sky out here never failed to amaze her, a vast dome that seemed to go on forever. Someone put on music, a Kasey Chambers song, 'Not Pretty Enough', and Ella started tapping her foot to the familiar rhythm, the melancholy lyrics somehow perfect for the evening. The atmosphere, the smell of meat cooking on the barbecue, and the cool evening breeze filtering across the yard gave her a warm, nostalgic feeling. Matfield would always be home. Everyone she needed was here. This was where she belonged.

Her peaceful thoughts were interrupted by the arrival of Eli and Dusty at the food table near where she and Cass sat. Both men were dressed in neat dark jeans and crisp shirts that looked freshly ironed, a definite improvement over their usual work clothes. She had to bite back a laugh when she noticed their new leather riding boots, still pristine without a single scuff mark, so obviously new they practically gleamed. Don't judge, she reminded herself. Be nice. You have a purpose tonight. He might be helpful if you play this right.

'Evening, ladies,' Eli said smoothly, dipping his head and flashing them both a charming smile that had probably worked on countless women.

Cass immediately straightened her shoulders and placed her empty plate on the table with exaggerated care, no doubt her movements requiring her full concentration. 'Good evening. How lovely to see you both.'

Dusty nodded in Ella's direction, his expression neutral but his eyes watchful. 'Evening. Nice to see you both here.'

Cass stood up a bit unsteadily, and Ella quickly shoved a fresh glass of water into her hands. 'Drink. Drink this, please.'

Cass closed her eyes, took a deep breath like she was balancing herself, then opened them before accepting the glass. 'Yes, Mum.' She looked at Eli and used her most demure voice, though the effect was somewhat undermined by her swaying slightly. 'I may have had too much champagne too quickly. Excuse me if I'm slurring. Thanks, Ella. You're always looking out for me.'

Ella made a low sound and frowned as she refilled the glass from a nearby jug. 'And more. Keep drinking.'

Cass smiled sweetly at both men, her most winning smile. 'Champagne. Three glasses of it on an empty stomach. Not my finest decision of the evening.'

Eli laughed, a genuine sound that lit up his face and made his eyes crinkle at the corners. 'Happens to the best of us. How about we walk it off a bit? Grab a water bottle and you can give me a proper tour of the town. I'm keen to stretch my legs after crouching down doing flooring all day. That's if you're feeling up to it.'

Cass's eyes looked like they would pop out of her head, and she nodded so energetically Ella worried she might fall over or give herself whiplash. Words seemed to have completely failed her, her mouth opening and closing without sound.

'Look after her,' Ella said to Eli as he hooked Cass's arm through his with gentle courtesy and led her back through the front gate and onto the street.

'He will,' Dusty said, grabbing a plate and loading it with food. 'He's a good bloke. She'll be safe with him.'

'Yeah, but will he be safe with her?' The words escaped before she could stop them, and she turned to Dusty with an apologetic grimace. 'Cass is wonderful, but she has had quite a lot to drink. And she tends to be very direct when she's had champagne.'

'I'm sure he can handle himself. Eli's been in worse situations.' He smiled, clearly not concerned. 'Now, what about you? Have you eaten?'

'I have, thanks.' She pointed to the chair Cass had vacated. 'You can sit here if you like. I'll just grab another drink and maybe one more sausage.'

'Sounds good. I'll hold down the fort.'

By the time she returned with a fresh glass of wine and more food, he looked completely settled, his legs stretched out in front of him, crossed at the ankles, a plate balanced in one hand and a beer in the other. His dark hair had grown back enough to show a bit of wave, and the evening light caught the angle of his jaw as he watched the other guests with casual interest, his expression relaxed and open. The shirt he wore was a deep blue that somehow made his features even more striking, and she noticed the way the fabric fitted across his shoulders. She looked down at her plate. 'So,' she said, settling into her chair and aiming for casual conversation, 'how's the pub renovation going? I heard you're nearly finished with the first stage.'

'Getting there. Should be done with the ballroom section by the end of next week. Then we start on the upstairs accommodation, which is going to be the trickier part. Lots of original features to preserve while modernising everything to current building codes. The regulations are a nightmare, but it's worth it to keep the character.'

'That must be challenging. Balancing the old with the new.'

'It is, but that's what makes it interesting. Anyone can throw up a new building. Bringing history back to life while making it functional for modern use takes actual skill.' He finished what food was left on his plate, then added, 'Your nephew's been a huge help, by the way. The kid's got natural talent. Best first-year apprentice I've ever worked with.'

She felt a small surge of pride despite her reservations. 'Liam's always been good with his hands. Just hated sitting in a classroom being lectured to. Couldn't sit still for five minutes.'

'Can't say I blame him. I was the same at his age.' Dusty took a sip of his beer, looking thoughtful. 'University nearly killed me. Sitting through lectures about astronomy while the sun was shining outside felt like torture.'

Her head snapped up. 'You studied astronomy?'

'Yep, and from what Oscar told me, you did too. Sounds like you went a lot further than I did though. I only lasted a year before I realised I was going to go mad if I stayed. Loved the subject, hated the academic approach to it. All theory, no practical application. Turned out I needed to work with my hands to stay sane. I take my hat off to you for finishing the course.'

'I didn't know that you studied.' She looked at him with renewed interest, seeing him in a completely different light. 'Oscar's good at sharing information. That's right though. I also decided that career path wasn't for me. That's why I'm back here in Matfield.' She took a long sip of her drink before looking back at him. 'So, all those quiz night answers weren't just lucky guesses.'

'No. Although I'm guessing you didn't think they were, even then.' His smile was knowing but not unkind.

'I thought maybe you'd read a lot.' She felt defensive suddenly, caught off guard. 'How was I supposed to know you'd actually studied it? You're a builder.'

'You could have asked instead of assuming I was just a builder who happened to know a few random facts.' He said it mildly, but the point landed.

She took a sip of her wine to buy herself time, the cool liquid doing nothing to ease her discomfort. 'You're right. I should have asked.'

'Why didn't you?'

'Because I'd already decided what I thought about you, and I didn't want to be wrong.' The honesty surprised her even as she said it, the words escaping before she could censor them.

He looked at her for a long moment, his expression unreadable. 'And what did you think about me?'

'That you were too good to be true. Too helpful, too involved, too perfect. People like that usually want something.' She met his gaze, refusing to back down.

'And you think I want something?'

'Don't you?' She kept her voice light, conversational, but she watched his face carefully for any tells.

'Maybe I just like it here. Isn't that a possibility?'

She answered him quickly. 'Or maybe your plans require local support first.'

He didn't react defensively, which surprised her. Instead, he smiled and set down his beer before responding. 'You're not entirely wrong. I am planning. But it's not what you think.'

'Then what is it?'

'If I tell you, will you listen? Or will you have already made up your mind before I finish talking?' The challenge in his voice was unmistakable.

The challenge hung in the air between them. Ella realised this was exactly the opportunity she'd been hoping for, but now that it had arrived, she wasn't sure she wanted to hear what he had to say. If he confirmed her worst suspicions about property development and commercial projects, she'd have to accept that her dream was dead. If he had some other explanation, she'd have to admit she'd been wrong about him. Neither option was appealing.

'I'll listen,' she said finally, meaning it despite her fears. 'I can't promise I'll like what you tell me, but I'll listen.'

He nodded slowly, as if considering whether to trust her with whatever he was about to reveal. Before he could speak though, someone turned up the music and Oscar appeared with a bottle of wine, insisting on refilling Ella's glass while launching into a story about a difficult customer at the pub who'd complained about everything. The moment stretched, then broke, and Dusty leaned back in his chair with a slight smile that suggested he knew exactly what had just been interrupted. 'Another time then,' he said, his voice carrying a note she couldn't quite identify. 'When we've got more privacy and fewer distractions.'

She wanted to argue, to demand he tell her now, but Oscar was still talking and Matt was calling people over to grab seconds before the food got cold. The opportunity had passed, leaving her with more questions than answers and the uncomfortable realisation that she'd actually been enjoying talking to Dusty Camilleri before his mysterious revelation had changed the mood.

'Fine,' she said, trying not to sound as frustrated as she felt. 'Another time. But soon.'

'Soon,' he agreed.

As the evening continued around them, with music and laughter and the comfortable chaos of a small-town gathering, Ella found herself hyperaware of Dusty's presence beside her. They fell into easier conversation after that, talking about nothing important; the weather, mutual acquaintances, funny stories from the pub and the produce store. He made her laugh with an impression of Ernie trying to give building advice, his voice and mannerisms so spot-on she nearly choked on her wine. She countered with a story about a customer who'd tried to return chook feed because his chickens didn't like the taste, insisting on a refund.

By the time Cass and Eli returned from their walk, both looking suspiciously pleased with themselves and holding hands, Ella had almost forgotten she was supposed to be extracting information from Dusty. Almost. Because underneath the easy conversation and unexpected laughter, she was acutely aware that he'd promised to tell her important details. And she was starting to suspect that whatever it was might change everything she thought she knew about why he'd come to Matfield.

CHAPTER 23

*E*lla resigned herself to the fact that tonight wasn't going to bring Dusty's revelation. She allowed herself to be drawn into the conversations swirling around her. Cass had returned and sat back down, though Dusty had quickly jumped up and offered her his chair when they'd arrived. She was subdued and kept drinking water, steering well clear of any alcohol. Ella noted that Eli seemed quite attentive, fussing over her in a way that suggested their walk had gone better than expected. He made sure she had more food and kept refilling her water glass. When she got up and said she felt ill, he immediately offered to walk her home. She must have really felt rough because she only nodded before saying a quick goodbye to those nearby.

Soon the group around Ella and Dusty were telling stories and reminiscing about days gone by. Most of the people her age had gone to school with her, creating that comfortable feeling that came from knowing someone's entire history. She wondered if Dusty felt like the odd one out, and she made sure to include him in the conversation, filling him in on gaps that he might not understand without being a local.

Rod, a mate she'd gone through school with told a funny story and the group erupted in raucous laughter. More stories followed, each one triggering another memory. Ella genuinely relaxed, laughing until her sides hurt at stories she'd forgotten about. She'd been foolish to isolate herself at home night after night. Tonight she was having a brilliant time, catching up with old friends and mixing with people she hadn't seen in ages. Even talking to Dusty had been surprisingly easy. She glanced at him, his head thrown back as he laughed at a story one of the other blokes was telling. He seemed to fit in naturally, and everyone except her had welcomed him into the fold without reservation. For a moment her guard slipped completely, and she enjoyed his company rather than analysing his motives. Then she remembered whatever it was he was planning to tell her, and the wariness crept back in.

The crowd gradually thinned as the night wore on. Parents with young kids left first, then the older residents who had early morning commitments. By the time Ella checked her phone, it was well after midnight. The full moon hung bright and low on the horizon, casting enough light to make the street visible without needing torches. She gathered her chair and said her goodbyes to the remaining guests.

Dusty appeared behind her as she was thanking Elsie and Matt. 'I'll walk you home,' he said, as though it was already decided.

'It's safe here. This isn't Melbourne.' She tried to keep her tone light, though the offer had caught her off guard.

He stopped walking, and she did as well, turning to face him. The moonlight cast shadows across his face, and he looked at her with an intensity that made her pulse quicken. 'May I walk you home?' he asked again, this time making it a genuine question rather than an assumption.

The way he asked was careful and respectful and made her previous refusal seem churlish. The moon was bright overhead, the street was quiet, and she was suddenly acutely aware that they were standing close enough that she could smell his cologne mixed with the faint scent of barbecue smoke on his clothes.

'I suppose it is on your way home,' she said finally, adjusting her grip on her folding chair. 'Yes, alright.'

Dusty grabbed the chair from her and they started walking down Somme Street together, their footsteps creating a rhythm on the footpath. For a while, neither spoke, and the silence felt surprisingly comfortable. The air had cooled significantly from the day's heat, and a light breeze rustled the leaves of the street trees. In the distance, a dog barked once, then fell silent.

'You were different tonight,' he said eventually. 'More relaxed.'

'I was just being myself.'

'That's what I meant. It was nice to see.' He adjusted his stride to match hers, his longer legs slowing to her pace.

They turned onto Fromelles Lane, and Ella was aware of how few houses they'd have to pass before reaching her cottage. Part of her wanted the walk to last longer, which was a dangerous thought she immediately tried to suppress.

'Can I ask you a question?' she said, needing to break the comfortable silence before she lost herself in it completely.

'Go ahead.'

'Earlier you said you'd tell me about your plans. About what you're doing here.' She kept her eyes on the path ahead. 'Will you actually tell me, or were they just more words to stop me from asking again?'

He was quiet for several steps, and she thought maybe he was going to deflect again. Then he stopped walking, and she stopped too, turning to face him beneath the massive fig tree that marked the corner of her parents' property, with her cottage further up the lane.

'I'll tell you,' he said. 'But not tonight. You've had a few drinks, and I want you to be completely clearheaded when we have that conversation.'

'I'm not drunk.'

'I didn't say you were. But this is important, and I don't want you to think I'm taking advantage of timing or circumstances.' His expression was serious in the moonlight. 'Plus, it's complicated, and we're both tired. Give me one more day to sort out the last details, and then I'll tell you everything. I promise.'

The fact that he was being so deliberate about when and how to have the conversation made her more nervous rather than less. 'That sounds ominous.'

'It's not. Or at least, I hope you won't think so.' He started walking again, and she fell into step beside him. 'Some of it you'll probably be angry about. But some of it might surprise you in a good way.'

'Now you're definitely making me nervous.'

'Don't be. Just give me until tomorrow night. Come to

the pub around seven. The ballroom section will be finished, and we can talk there without interruptions.'

They reached her gate, and she paused with her hand on the latch. The cottage looked small and welcoming in the moonlight, her porch light casting a warm glow across the front garden. She should go inside, end this conversation before it became more complicated than it already was. But she hesitated, not quite ready to walk away.

'Tomorrow night then,' she agreed. 'But if you're just stalling, I'm going to be seriously annoyed.'

'I'm not stalling. I'm trying to do this right.' He reached out and opened the gate for her before leaning her chair against the fence.

The gesture was simple but considerate, and it caught her off guard more than all the grand community projects he'd been involved in. 'Thanks.'

'You're welcome.' He stepped back, creating distance between them. 'Goodnight, Ella. Thanks for tonight, for including me in those stories and not making me feel like a complete outsider.'

'You're not a complete outsider,' she said before she could stop herself. 'Maybe partial, but not complete.'

His smile was visible even in the dim light. 'I'll take partial. It's better than I had this morning.'

When he leaned forward, her skin tingled. His lips brushed gently across hers, soft and questioning, before pulling back. Their eyes met and held, and she saw her own surprise reflected in his gaze. She closed her eyes and took a step towards him, closing the distance between them. This time when his mouth found hers, the kiss lingered, warm and certain, making her pulse race.

They stood staring at each other afterwards, neither

quite knowing what to say, until his hand rose to brush tenderly across her cheek. 'Night, Ella.'

Her words barely came out. 'Night, Dusty.'

She watched him walk away down the lane, his hands in his pockets and his pace unhurried. When he turned the corner and disappeared from view, she finally opened her gate and walked up to her cottage, her fingers touching her lips where the warmth of his kiss still lingered.

Inside, she leaned against the closed door and tried to process everything that had happened. She'd gone to the barbecue planning to extract information from him, to use him to further her own goals regarding the properties. Instead, she'd found herself enjoying his company, laughing at his jokes, and agreeing to meet him tomorrow for what sounded like a serious conversation that could change everything.

As she got ready for bed, she couldn't shake the feeling that tomorrow night was going to be significant in ways she couldn't quite predict. And the fact that she was more excited than anxious about it was perhaps the most unsettling realisation of all.

CHAPTER 24

Dusty appeared at the store just after nine in the morning, the bell above the door announcing his arrival while Ella was restocking shelves in the back corner. She heard his voice asking Tyson where she was, and her stomach did that annoying flip that had kept her awake half the night. She'd replayed that kiss a hundred times, analysing every second of it, wondering what it meant and whether he'd been thinking about it too.

'I'm back here,' she called out, wiping dust off her hands onto her denim shorts. She'd dressed for a day of heavy lifting and stock rotation, which meant practical clothes and hair thrown up in a messy ponytail. Not exactly the image she wanted to present after kissing someone the night before, but here she was.

He walked down the aisle towards her, looking completely at ease in his work clothes; dusty jeans, a faded shirt with the sleeves rolled up, and sturdy work boots. If he was thinking about last night, his face gave nothing away.

'Morning,' he said, as casual as if they'd never touched. 'Got a minute?'

She set down the bag of stock feed she'd been holding. 'Sure. What's up?'

'I've been thinking about our conversation last night. About telling you what's going on with the properties.' He leaned against the shelving unit, completely relaxed. 'I reckon it'd be better if we talked out at that block instead of at the pub. More private, and you can actually see what I'm talking about.'

'The property out of town?' She tried to keep her voice neutral.

'Yeah. I was thinking I could pick you up this afternoon if that suits you. I'll bring some food so we don't have to rush back for dinner.'

The casual way he said it, like he was proposing a business meeting rather than addressing the elephant in the room from last night, threw her completely off balance. 'You want to drive me out there?'

'Makes more sense than trying to explain it all in the abstract. Plus, you know the place better than I do. You can tell me if I'm missing the obvious.' His dark eyes held hers steadily, no hint of awkwardness or acknowledgment of what had happened at her gate.

She searched his face for any sign that he was thinking about the kiss, but found nothing. Maybe it had meant less to him than it had to her. The thought stung more than it should have.

'Alright,' she said finally. 'I can get away from here at three. I'll be ready.'

'Good. I'll see you then.' He straightened up and started to leave, then paused. 'Oh, and don't worry about getting changed or anything. We're just going to be walking around in the dust.'

After he left, she picked up the bag of stock feed and just stood there, trying to process what had just happened. He'd completely ignored the kiss, acted like they were just two acquaintances arranging a meeting. Meanwhile, she'd spent the entire morning rehearsing what she'd say if he brought it up.

Tyson appeared at the end of the aisle. 'What did he want?'

'Just to arrange a time to talk about some building project.' She hoisted the feed bag onto the shelf with more force than necessary.

'Right. And that's why you look like you want to throw something?'

'I don't want to throw anything.'

'Sure you don't.' Her brother grinned knowingly. 'For what it's worth, I like him. He's good to Liam, and he knows what he's doing with a hammer. That's more than you can say for most blokes these days.'

She didn't respond, just moved on to the next bag. The fact that even Tyson had an opinion about Dusty, reminded her of how thoroughly he'd integrated himself into their community. Which made whatever he was about to tell her this afternoon even more significant.

BY THE TIME three o'clock arrived, Ella had worked herself into a state of nervous anticipation that she tried desperately to hide. She'd told herself a hundred times that this was just about the properties, about getting information she could use. But the memory of that kiss kept surfacing, along with the uncomfortable awareness that she really did want to see him again, regardless of what he had to tell her.

His white ute pulled up exactly on time, and she locked the store's front door before walking out to meet him. He'd showered since this morning, his dark hair still slightly damp, though he was wearing similar work clothes. When she climbed into the passenger seat, the confined space immediately made her aware of how close they were sitting, and the faint scent of his soap mixed with something distinctly him.

'Ready?' he asked, starting the engine.

'As I'll ever be.'

The chemistry between them was undeniable now. She could feel it in the way he glanced at her when he thought she wasn't looking, in the careful way he kept his hands on the steering wheel, and in her own hyperawareness of every movement he made. It made her nervous in a way that had nothing to do with property disputes and everything to do with the fact that she couldn't trust her own reactions around him anymore.

She needed to stay focused. Whatever he was about to tell her could affect her entire future, her plans, and her family's business. She couldn't let physical attraction muddy her judgment.

They drove out of town in silence for the first few minutes, the landscape opening up around them as houses gave way to paddocks and scrubland. The late afternoon sun cast everything in golden light, making even the drought-stricken country look beautiful in that particularly Australian way. Dry grass stretched in every direction, punctuated by stands of eucalyptus and the occasional windmill catching the breeze.

'You're quiet,' he observed.

'Just thinking.'

'About last night?'

The question caught her off guard. 'I thought we were pretending that didn't happen.'

'I wasn't pretending. I just didn't think we should talk about it until after we dealt with the property situation.' He kept his eyes on the road. 'Seemed like adding that complication wouldn't help either of us think clearly.'

'So you have been thinking about it?'

'Of course I have. Have you?'

She didn't answer immediately, watching the landscape roll past. 'Maybe.'

'That's what I thought.' There was a tone in his voice that might have been amusement or satisfaction. 'For the record, I'm not sorry it happened. But I am sorry about the timing.'

Before she could formulate a response to that, he turned off the main road onto the rough track that led to the property. The ute bounced over ruts and stones, and she grabbed the 'oh shit' handle to steady herself. Within minutes, the boundary fence and old windmill came into view, rusting and motionless against the backdrop of hills.

He parked near the gate and when he got out, she saw he'd come prepared. In the back of the ute was a small folding table, two camping chairs, and what looked like a proper picnic basket. 'You went to some trouble,' she said, following him towards the shade of small trees and bushes that lined a gully nearby.

'The pub put the basket together. I just had to pick it

up.' He arranged the chairs in the shade, then started unpacking food. There was fresh bread, cheese, cold chicken, salads, and even a bottle of wine with proper glasses. 'Patricia insisted on the wine. Said any serious conversation requires decent refreshments.'

Despite her nerves, Ella felt her appetite respond to the sight and smell of the food. He'd gone to considerable effort, which meant he was either trying to soften bad news, or he actually cared about making this comfortable for her. She wasn't sure which option unsettled her more.

'This looks amazing,' she admitted, taking a seat. 'Thank you.'

'You're welcome.' He poured wine into both glasses and handed her one. 'To honest conversations.'

She clinked her glass against his, although the toast felt ominous. 'To honest conversations.'

They ate for a while, the food providing a distraction from the tension humming between them. The chicken was perfectly seasoned, the bread was fresh from the bakery, and the wine was surprisingly good. Patricia clearly knew what she was doing. 'So,' Ella said finally, unable to wait any longer. 'Are you going to tell me why we're really here? What your plans are for this place?'

He set down his wine glass and leaned back in his chair, his gaze sweeping across the property before returning to her face. 'I am. But first, I need you to understand why I came to Matfield in the first place.'

She waited, her heart beating faster.

'And I need you to listen to the whole story before you make up your mind about what it means. Can you do that?'

'I can try.'

'That's all I'm asking.' He took a breath, and she could see him gathering his thoughts, deciding where to begin. The afternoon sun was lowering behind them, casting long shadows across the dry grass, and somewhere in the distance a crow called out into the stillness.

This was it. Whatever he was about to tell her would no doubt change everything. And judging by the serious expression on his face, she had a feeling it was going to be complicated in ways she hadn't anticipated.

CHAPTER 25

*D*usty took a long breath and looked out across the property, as if gathering the right words from the landscape itself. 'My grandmother died two years ago. Mina. She was ninety-two when she passed, sharp as a tack right until the end.' He paused, his fingers tracing the rim of his wine glass. 'Before she died, she asked me to do a task for her. A burden she'd been carrying for over fifty years.'

Ella leaned forward slightly, caught by the shift in his tone. This wasn't what she'd expected.

'Mina was born in inland Queensland in 1930. Her grandfather came out from Afghanistan in the 1890s as a cameleer. You know about the Afghan cameleers?'

'A bit. They brought supplies into the outback before trucks took over.'

'That's right. Her grandfather worked the camel trains through Central Queensland, then settled near Marree when the camel trade died out and motor vehicles made them obsolete. He married an Aboriginal woman from the area and together they had a large family.

Mina's father was part of that family and grew up on the camel trails. He married a woman who was also a descendant of the cameleers and they had a property at Marree. By the time Mina was born, her family was running a small market garden, trying to make a go of it on land that fought them every step of the way.' He picked up a piece of bread but didn't eat it, just turned it over in his hands. 'Mina grew up caught between worlds. She was a mixture of her Afghan heritage and the Indigenous culture around her. The Aboriginal families were their only real support. She had fond childhood recollections of that time spent with them, learning stories and sharing meals. But they were all outcasts together. The white town people never accepted any of them.'

He set down the bread and picked up his wine glass, staring into it. 'Then she met my grandfather. Antonio Camilleri. Everyone called him Tonio. He was Maltese. Came out after the war under one of those assisted migration schemes that promised opportunities if you were willing to work hard enough. He worked cane up north first, which was brutal labour in brutal heat. Then he drifted south and inland, looking for a better job. He was Catholic, spoke with an accent, and looked Mediterranean. The locals called him a dago.'

'That must have been rough,' Ella said quietly.

'It was. Mina met Tonio when she went into town to buy supplies with her father. He was helping to build a store and her father, impressed by his work, asked him to come out to their place and fix the roof of their shack.

Tonio refused to charge them anything, only asking to share a meal with them in return. They became friends, but when he fell for Mina, both families lost their minds. Her relatives wanted her to marry within their community. By then some of Tonio's family had migrated and were living in Melbourne, and they wanted him to marry a good Catholic Maltese girl from a respectable family. They did it anyway. Went against everyone and got married in 1948. She was only eighteen.'

The way he told it, with such careful detail, made it clear this wasn't just family history. This mattered deeply to him.

'They moved away from everything she knew and scraped together enough money to buy a small property.' He gestured around them. 'This property. Plus after a while they also purchased the block in town next to your family's store. They were going to make a life for themselves despite everyone telling them they wouldn't last.'

Ella felt her stomach drop. 'This property? Your grandparents owned this place?'

'Yeah. They lived here from 1950 until 1966. Sixteen years of trying to belong in a town that never wanted them.' His voice was matter-of-fact, but she could hear the weight behind it. 'The locals tolerated them for business. They'd employ Antonio when they needed a structure built or fixed. But socially? They were always outsiders. Too dark, too foreign, too different. She said the only people who treated them like actual human beings were the Indigenous families in the area.'

'I had no idea.' Ella was reeling, trying to reconcile this history with what she thought she knew about the property.

'My dad was born here in 1958. He was their first child, and for a while, things were okay. Hard, but okay. Then in 1963, they had a baby girl.' He stopped, and Ella could see him working to keep his voice steady. 'Amira Elena. My grandmother named her after both her Afghan heritage and my grandfather's Maltese one. A bridge between their worlds.'

He stopped and took a deep breath. 'Amira was three months old when she died. She got sick, probably pneumonia or something similar. By the time they got her to a doctor, it was too late.' He paused, his jaw tightening. 'Medical care out here was basic at best back then, and for a family like theirs, who half the town thought shouldn't even be here...' He trailed off, shaking his head.

'God, that's awful.'

'It destroyed them. My grandfather buried her here on the property. He carved a wooden cross and marked the spot. But the town...' His jaw tightened. 'The town said they'd buried her "out back like an animal" because she wasn't baptised properly.'

Ella felt sick. 'People actually said that?'

'They did. My grandmother told me about it before she died. She remembered it word for word. How the whispers followed them everywhere. How the grief was bad enough without having to hear people talk about her baby like that.' He finally ate the piece of bread he'd been holding. 'A few days after the burial, they couldn't take it anymore. They dug her up in the middle of the night, wrapped her carefully, and drove her to Melbourne. Antonio's brothers helped them arrange a proper Catholic burial in consecrated ground.'

'They took her body to Melbourne?'

'They did. Left the cross here and a few small things buried at the site. A baby bonnet and a rosary that had belonged to Antonio's mother. Then they came back and tried to keep living here, knowing their daughter was hundreds of kilometres away in a cemetery they couldn't visit regularly.'

Ella sat back in her chair, trying to process everything. 'How long did they stay after that?'

'Another three years. They hung on until 1966, trying to prove they belonged and trying to make their son's life better. But the grief never left them, and the town never warmed to them. Eventually they moved back to Melbourne to be near Antonio's family. My dad was eight years old.'

'That's heartbreaking.'

'It shaped everything about our family. My grandmother never got over losing that baby. She pushed her only son toward medicine, believing that education and medical knowledge could have prevented the kind of helplessness she'd felt.' He took a breath. 'That's why my dad became a cardiac surgeon, and why he in turn encouraged his children to go into medicine. He made sure we all had the best education and opportunities.' He smiled sadly. 'It's why all my siblings went into medicine or dentistry. Fortunately, they were all passionate about their vocations.'

'And you?' Ella asked softly.

'I'm the odd one out. The only one who didn't follow that path.' He smiled. 'Turns out I inherited my grandfather's hands instead. He was a carpenter before he bought this place. I think that's why Nonna asked me to do this for her instead of my siblings. She knew I'd understand what it meant.'

'What did she ask you to do?'

He was quiet for a moment, and when he spoke again, his voice was thick with emotion. 'I sat with her in the hospital three days before she died. She was so small by then, frail in a way I'd never seen her. But her mind was clear, and she had things she needed to say.' He set down his wine glass and rubbed his face. 'She took my hand and said...' His voice broke slightly. '"Dustin, until the echoes of that baby girl are put to rest, I cannot rest. Even after I'm gone, they will haunt me. I need you to put it all to rest and make the echoes good ones. Ones that carry love and family and tradition, not just grief and shame."' He paused. 'I wrote it down so I would remember it word for word.'

Ella felt tears spring to her eyes. The raw pain in those words, the weight of decades of unresolved grief, hit her like a physical blow.

'She wanted me to find the grave site,' Dusty continued, his voice barely above a whisper. 'The place where they first buried Amira. My grandmother needed to know if the cross was still there, if any trace remained of that spot where she said goodbye to her daughter the first time.' He stared at his hands. 'She gave me all the details she remembered. The direction from the old house, the trees nearby, the way the land sloped. But she was twenty-nine when she left here. She carried that grief for over sixty years without ever coming back. I'm not sure how accurate the description is.'

He looked directly at Ella now, and she could see the moisture in his eyes. 'She made me promise. On her deathbed, she held my hand so tight and made me swear I'd find that place and honour it properly. Make it mean something other than loss and exclusion. Turn those echoes into a beautiful memory. Just one day do that for me, she said.'

Ella wiped at her own tears, completely undone by the depth of love and commitment in his quest. All her suspicions, all her judgments, felt petty and small in the face of this.

'How did you end up working here in Matfield?' she asked. 'Was that why you came?'

'That's where Oscar comes in.' Dusty's expression softened slightly. 'He and my dad met at King's College in England. My father was sent there on a scholarship for medical studies, and they became friends. Oscar had just been awarded a Rhodes Scholarship.' He paused. 'When my father came back to Australia to complete his studies in Melbourne, they lost contact. It wasn't until Oscar showed up on Dad's doorstep many years later that they reconnected.' He smiled at the memory. 'Oscar didn't follow his original plan of study and somehow ended up here owning the pub. He and my father remained the best of friends. Oscar and his wife often visited them in Melbourne, though my parents never made it out here. My father was always working, and we rarely, if ever, went on a holiday.'

Last year, when Oscar and Patricia were visiting Melbourne, Oscar mentioned he was looking for a builder to renovate the pub. He wanted someone reliable who could handle historical restoration work.'

'And you volunteered?'

'The moment my dad told me it was in Matfield, I

practically begged for the job.' He gave a slight laugh. 'He thought I was mad, wanting to come all the way out here for months of work.' He looked down at his hands. 'The family, mainly my siblings, always talked about the two properties out here. Everyone was busy though, and I know it sounds terrible, but I always had an excuse not to come out this way. When the opportunity presented itself, it felt like it was meant to be.'

His expression grew serious. 'But I couldn't tell Dad why I was so eager. Nonna had made me promise not to tell the family until I'd found the grave. She didn't want them to know she was still carrying that pain if I couldn't fulfil her wish.'

He rubbed his face. 'I'd often looked at where the town was on a map but hadn't quite found the time or inclination to get there. I'd decided I would search for it if I ever travelled around Australia. With this opportunity, it looked like fate was playing a hand. It was meant to be that I come here, work and look for what Nonna had lost.'

'So Oscar doesn't know either?'

'Oscar thinks I'm just here for the building work, although he knew years ago about the connection to Matfield. Eli knows most of the story but not everything. I couldn't risk word getting around town before I'd completed what I came to do.'

The revelation sat between them, changing everything Ella thought she'd understood about his presence in Matfield. This wasn't about development, or profit, or taking advantage of cheap country land. This was about a grandson's love for his grandmother, about honouring a family's pain that had been ignored and dismissed for decades.

'The property's still in the family trust my dad set up after my grandparents passed away and he inherited the property,' he continued. 'It's taken us years to get to where we are with our plans for it and the other one they owned.'

'The block in town? Next to our store?'

'Yes. Same thing. Still in the family trust. My siblings and I do have plans for it, but it's not what you think. That's what I've been doing here, Ella. Not scheming for a developer. Not looking at how to make a lot of money. Just trying to find a grave so I could tell my grandmother's spirit that her baby's memory hasn't been forgotten. That Amira Elena matters, that her short life had meaning and that the echoes she left behind are about love, not shame.'

Ella felt tears streaming down her face now, unable to hold them back. All this time she'd been convinced he was some opportunistic developer, and instead he'd been on a deeply personal quest to honour his grandmother's grief and transform decades of pain into a meaningful memory.

'You've been walking around this property for weeks,' she said, her voice breaking. 'Covering every inch of it.'

'I have. And I still haven't found it. The old homestead has shifted, trees have grown or died, and the landscape has changed. What she described doesn't match what's here now, at least not that I can find.' His frustration was evident in every word. 'I've been out here dozens of times, in different light and weather conditions, trying to see what she saw sixty years ago.'

He looked at her with an expression that was raw and vulnerable. 'You said you've been coming here since you were a teenager, that you know this land better than anyone. Have you ever seen anything that might be...' He trailed off, as if asking was almost too much. 'A wooden cross, maybe fallen over? A pile of stones that seemed deliberate? Anything that might mark a grave?'

Ella's mind raced back through all her walks across this property. The hours spent exploring, imagining building her house here, finding peaceful spots to sit and think. Had she ever noticed anything like what he was describing? She thought about the overgrown areas she avoided, the rocky sections she assumed were just natural formations and the spots near the creek where vegetation grew thick.

'I don't know,' she said honestly. 'It's strange that you say she was a descendant of Afghan cameleers. I remember seeing two camels here, back before I went to uni. They followed me once, at a distance. For about an hour they walked behind me before they stopped. When I turned back to look at them they'd turned around and were headed back towards the creek. I wonder if your grandparents had camels on this property when they lived here.'

'They did. She told me, but I can't remember their names. I'd have to check the story with Dad, but I think they had them when they first moved here but then they let them go. I guess with the use of the car they weren't needed anymore. Nonna said they were her pets and they used to follow her all over the property. Dad says he can remember them too. It's amazing that they, or maybe their offspring, might still be around.'

'I haven't seen them for a long while. Now I'm also thinking about another place here on the property that might match the spot you're talking about. There's no cross or anything but it's an unusual area.'

She thought for a while. 'I've never been looking for a spot like that. But now that you've told me...' She paused, trying to remember every detail of the landscape she thought she knew so well. 'There's an area beyond the back creek, where there's a strange circle of rocks. I always thought it was just natural formation, but maybe...'

His face lit up with hope so intense it was almost painful to witness. 'Could you show me? Would you be willing to help me look?'

The question hung in the air between them, loaded with more meaning than just searching for a grave. He was asking her to be part of a deeply personal quest, to help him complete a promise to his grandmother. After weeks of suspecting him, judging him, keeping him at arm's length, he was inviting her into the heart of why he'd really come to Matfield.

'Yes,' she said, surprising herself with how quickly and decisively she answered. 'Yes, I'll help you look. We'll find it together.'

He reached across the small table and took her hand, squeezing it gently. 'Thank you. You have no idea what this means to me.'

But she thought maybe she did. She could see it in his eyes, in the way his shoulders tensed when he talked about his grandmother's dying wish, in the reverence with which he spoke about Amira Elena. This wasn't just about finding a grave. It was about honouring love that had been dismissed, recognising grief that had been mocked, and transforming echoes of pain into echoes of remembrance and respect.

As they sat there in the fading light, their hands still clasped across the table, Ella realised that everything had shifted between them. The property wasn't what she'd thought. Dusty wasn't who she'd assumed. And the future she'd been so certain about suddenly looked completely different, shaped by a story that had begun before either of them were born.

CHAPTER 26

$\mathcal{D}$usty helped Ella pack up the remains of their meal as the last light faded from the sky. The sunset painted everything in shades of orange and gold that would have been spectacular if he'd been paying attention. But his mind was elsewhere, caught between relief and vulnerability. The relief of finally telling someone the truth sat warm in his chest, easing a tension he'd been carrying since arriving in Matfield. But more than that, it was her reaction that had undone his emotions. The way she'd cried for his grandmother, for a baby she'd never known and for a family's grief that had nothing to do with her own life. It wasn't a reaction you could fake or perform. It was real.

'We should head back,' she said, folding the tablecloth with careful movements, her fingers smoothing out each crease with unnecessary precision. 'It'll be dark soon, and there's no point trying to search now.'

'When can we come back? When do you have time to help me look properly?' He tried to keep the urgency out of his voice but couldn't quite manage it. He'd been searching for months, walking this property in heat and wind, with the particular kind of loneliness that came from carrying a secret, and now, with her help, he felt closer than he'd ever been. So close he could almost taste it.

'Saturday? I've got the whole day off. My brother's managing the store.' She looked towards the hills, her eyes narrowing in the gathering darkness. 'It's a fair way in, up on a bit of a rise on those hills. I'm not certain it's what you're looking for, but I've always been drawn to that spot. There are these strange circles of rocks that never quite made sense. Too deliberate to be natural, but I could never work out what they were for.'

'Saturday works. I'll pick you up early. What time?'

'Six? That'll give us a fair few hours before the heat gets unbearable.'

They loaded everything back into the ute, and as they drove away from the property, Dusty felt the atmosphere between them had fundamentally changed. The antagonism that had defined their interactions for months had dissolved, replaced by a connection he didn't quite have words for yet. Trust, maybe. Friendship, certainly. And underneath it all, that awareness that had been there since the barbecue, now impossible to ignore, palpable in the confined space of the ute cab.

'Thank you for telling me,' Ella said quietly as they hit the main road back to town, the ute's headlights cutting through the darkness. 'For trusting me with your family's story.'

'I should have told you weeks ago. Would have saved us both a lot of trouble.' He glanced at her, catching her profile in the dashboard lights, the way shadows played across her face. 'I'm sorry I let you think I was someone I wasn't.'

'I never gave you the chance to explain.' She turned to look at him, and even in the dim light he could see the regret in her eyes. 'I jumped to conclusions about who you were and what you wanted. That wasn't fair to you.'

The apology hung between them, genuine and necessary. He reached over and briefly squeezed her hand where it rested on her knee, then returned his attention to the dark road ahead. The touch lasted only seconds, but it felt significant in a way that quickened his pulse and made him hyperaware of the small space between them.

When he pulled up outside her cottage, neither moved to get out immediately. The engine ticked as it cooled, and somewhere down the street a dog barked twice then fell silent.

'Saturday then,' she said, but she didn't reach for the door handle.

'Saturday. I'll bring water and snacks. And proper sun protection.'

She smiled at that, and he noticed how it changed her whole face, softening the guardedness she usually wore like armour. 'You're learning.'

'I'm trying.' He wanted to say more, wanted to acknowledge what was building between them, but the words felt too big for the moment, too weighty for this fragile new understanding they'd reached. Instead he just said, 'Goodnight, Ella.'

'Goodnight.'

He watched her walk to her door, waited until she was safely inside with the light on, then drove the short distance back to his cottage. Inside, he sat on the small couch that sagged in the middle and let himself really feel what had happened. He'd told her everything, stripped himself bare of pretence and defensiveness. Instead of judgment or pity, she'd offered understanding and help.

* * *

THE NEXT FEW days crawled by with agonising slowness. Work on the pub kept him busy, and Liam's eager questions about technique provided a welcome distraction, but his mind kept circling back to Saturday. To searching with Ella. To the possibility of finally fulfilling his grandmother's last wish.

Eli noticed his distraction. 'You alright, mate? You've measured that beam three times and gotten three different numbers.'

'Fine. Just thinking.'

'About Ella?'

Dusty looked up sharply. 'How did you know?'

'Because you've been checking your phone every five minutes and smiling at nothing. Plus, you're whistling. You never whistle.' Eli grinned, clearly enjoying himself. 'So, what happened? You finally tell her about the property?'

'I did. She's going to help me search for the grave on Saturday.'

'That's good. That's really good, Dusty.' Eli's expression turned more serious, the teasing falling away. 'She's a good sort. Bit prickly at first, but genuine once you get past the defensive walls. Takes some work to get there, but worth it.'

'Yeah.' Dusty returned to his measuring, getting it right this time. 'She is.'

By Saturday morning, he'd worked himself into a state of nervous anticipation that felt ridiculous for a thirty-two-year-old man. He'd packed and repacked his backpack twice, making sure they had enough water, food, a first aid kit in case of snakebite or falls, his grandmother's notes about the location, and a small trowel in case they needed to dig carefully around anything they found. Then he'd unpacked it all and started again, convinced he'd forgotten essential items.

The morning was already warm when he pulled up outside Ella's cottage at exactly six. She emerged wearing practical clothes for a day of rough walking: long pants to protect against scrub and snakes, sturdy boots that had clearly seen plenty of use, a long-sleeved shirt, and a wide-brimmed hat. She carried her own backpack and a walking stick he assumed she'd need for the terrain.

'Morning,' she said, climbing into the passenger seat with an easy smile that made his heart skip in a way he hadn't felt in years.

'Morning. Ready for an adventure?'

'As ready as I'll ever be.'

* * *

THEY DROVE out of town as the sun was still climbing, painting the landscape in shades of gold and pink. The heat hadn't built to its full oppressive weight yet, and the morning light made everything look softer, more forgiving and full of promise. Dusty found himself acutely aware of her presence beside him, the way she pointed out landmarks as they drove, the easy comfort of her company.

'We'll park on the north side,' she said as they approached the property. 'There's a better track in from that direction, and it'll take us straight towards the area I was thinking of. Your property incorporates those hills so we'll park as close as we can to them.'

He followed her directions, pulling off onto a rough track he'd never noticed before. It was overgrown but still passable, suggesting it had been used occasionally over the years, maybe by kids looking for adventure or farmers checking for wandering stock. When they parked and got out, the morning air was fresh and clear, carrying the scent of eucalyptus and dry grass in a landscape indefinably Australian that he'd never quite found words for.

'It's about a forty-minute walk from here,' Ella said, adjusting her hat and shouldering her pack. 'The terrain gets rougher as we go, but nothing too difficult if you watch your footing.'

They set off together, falling into a rhythm that felt natural despite the importance of their mission. Dusty found himself watching her as much as the landscape, noting how confidently she moved through the bush and instinctively found the easiest paths through scrub and around obstacles. This was her natural environment, and seeing her like this, completely at ease and in command, made him realise how much of herself she'd been holding back in town.

'You really do know this place,' he observed.

'I've walked every inch of it over the years. It always worried me that no one else cared for it.' She glanced back at him, and an understanding passed between them, an acknowledgment of how those dreams had shifted. 'Never knowing it already had so much life and loss attached to it.'

'Does it change how you feel about it? Knowing my family's history here?'

She was quiet for a moment, navigating around a fallen log that was half-rotted and crawling with ants. 'It makes it more real somehow. Less like an empty canvas and more like a place with stories that matter. I've always felt like there were unanswered mysteries to this place, echoes I couldn't quite hear but knew were there, and now I know some of them. I think I like it better this way, actually. It's more honest.'

Her answer settled him. He'd worried that his family's tragedy might taint the land for her, but instead it seemed to have deepened her connection to it, made it sacred rather than cursed.

They walked in comfortable silence for a while, the only sounds their footsteps, birdsong, and the occasional rustle of small animals fleeing their approach. The sun climbed higher, and even with the morning coolness, Dusty could feel sweat beginning to gather under his hat, trickling down his back.

'There,' Ella said eventually, pointing towards a slight rise ahead. 'That's the area. See how the land lifts slightly and then drops away towards the creek? And there's that old river red gum that must be hundreds of years old.'

His heart rate picked up, pounding in his ears. The description matched elements of what his grandmother had told him, though so much had changed over sixty years. They climbed the gentle rise together, and as they crested it, Ella led him towards a cluster of rocks that did look deliberately placed rather than naturally fallen.

'This is it,' she said softly. 'This is the spot that always felt different to me. Sacred somehow.'

Dusty stood there, looking at the circles of rocks, at the old tree providing shade and at the way the land rolled away towards the creek. His chest tightened. This could be it. After months of searching, weeks of doubt, this could actually be where his grandmother had said goodbye to her baby daughter so many years ago.

He looked at Ella. There was hope and concern in her eyes, and he felt an overwhelming gratitude that she was here with him for this moment. Whatever they found or didn't find, at least he wasn't doing this alone anymore.

CHAPTER 27

*D*usty approached the rock circles slowly, almost reverently, as if sudden movement might somehow disturb whatever remained of his grandmother's grief. Ella hung back slightly, giving him space for this moment. She understood instinctively that this was his journey, his promise to fulfil, and she was here as witness rather than participant.

The rocks were weathered grey stone, arranged in two concentric circles with a gap on the eastern side. They'd settled into the earth over decades, half-buried now, but the deliberate pattern was unmistakable once you knew to look for it. Native grasses had grown up between them, soft and silvery in the morning light, and a small wattle tree had taken root just outside the outer circle, its delicate leaves providing dappled shade.

'This is it,' Dusty said, his voice rough with emotion he was barely holding in check. 'This has to be it.'

He knelt beside the inner circle, running his hands over the stones with infinite care, almost like each one held memories he could somehow access through touch. Ella watched his shoulders tense as he took several deep breaths. She moved closer, offering silent comfort as she kneeled beside him and placed a hand on his back.

'My grandfather would have placed these rocks,' he said, touching each one as if greeting old friends. 'This is exactly the kind of work he'd do, even in grief. Even when his heart was breaking, he'd make a beautiful and permanent spot.'

'The pattern is deliberate,' Ella observed, studying the careful arrangement. 'And look,' she gestured to the well-worn larger rock that she had sat on so many times over the years. 'I've always thought that rock had been placed there for someone to sit on. It's too perfectly positioned to be natural.'

Dusty pulled his grandmother's notes from his pocket, the paper worn from being folded and refolded countless times, the creases threatening to tear. 'She said there was a large gum tree to the west, rocks marking the boundaries, a place to sit, and words. She couldn't remember what, just that Antonio had carved letters into wood. Look behind us. That could be the dip in the hills that she said you could see from here. Like a v shape. Her memory was so clear about some details and fuzzy about others.'

They searched carefully, not wanting to disturb anything but desperate to find proof they were in the right place. Ella moved around the perimeter while Dusty focused on the centre of the circles. The morning sun climbed higher, making the shadows shift and change, revealing and concealing in turn.

'Dusty.' Ella's voice was quiet but urgent. 'Look at this.'

He moved to where she crouched near the base of the

old river red gum. Partially buried in accumulated leaf litter and soil, a piece of carved wood was visible. It was weathered almost smooth, but as Dusty carefully brushed away the debris with trembling hands, letters began to emerge.

'Amira Elena,' he read, his voice breaking on each syllable. '1956. Beloved daughter.'

The carved marker was simple. Time and weather had faded it, embedded it into the earth itself, but it had survived. His grandfather's hands had shaped this, pouring love and grief into every careful cut, creating a permanent memorial when everything else felt unbearably temporary.

Dusty sat back on his heels, tears streaming down his face, not bothering to wipe them away. 'She was right. It's still here. All these years, and it's still here.'

She felt her own tears fall as she watched him process the discovery, putting to rest decades of family grief. This wasn't just finding a grave marker. This was connecting across generations, honouring a promise, and validating grief that had been dismissed and mocked. This was proving that Amira Elena had mattered. She still mattered, her short life leaving marks that endured even when everyone who remembered her was gone.

'Should we dig?' she asked gently. 'Your grandmother mentioned they left items here. A bonnet and rosary?'

'Carefully. Very carefully.' He pulled the small trowel from his backpack, and together they began to excavate around the wooden marker with archaeological precision, working slowly and methodically.

It didn't take long. About twenty centimetres down, wrapped in what had once been oiled cloth but was now mostly disintegrated, they found a small metal box. Dusty lifted it out with trembling hands, brushing away decades of soil with infinite care.

Inside, preserved by the sealed tin, were the items his grandmother had described. What had once been a tiny white bonnet fell apart as he lifted it out, the old fabric destroyed probably from the heat and conditions. A rosary with wooden beads worn smooth from use was still intact though, and he passed it slowly to Ella to hold. There was also an unexpected item; a photograph, faded and water-damaged but still just visible. A young woman with dark hair and striking features held a baby wrapped in white. Mina and Amira, captured in one of their few moments together.

'Oh God,' Dusty whispered, staring at the photograph. 'I've never seen this. The family doesn't have any photos of the baby. They must have destroyed them all when they left, unable to bear looking at them.'

'Your grandmother was beautiful,' Ella said softly, looking at the young woman whose pain she now understood so intimately. The photograph showed Mina smiling at the camera, but there was a look in her eyes, some shadow that suggested she already knew happiness was fragile.

'She was so young when she left her family and came here. Same age as some of the kids Liam goes to school with.' He carefully lifted the photograph, and underneath it was a rectangle shaped piece of metal, a short message etched onto its surface.

He read aloud, his voice shaking with each word: 'You were loved. You will always be loved. We will meet again.'

The grief in those words, raw and immediate even

after sixty years, undid them both. Dusty bent forward, letting go of tears he'd had been holding back since his grandmother died, maybe since he'd first heard this story and understood the weight of what he'd been asked to do. Ella wrapped her arms around him, crying for this family she'd never known. This place was a symbol of grief that had shaped generations and showed a love that had survived, even when everything else was taken away.

They stayed like that for long minutes, kneeling in the dirt beside a grave that held no body but contained so much memory and pain. Around them, the bush was silent except for the wind in the leaves and the distant call of crows. The land out here could be harsh and it had held its secrets close.

Eventually, Dusty straightened, wiping his face with the back of his hand. 'Thank you,' he said to Ella, his voice raw. 'Thank you for helping me find this. For being here. For not making me do this alone.'

'I'm honoured you let me be part of it.'

He carefully repacked the items in the tin box, handling each one with reverence. 'I need to take these to Melbourne. To show my dad, to let the family know what we found. They need to see that their sister, their aunt, was loved and honoured even in this place that rejected them. They need to know the story hasn't ended.'

'What will you do with the site?' Ella asked, looking around at the peaceful clearing.

'I want to restore it properly. Clear around it, maybe add a small headstone, acknowledging that she was buried here first. Create a memorial that tells the full truth. Amira was buried here with love, then moved to be with family, but this spot remains sacred. A memorial to a baby girl and the family who loved her despite everything.'

Ella looked around the site, imagining it cleared and tended, with a permanent and beautiful marker. 'It would be a way to make the echoes good, like your grandmother wanted.'

'Exactly.' He stood, helping her to her feet, his hand lingering in hers. 'And maybe, if my family agrees, we could do more. An addition that benefits the community.'

The vision he was describing transformed the property from personal into communal. Ella felt her own dreams of building here shift and change, the image she'd held for so long dissolving and reforming into a different purpose. How could she claim this land for herself when it held such significance? When it could mean so much to people who had history here?

'That's a beautiful idea,' she said honestly, her mind settling on the reality that this land belonged to Dusty and his family. It wasn't her plan, and it meant that all her time had been wasted dreaming about what could have been for her, a place to call home. But she knew it felt right. It was family history. It was decades and decades of time and honour for those families who had struggled through the early years of settlement and tried to live in a land that was not only unforgiving and harsh but also battled against the minds of local settlers who mostly distrusted and ostracised anyone who was different, particularly if their skin was darker and their features those of a foreigner.

They spent another hour at the site, photographing everything carefully from multiple angles, measuring distances, making notes about the condition of the marker and the surrounding area. Dusty wanted to be able to describe it all precisely to his family. He wanted to show them that their history hadn't been erased or forgotten and that love that had begun with the story of Mina and Antonio had filtered down to the current generations, the connections and beliefs of family, love surviving even when everything else was stripped away.

As they finally prepared to walk back to the ute, Dusty paused and looked at her with an intensity that made her breath catch. 'I know you wanted this property for yourself and that this changes your plans completely.'

'It's alright,' she started, but he shook his head, stepping closer.

'No, let me finish. There's the other block too, the one in town next to your family's store. The one you thought I was developing.' He took a breath. 'My family does have plans for it, and they've been working through the details for months, actually closer to a year. That's part of what I couldn't tell you before.'

Ella's nerves tightened, that familiar anxiety creeping back. 'What kind of plans?'

'I can't tell you the specifics yet. The family needs to make some final decisions, and there are a few legal things to sort through first.' He stepped closer to her. 'But I can tell you this, it's a project this town desperately needs. A facility that would have meant so much to my grandparents and a project my family will create as a way of giving back, of making those echoes good.'

She searched his face, trying to read what he meant. 'That's very cryptic. For me the worst thing would be if some large building went on there. An industry or shop that wasn't in keeping with the town's heritage look. If you look at our produce store, it's pretty much the same front façade as it was a hundred years ago. I just don't want the town to look like an ugly concrete or brick suburban place. I don't want progress to destroy what makes us special.'

'I get it and I know. I'm sorry I can't tell you yet. I don't feel that it's a development that would change the character of the main street.' He reached out and gently wiped a tear from her cheek, his thumb lingering for just a moment, rough and warm against her skin. 'Trust me a bit longer? Just until my family makes the final decision?'

Ella wanted to push for more information, but the earnestness in his eyes stopped her. After everything he'd shared today, after the way he'd trusted her with his family's deepest grief, she could give him this. 'Alright. I'll wait.' She noticed however that he hadn't confirmed that it would match what was already in the town or that it wouldn't be some monstrosity that would tower over the produce store or the small butcher's shop on the opposite side.

'Thank you.' His hand was still on her face, and she leaned slightly into his touch. 'I want good things for this town, Ella. And I especially want good things for you.'

The way he said it, looking at her like she was precious, made every nerve in her body come alive with awareness. They were standing close enough that she could feel the heat coming off his body despite the morning air. She decided she had to trust him. She couldn't do much else anyway. The block belonged to him and his family. She and her family had no say in what might go there.

'We should head back,' she said, though she didn't move. 'It's getting hot.'

'We should,' he agreed, also not moving.

For a long moment they just stood there, the found grave behind them, the morning sun warming their backs, and everything between them feeling charged with possibility. Then Dusty smiled, that slow smile that transformed his whole face, and stepped back, breaking the spell.

'Come on. We've got a long walk back, and I promised to feed you properly when we got done.'

They walked back to the ute in companionable silence, both processing everything that had happened. The weight of the morning, the significance of what they'd found, settled over them like a blanket. But when they reached the vehicle and he opened her door, their hands brushed, and Ella felt that same electric awareness from the night of the barbecue. A connection was building between them, moving beyond simple attraction into genuine emotion.

As they drove back towards town, Dusty reached over and took her hand, linking their fingers together naturally, as if they'd been doing it for years. She didn't pull away. Instead, she squeezed gently, acknowledging what they both knew. Finding the grave had changed everything, but not in the way either of them had expected.

CHAPTER 28

After that day, Ella's life shifted. She no longer had the dreams she once had, and that left a huge gap in her daydreaming and the momentum in everyday things. The property out of town, the block next door to the store, the neat little plans she'd sketched out in her mind during quiet moments behind the counter, all of it had dissolved the moment she learned the truth about who owned them. It wasn't just disappointment that sat heavy in her chest. It was more complicated, tangled up with the way Dusty had looked at her when they'd stood together at that tiny grave, the air between them charged with grief and possibility.

'What are you going to do?' Tyson asked as they both leaned over the counter, grateful that there were no customers in the store. Outside, the heat shimmered off the road in waves. The usual afternoon quiet settled over Matfield like a blanket, that particular stillness that came with temperatures above forty.

'I'm not sure,' she replied, running her finger along a

worn groove in the wood that her grandfather's elbows had probably carved out over decades of leaning in exactly the same spot. 'I think I'll start having a look at what else is available in the area. Somewhere I can build a small house, or maybe a property that already has a building on it I can renovate.' Even as she said it, the words felt hollow, as if she was reading lines from a script she didn't believe. Nothing else would have the history of Pazhvak Station. She'd driven past it so many times and imagined herself living there. No other property would have that view of the ranges, or that particular quality of light at sunset that turned everything golden.

'I think once Mum and Dad are back, we'll have to discuss more about this men's shed Dad's so keen on. Surely we can find somewhere else to put that in play.' Her brother straightened up, stretching his back with an audible crack. 'I noticed yesterday there were a couple of surveyors next door, marking out that block for who knows what. Had fancy equipment and took measurements for hours.'

She sighed, the sound carrying all her accumulated frustrations. Everything seemed so complicated, and she wasn't sure she had the energy to think further than tomorrow. The surveyors only confirmed what she already knew. Dusty would do whatever he needed to do with his family's land, and she'd have to let go of plans that had never really been hers to make. 'I've lost my mojo,' she told her brother, hearing the defeat in her own voice.

He straightened up properly then, fixing her with the kind of look that older brothers perfected, equal parts sympathy and impatience. 'You'll get it back. You always do. Get cracking because there's customers coming in.' He nodded towards the door where a ute was pulling up outside, dust billowing behind it. 'Everyone's after feed for their stock. We need that bloody rain soon, or there'll be nothing left to sell them.'

* * *

THAT NIGHT ELLA lay in bed watching the ceiling fan doing little more than push hot air around. She mulled over the events of the past weeks. Dusty had been busy at the pub, and with the produce store also being busy, she hadn't crossed paths with him since the day they'd found the grave. She'd thought about him more than she cared to admit, though, lying awake in the heavy darkness, listening to the wind rattling the corrugated iron on the shed out the back. She kept seeing the way his hands had been so gentle, clearing the earth from that tiny head-stone, the way his voice had cracked when he'd read his grandmother's words. When she woke properly in the middle of the night, restless and unable to settle back to sleep in the oppressive heat, an instant thought crossed her mind.

At the other end of town, there was a building that was designated for historical items and memorabilia. The community had always talked about creating a heritage village, collecting all the old farming gear and replicating some of the buildings from the pioneering days. That had not come to fruition, however. Plans and good intentions only went so far in a town where everyone was too busy just keeping their own properties going, fighting drought and debt and the constant erosion of rural services. Mrs

Walton, however, had devoted her life to keeping alive the history of Matfield and the surrounding areas, and she was excited when Ella rang early the next morning and asked her if she thought there might be anything there that connected to the property out of town.

'How about you come over tomorrow. It's Saturday, so I can unlock the place for you. I have a feeling there might be some photos or diary entries that relate to the people who once lived out there. It's a long while since I've seen them, but it rings a bell. The family that lived there lost a child and then a few years later moved away. Come and have a look, dear. I'm sure we can find something.'

And they did. In amongst a room that was filled from floor to ceiling with every different kind of memorabilia, photos and artefacts that you could ever imagine, Mrs Walton pulled out a large box filled with notebooks and photos. The room itself was a testament to her dedication, every shelf and surface crammed with the accumulated evidence of lives lived and lost in this harsh, beautiful country. Dust specks danced in the shaft of light coming through the high window, and the air smelled of old paper and time itself. It wore that particular mustiness that comes from decades compressed into cardboard and leather.

'Everything in this box belonged to the White family. The eldest son, Patrick, he's long gone now, well he was an avid photographer. Most of the photos we have of that era in Matfield were taken by him. And to make it even better, his Aunt Betty, who was his mother's sister, lived with his family. She spent most of her life in a wheelchair. Polio, poor thing. Betty kept journals and was an avid historian and storyteller. She died, let me think...' Mrs

Walton looked up at the ceiling as if it held the answer, her fingers tapping against the box. 'Ah yes, only a few months after my Bert died. That was 2001.'

Ella listened while Mrs Walton rattled off some more names and stories about those who had contributed to the town's historical collection, her weathered hands moving lovingly over the boxes and folders, as if greeting old friends. The old woman's passion was infectious, and Ella was drawn into the narrative of Matfield's past, seeing it not as a collection of dates and facts but more like a thread connecting all of them to the people who had struggled and survived before them.

'I just seem to remember some photos here of that family who lived out there, and I'm not sure what note-book it's in. I've read them all, but there's a mention of them in one of these journals. I don't remember what it said exactly, but I remember it talked about that small child or maybe it was a baby, dying. Tragic. Anyway, you're welcome to sit here in that chair and go through it all. I've got washing to hang out and a cake to put in the oven. I'll come back in a while and answer any questions you have.'

Ella decided to go through the photos first, which she thought would be quicker than reading all the journals. However, there were so many interesting pictures of the area that it took a lot longer than she intended. She pored over the black and white photos, gasping aloud when she found some of her family's produce store dating back to the 1940s. There were quite a few she had never seen before, and it was obvious that the photogra-pher was fastidious in capturing everyday life. They were candid rather than posed, capturing genuine moments of life in a way that made the past feel tangible and real.

There was one of her grandfather leaning over the very same counter where she'd served customers just yesterday. His long droopy moustache distinguished him immediately, and she held it up, noting all the produce behind him and the array of farming tools on the shelves to the side. The detail was extraordinary. She could see the labels on tins, the way the light fell through the front window, the worn patch on the floor where generations of boots had scuffed the boards smooth. She would take photos on her phone of these and get them printed. They would be perfect to put up in the store, a visual reminder of the history of the place. Quickly she had about fifteen photos of the produce store set aside, a small treasure trove of family history.

Then she came upon what she had come for. They were tied up in string, the kind of rough twine that people didn't use anymore, and the bundle had been tucked into a corner of the box to keep them separate. A collection of twenty-nine photos all up. Black and white and all the same size, about half the size of an A4 piece of paper. The first one had no people in it. There were just two camels standing, looking straight into the lens of the camera, their expressions patient and knowing. She held it up and turned it around, her heart beating faster. *Camilleri family and camels. 1963. Outside Matfield.*

Slowly she picked out some more photos, her hands trembling slightly. When she came to one that showed the family standing outside their hut, she gasped. In the mother's arms was a baby, small and dark-haired, wrapped in what looked like a pale shawl. On the back the description stated: *Mina and Antonio Camilleri. David Camilleri (8) and baby Amira (2 months) Pazhvak Station.*

There were more. Photos of Mina leading a camel across a paddock, her slight figure dwarfed by the animal's height, but her posture confident and easy. Antonio building a porch on the front of the house, his hands gripping a hammer. Antonio sitting on the edge of the newly built porch, swinging his legs, his face tilted up towards the camera with a shy smile that reminded her so much of Dusty she had to catch her breath. The photo she loved the most was one of Mina sitting on the front steps of the house, the newly erected verandah now having chairs on it. In her arms was the baby again, and Antonio stood beside her, his arm wrapped around her shoulders in a gesture so tender it made Ella's throat tighten. She peered closer into Mina's face. She had been a beautiful young woman, with dark hair and strong features. Her expression was of pure love for her son and the baby in her arms.

Another similar picture, showed her smiling down at the baby, her husband standing behind them, his eyes also cast down upon the children. She noted his stance, protective and proud, a fleeting image of a man who would have done anything for his family. Ella could see Dusty in him, the same set of the shoulders, the same way of holding himself, the same intensity in the eyes, even captured in black and white.

She stopped and thought hard as she read the writing on the back. This time the photographer had referred to the property as 'Camel Place.' She peered closer. They looked just like any family today. Trying to make a more comfortable home, trying to create the best for their family despite being strangers in a strange land. These were invaluable, and she couldn't wait to show Dusty. This was his history. Photos of his grandmother as a young woman, vital and happy, before grief had marked her. This was proof that his family had been here, had mattered, and had built a family life, even if it hadn't lasted.

When Mrs Walton returned, bustling in with the scent of baking following her, Ella showed her all the photos, spreading them carefully across the desk. The old woman's face softened as she looked at them, her gnarled fingers touching each one with reverence. 'You know, dig through those notebooks. I have a feeling there's a hard-cover one in there that might have the information that you're looking for. It's not much from memory, but there are words written. Betty was thorough, bless her.'

After flicking through the pages and skimming over the calligraphy style writing, Ella finally found what she was looking for. Betty's handwriting was beautiful, each letter formed with care, and reading it felt like eavesdropping on the past. Amidst the stories of local farmers, there was a reference to the woman Mina, who was descended from Afghan cameleers, and her husband, Antonio, a Maltese immigrant who had come to Australia after the war and was known for his building abilities.

He can build anything. Not only has he built new stairs for the local pub but he has also mended the verandah posts that showed every sign of collapsing. Regardless of what the locals say about his foreign ways, they often now employ him to build or fix what others can't. His wife, although she comes to town, is quiet, and some say she can't speak. I have, however, heard her talk in her own language to the young boy and now a new baby.

They come to town sometimes, but have made no effort to make friends or be part of the community. Some say that they are friends with the Aborigines who live out near them. This has not helped them settle in.

Ella paused, feeling the weight of those words. The casual prejudice, the isolation, the way the Camilleris had been marked as different and therefore suspect. She read on, her chest tightening with each paragraph.

A later entry said: *Today I spoke to the lady who waits in the car while her husband gets the groceries. The baby was crying and she said they needed help. Her English is not very good but I tried to explain that the doctor only came on the first Friday of the month which had just gone. She was concerned, and when her husband came back to the car he was also upset. He asked me again where they could get a doctor. Even the retired midwife was away and there was no one who could help. They had been to the chemist for some medicine and they were going to try that. The chemist told them if the baby was still sick tomorrow to come back into town and they'd try and get someone else to help them.*

Ella had to stop reading for a moment. She could picture it all too clearly, the desperate parents in a town where they had no real connections, where the language barrier made everything harder, where help came once a month if you were lucky and the calendar had just turned against them.

The next time I heard about them was from the chemist who said he had called the flying doctor for them the next day, but by the time they got there, the baby had died. This upset me for a very long time as I should have helped more that day. The chemist felt the same and told me it seemed that the baby only had a cold. This is a dreadful thing to happen to people who don't have family to help out and barely know the language. It highlights the difficulties of those who come from across the ocean, and after this happened I made a point of getting Patrick to drive me out and check on the family. We often took some fruit or other foodstuffs, and a couple of times Patrick bought a ball and a cricket bat for the small boy. The lady, Mina, would always make us a cup of tea and offer us sweet biscuits that her husband told us was from her traditional land of Afghanistan. He talked about how his wife was a descendant of the Afghan people who had come across the oceans in the late 1800s. They seemed like very nice people and Mina made us take some extra biscuits back with us. Mother loved them.

I could tell that she was pining for her baby, and although she was only young, she hardly smiled. It was difficult because she had very little English, but I think she knew that we cared and were worried about her. Others weren't so sympathetic and terrible rumours ran around town. Those of us who talked to the family knew better though, and I often sat and talked to Antonio when he came in for supplies. Mina never came into town again, and the last time I saw them they told me they were moving back to Melbourne to be near their family. I wasn't home the day they left but Patrick said the man, Antonio, came to the door and handed him a tin filled with Mina's biscuits. There was a note that just said, thank you. Nothing more. We did not see the family again and we do not know where they went. The property was closed up and, up until the date of writing this, no one has ever come back or lived there. I do not know what happened to this family once they left Matfield.

Ella kept looking through the journal but there was nothing more, and she didn't really expect there to be. If Dusty's account was right, the family had never returned and had spent the next fifty years paying rates on land they couldn't bear to visit. Her heart felt heavy, and sorrow filled her as she took photos of all the parts in the journal that related to the family. She photographed each page carefully, making sure the text was clear and legible, then moved back to the photos. Copies of the back and front of each photo were also taken, her phone's camera clicking over and over in the quiet room. Then she carefully tied the string back up and put everything back where it had come from, treating the bundle with reverence.

She would bring Dusty here so that he could see everything for himself. For now though, she just wanted to go and see him and show him what she had found. This discovery felt too important to wait. She knew these photos would mean everything to him, she knew that with a certainty that made her hands shake as she gathered her things. This was his grandmother as a young mother, alive and hopeful before tragedy had left its mark. This was proof that the Camilleris had existed, had mattered. They had been seen and remembered by at least some people in this town.

She thanked Mrs Walton profusely, promising to return with Dusty soon, then practically ran to her car. She needed to find him. She needed to give him this gift of his family's history, this tangible proof that they hadn't been entirely forgotten or erased from Matfield's story.

A knock on the door greeted Dusty as he emerged from the shower. Eli must have locked himself out again. Neither of them could get out of the habit of locking the front door when they went out, even though it seemed no one locked doors here. People left keys in utes, and houses open in ways that would be insane in Melbourne. He wrapped a towel around his hips and shook his head, getting any excess water off. Droplets scattered across the bathroom mirror and he swiped at them with his hand. Tucking the towel tight, he walked to the front door and opened it, about to tell Eli that this was the third time this week he had locked himself out.

'Whoa. You're not Eli,' he said as he stepped backwards. Ella stood in front of him, her long hair loose, her large green eyes wide as she looked him up and down. He watched her gaze travel from his face down to his chest, lingering there for a moment before dropping lower, and he felt suddenly, acutely aware of how little the towel actually covered.

'Um. No, I'm not. Sorry if you're disappointed.' She grinned at him, and he noticed her eyes roaming over his body again, slower this time, more deliberate. Her expression made his skin feel hot, and it had nothing to do with the shower.

For some stupid reason he felt his face burning. She didn't drop her gaze, her eyebrows rising in a humorous way as if she knew he was feeling awkward and was thoroughly enjoying it.

'Are you going to ask me in?' she questioned, her voice teasing. 'I have some items I'd like to show you.'

'Um, yes, sure. Come in.' He tightened his grip on his towel, suddenly paranoid about the way he'd tucked it. That was the last thing he needed, it coming loose in front of her. 'Give me a sec and I'll throw on some clothes.'

She looked like she was about to burst out laughing as he walked quickly to the bedroom, very conscious of her eyes on his back. Emerging wearing shorts and a T-shirt, his hair still damp and sticking up at odd angles, he smiled as she laughed outright. 'Surprise. It's me.'

'So funny,' he replied, but he was grinning too. She was different today. Her manner was lighter. The tension that had been between them since they'd found the grave seemed to have eased, replaced by a mood that felt almost playful. 'Cup of tea, or is it too early for a beer? They're light beers. Three o'clock. Not too early.'

'Not at all. Yes, I'd love one.'

They sat at his small kitchen table and she surveyed the room. She'd been in this cottage before. Some of the teachers had once lived here and she'd been friends with them. Basic but comfortable, and it looked like the same furniture that had been here years ago. The same mismatched chairs were spread around the same laminated table top with its fake wood grain pattern. He noticed her looking around. 'It's not the Taj Mahal, but it suits Eli and me. The kitchen works well and we can walk most places, so it pretty much satisfies our requirements. You'd pay a fortune for a rental house like this in Melbourne.'

'Different world here, isn't it?' she said.

He took a sip of his beer and she couldn't help but smile back at him when he gazed at her over the top of it. He had a way of looking at her that made her feel nervous but also excited. It was a long time since she'd felt like that, and she wasn't sure if the attraction she was feeling was simply a reaction to seeing that body with hardly any clothes on, or a deeper connection, a connection that had been building between them since that first antagonistic meeting.

She fanned her face with a magazine that was nearby. 'Is it hot in here?'

He grinned broadly. 'It is. Very hot, but I don't think it's the weather.'

'Very funny. Well, you shouldn't parade around half naked. It's not what I was expecting when you opened the door.'

He held up his beer to clink against hers. 'What have I done to gain the pleasure of your company this afternoon? It's not every Saturday that a beautiful woman appears on my doorstep.'

'Save your charm, Dusty. You won't win me over with those charismatic words.'

She could tell he was not offended by her reply, but rather amused. Her once hostile replies were now laced with affection, and no matter how much she tried to retain her distance from him, she knew she was failing miserably. Sitting so close to him, she could smell whatever soap he must have just used. Rugged stubble lined his face, and his hair was dishevelled, as though he had just rubbed the towel over it and not bothered to check a mirror. She shivered, a delicious feeling of awareness running through her, which didn't help when his eyes locked with hers and held them for a beat too long.

Gathering her thoughts and reminding herself to get a grip on her feelings, she pulled out the folder that Mrs Walton had so carefully placed the photos in. The old woman's words echoed in her mind as she held it. 'Take them, dear. I know you'll look after them and really no one else has bothered with them all these years. In fact, if the family wants them, they can take copies and give the copies back to me. They might like to keep these originals for themselves. You've got photos of the journal entries, so you have everything you need to take to your friend.'

Now, holding the folder in her hand, Ella felt the weight of what it contained. 'I remembered that Mrs Walton runs a small community group that has collected anything related to the local history of the area. It's been collected over many years and I wondered if there was anything in there about your family.'

His eyes widened and he leaned forward, suddenly intent. The scent of his body, or that damn soap, or whatever that pleasant lingering scent was, filled her nostrils and she stopped herself from wallowing in the pleasant aroma. He stared hard at her and then down at the folder.

'I went there this morning and asked Mrs Walton. She knows pretty much where everything is about anyone.

There was a local photographer, Patrick White, who took thousands of photos over the years, and he apparently loved just taking random pictures of the way people lived. So not so much posed portraits. The photos are amazing and show what life was really like out here back in the day.'

'Are you going to tell me you found a photo of someone in my family?'

'Better than that.' She eased open the folder and pushed it gently towards him, watching his face. 'The descriptions are on the back. There are twenty-nine photos of your grandparents with your dad and the baby girl, Amira.'

For a long while neither spoke. Dusty picked each photo up and studied it before moving onto the next, his fingers gentle on the aged paper. She watched his face as he looked at them, saw the moment recognition hit him. 'This is Nanna and Nannu. They're the Maltese names for grandparents. It's what we always called them. Wow, they look so young, but I can recognise their faces. The way Nanna's standing, that's exactly how she used to stand when she was looking at a person or place she loved.' He stopped talking and peered closely at the photo of the family sitting on the front steps. 'And... photos of the baby. I don't think Nanna had any, maybe apart from that little one she buried at the grave site. My God, Ella. These show not only them, but the baby.' He stopped and looked up, and she saw tears brimming in his eyes. 'If only she'd seen these. She wouldn't have known they existed because they never came back here.'

He spread the photos out on the table in front of them, both of them leaning in close, their heads nearly touching as they looked at them, pointing out different elements of interest. Dusty pointed to one that showed his grandmother standing on a platform. It was a lookout over a vast valley, with a line of mountains rising on the horizon. Although it was black and white, you could tell the sun was setting, and the look on Mina's face was one of beauty and wonder.

'She's beautiful,' Dusty said as he ran his finger over the picture, tracing the outline of her figure. 'I wish you could have met her. She was an amazing person. If I had one word to describe her, it would be kind.'

Ella peered closer, aware that her face was so close to Dusty's, that she could feel the warmth radiating from his skin. 'She went through so much.' For a moment she froze, caught by the intensity of his gaze, before sitting back up again. 'There's more.'

'More photos?' He was still looking at the image of his grandmother, drinking in every detail. 'Hang on a minute. Where is this last one taken, do you think? It's not somewhere I'm familiar with. Is this on their property?'

Ella picked it up, studying the landscape. 'That's the lookout further out here to the west. It was always known as Kissing Point. Kids from school would drive out there and park. You know.'

He laughed, and the sound eased some of the emotion in the room. 'I'm not sure how romantic Nannu would have been. Look at Nanna though. I reckon she would have only been about eighteen in this photo. So young.'

'So brave to come to a place like this back then, where she wouldn't have known anyone.' Ella thought about being that age and that isolated, carrying a baby in a place where people looked at you sideways because of your accent, or the colour of your skin. 'I can't imagine how lonely it must have been.'

'I need another beer,' he said, standing up and going to the fridge to get them another beer each. When he placed the cold bottle down in front of her, their fingers brushed, and neither of them moved for a second. The touch sent electricity up her arm, and she heard his breath stop before he pulled away. 'You said you have more?'

Sitting back in the chair, closer this time, he waited. 'Not photos,' she replied. 'I have diary entries.'

She told him about Betty White, Patrick's aunt, who happened to be in a wheelchair and who had loved recording the area's history. 'Her journals are all in a box in Mrs Walton's history room. She wrote down every-thing from about 1940, all through the war and then up to about 2002, when she passed away. It's a written story of Matfield and the people in it. I found some entries about your family. There could be more, but this is what I found today. Mrs Walton remembered reading them years ago. She didn't think there were any others.'

She passed him her phone, the screen showing the photographed pages. Sipping her beer as he read, she watched his face. She could tell that reading the sadness in the story was difficult for him. His jaw tightened and his eyes moved quickly over the words, then slowed, then stopped. When he finished, he passed the phone back to her, his hand gripping his beer hard enough that his knuckles showed white. 'They were misunderstood. If only they'd had someone close to them, to help them get decent medical help at least.'

'When I read it, I got the impression that the writer,

Betty, and some of the others did care about them, but the language barrier wouldn't have helped.'

Dusty wiped the tears from his eyes. 'It's just so sad. I know there would have been plenty who judged them because of where they came from, but there would have been others like this Patrick and Betty, who were good people, but there was no real connection between them. That's what kills me. They were here, they were trying, but no one really saw them.'

'It's interesting how your grandfather was known as a good carpenter and now here you are back in the same town doing similar work.' She said it gently, wanting to give him a link to hold onto, some thread of continuity.

He looked up at her, and his expression shifted. 'I never thought about it that way. Nanna used to tell me stories about him, about how he could fix anything or build whatever was needed. I just thought she was exaggerating a bit, you know? Making him sound better than he probably was.' He paused, running his thumb over the edge of one of the photos. 'But here it is in writing. Someone else saw it too.'

'He was real. They were real. They mattered here, even if it didn't feel like it to them at the time.' Ella reached across and touched his hand briefly. 'She felt the warmth of his skin. Mrs Walton said you can keep the originals if you want. Take copies for her records, but these should be with your family.'

'I don't know what to say.' His voice was rough, and he turned his hand over so their palms were touching. 'You didn't have to do this. Go digging through all that history for me.'

'Yes, I did.' She meant it, and she didn't pull her hand

away. Somewhere between resenting him for owning the land she wanted, and standing with him at that tiny grave, her feelings had changed. She cared about this, about him, about making sure his grandmother's story wasn't forgotten. 'Everyone deserves to know where they come from.'

They sat in silence for a moment, their hands still touching on the table, the photos spread between them like a bridge across time. Outside, the late afternoon light was starting to soften, and in the distance a dog barked. She thought to pull her hand away and break this moment before it became something she couldn't take back, but she stayed still, caught in the warmth of his palm against hers.

'That lookout in the photo,' she said finally, her voice quieter than usual. 'The one where your grandmother's standing. I was thinking...' She hesitated, not sure if she was overstepping. 'Would you want to go out there? See it for yourself? It's only about twenty minutes from town.'

Dusty looked at the photo again, his grandmother's young face turned towards that vast horizon. He looked back at Ella. 'You'd take me?'

'I'd like to.' She felt her cheeks warm. 'I mean, it's part of the story, isn't it? Might be nice to see where she stood. The view's still the same.'

He studied her for a long moment, and she wondered what he saw. His thumb moved slightly against her palm, whether consciously or unconsciously, she couldn't tell, but the small movement sent heat through her entire body. Finally, he smiled, and it reached his eyes properly for the first time since he'd started looking at the photos. 'When?'

'Now?' The word came out before she'd really thought

about it. 'We've still got a couple of hours of daylight left. Perfect time, actually. The sunset from up there is...' She stopped herself before she said something ridiculous about it being romantic. 'It's worth seeing.'

He let go of her hand and she felt the loss of contact like a physical jolt. 'Now sounds good.' He said as he started gathering the photos carefully.

She watched him stand. 'Dusty?'

He turned back. 'Yeah?'

'I'm glad you came to Matfield.' She said it simply, meaning every word.

His smile was slow and warm, and the way he looked at her made her breath catch. 'Yeah. Me too.'

CHAPTER 30

*D*usty insisted that he drive. 'But I asked you to come out there,' she joked as she got into his ute, the cabin still holding the warmth of the afternoon sun. The seats were worn but clean, and there was the faint smell of timber and sawdust that seemed to follow him everywhere, mixed with the scent of soap that was becoming dangerously familiar.

'Lucky they were only light beers otherwise we wouldn't be going anywhere.'

With Ella that close to him in the cottage, their heads bent over those photos, he had found it hard not to reach out and take her in his arms. It was overwhelming, and he spoke sternly to himself about the need to restrain himself from throwing himself at her. He had stopped pretending weeks ago that he didn't have strong feelings for her. At night, she was all he could think about, lying in the darkness listening to Eli snoring in the next room, replaying every conversation they'd had, every look she'd given him.

Every time someone came through the door at work, he hoped it was her, feeling that stupid leap in his chest, only to feel it deflate when it was just Oscar or another local having a look.

Usually it was Cass. Eli and Cass had become inseparable since Eli had come back. Dusty watched his mate, noticing the same dopey look that Dusty suspected he himself wore whenever Ella was around. Cass asked him not to mention it to Ella. 'She just worries about me, that's all,' she told him. He understood. Best friend, protective instincts, all of that.

Now he was on the edge of falling into the same trap. Love. A beautiful woman. An isolated outback town. It wasn't what he'd planned. He wasn't going to do anything about it though, unless she clearly wanted it too. Sure, they'd kissed, and the memory of it still made his pulse quicken, but the fact that she seemed to be losing her hostility towards him didn't mean he should assume she wanted anything more. He wasn't up for a short-term fling. That was the last thing he needed. If he was going to do this, it had to be something they both wanted.

* * *

They talked all the way out, easy conversation flowing between them now without the earlier antagonism. She told him stories about growing up in Matfield, about her grandfather, the produce store, and how the creek had flooded, cutting the town off for three weeks. He told her about Melbourne. She laughed when he explained how he learnt carpentry from an old Italian bloke who'd sworn at him constantly in a mixture of English and Italian, but had taught him everything worth knowing.

The kilometres disappeared beneath them, the landscape opening up into that vast emptiness that still took his breath away. He followed her instructions when they turned onto a dirt road he hadn't been down before. Hills rose in the north, and before long they reached the bottom of them, their dark red shapes with boulders stacked up making for a striking formation in the otherwise flat and broad land. It was beautiful in a harsh way, unforgiving and ancient. The sun still had a while to go before it set, and they both climbed out of the ute, the heat of the day finally starting to ease.

They set off along a well-worn track that led up the hill. The path was narrow in places, and more than once his arm brushed against hers as they walked. Each time it happened he felt that jolt of electricity, that awareness of her beside him, and he had to force himself to keep his breathing steady. She didn't seem to notice, or if she did, she gave no sign of it.

'No teenagers around this afternoon,' she quipped, looking around the empty hillside. 'Maybe they've found a better spot since I was that age.'

'Did you kiss a few boys up here?' he asked, a faint smile crossing his face as he considered what she must have looked like as a teenager. All green eyes and defiance, probably. Breaking hearts without even trying.

'Maybe a few. Nothing too serious, but we were teenagers in a town with nothing much else to do.' She glanced at him, her expression playful. 'The trouble was most of those boys are the men you now see at the pub.

They're more like brothers to me. I guess that's why I never felt serious about any of them.'

'Yeah, I'm surprised you're not married or with someone. How come you're still single?' He wondered if he'd gone too far with the interrogations when she frowned at him, her eyebrows drawing together in a way that was both intimidating and adorable.

'Same for you? Why are you still single?'

'Haven't met the right person.' He said it with a wry smile, but he was looking right at her when he said it, and he wondered if she caught the implication. Hadn't met the right person until now, maybe.

She flicked him a look, something unreadable passing across her face, colour rising in her cheeks. 'Ditto.' Then she turned away, pointing up the path. 'Come on, let's climb this last bit before the sun sets.'

The track steepened and he found himself behind her, watching the way she moved over the uneven ground with the confidence of someone who'd walked this path a hundred times before. When they reached a particularly rough section, loose rocks scattered across the narrow trail, he reached out instinctively to steady her. His hand found the small of her back, warm through the thin fabric of her shirt, and he felt her pause for just a second before she kept moving. He didn't take his hand away immediately, and neither of them said anything about it. The contact felt natural, necessary even, and when the path widened again and his hand fell away, he felt the loss of it.

'Almost there,' she said, slightly breathless from the climb. 'Just around this bend.'

They rounded the corner and suddenly the viewing platform was in front of them; a simple wooden structure that looked like it had been there for decades. But it was the view that made them both stop. The valley spread out below them, vast and empty and beautiful. The hills rolled away into the distance, layers of red, ochre and purple below a sky that was starting to turn that particular shade of gold that only happened in the outback. The sun hung low on the horizon, still fierce but beginning to soften, the whole landscape glowing with it.

'This is where she stood,' Ella said quietly, and he knew she was imagining his grandmother, young and hopeful, looking out at this same view.

He moved to stand beside her at the railing, their shoulders almost touching. 'It's beautiful. I can see why she would have come here.'

'They say it's the best view in the district. On a clear day you can see for miles.' She turned to look at him, and the golden light caught her face, making her eyes look impossibly green. The air between them felt charged suddenly, heavy with things unsaid. They were standing so close now, close enough that he could see the faint dusting of freckles across her nose, and count her eyelashes if he wanted to.

'Dusty,' she said, and his name on her lips sounded different somehow, softer.

'Yeah?'

'I think...' She paused, seeming to gather courage. 'I think we should probably talk about what's happening here.'

'What is happening here?' He kept his voice gentle, not wanting to spook her.

'You know what.' She said it quietly, but there was certainty in her voice. 'This. Whatever this is between us.'

'And what do you think it is?'

She took a breath. 'I think it's something I wasn't looking for and don't know what to do with.' Her honesty was disarming. 'I think you scare me a bit, if I'm being completely truthful.'

'Why?' He turned to face her fully now, giving her his complete attention.

'Because I didn't want this. I came back to Matfield to build a life on my own terms, to not need anyone, to be independent and self-sufficient.' She was talking faster now, words tumbling out. 'And then you showed up and ruined all my plans, and now I can't stop thinking about you, and that terrifies me because the last time I let someone in like this it ended badly.'

He reached out slowly, giving her time to pull away if she wanted to, and tucked a strand of hair behind her ear. His fingers lingered on her cheek. 'I'm not him.'

'I know that.' Her voice was barely above a whisper. 'That's what scares me most. Because if you were, it would be easier to keep my walls up.'

The sun was sinking lower now, painting everything in shades of amber and gold. The world felt suspended, holding its breath. He could feel her trembling slightly under his touch and see the conflict in her eyes.

'Ella,' he said softly. 'I'm not asking you to tear down all your walls at once. I'm just asking for a chance. A real one, not you deciding I'm the enemy before you even know me.'

'I know you now,' she said. 'That's the problem.'

'Is it?' He moved fractionally closer. 'Because from where I'm standing, that sounds like the opposite of a problem.'

She laughed, a breathless sound. 'You're very sure of yourself.'

'I'm not sure of anything except that I haven't been able to stop thinking about you since the night I arrived in this town.' His thumb traced along her jawline, and he felt her sharp intake of breath. 'And I'm pretty sure you've been thinking about me too.'

'Pretty sure?' Her voice held a challenge now, that spark he loved. 'After what I just said?'

'Well, there was that kiss at the barbecue. That gave me a few clues before this.' He was smiling now, and so was she, the tension lightening.

'That was...' she started, but he cut her off.

'Amazing? Unexpected? Something we should probably do again?'

'I was going to say a mistake, but...' She looked up at him. 'But I'd be lying.'

The sun touched the horizon, sending up a final blaze of colour. They stood there in that golden light, the world spread out below them, and Dusty knew this was the moment. He could feel it in the way she was looking at him, and the way she swayed slightly towards him. 'Tell me to stop,' he said, moving closer still, 'and I will.'

'I'm not going to do that,' she whispered.

He kissed her then, slowly and carefully, giving her every chance to change her mind. But she didn't pull away. Instead, she leaned into him, her hands coming up to grip his shirt before she kissed him back with an intensity that stole his breath. This wasn't like that brief kiss at the barbecue. This was deliberate, intentional, with no hesitation from either of them.

When they finally broke apart, both breathing hard, he

rested his forehead against hers. 'So,' he said, his voice rough. 'Where do we go from here?'

'I have absolutely no idea,' she admitted, but he could hear the smile in her voice.

The sun had set properly now, leaving them in the soft twilight that came before darkness. Around them, the bush was settling into evening sounds, and the air had finally cooled to a comfortable temperature. They stood there together, hands entwined, looking out at the darkening landscape, neither of them saying anything for a long time.

Finally, Ella spoke. 'We should probably head back before it gets completely dark.'

'Probably,' he agreed, but neither of them moved.

She turned to look at him, her face serious now. 'Dusty, I need you to understand something. I'm terrible at this. As in really bad at relationships, letting people in, or trusting that things will work out. I'm probably going to panic and push you away and be difficult.'

'I know.' He squeezed her hand. 'I'm okay with that.'

'You say that now, but...'

'No buts.' He turned her to face him properly. 'I'm not asking you to be perfect, or anything other than yourself. I'm just asking you to try. To give this, us, a real chance instead of running because it might be hard.'

She studied his face and he let her look. He wanted her to see everything he was feeling. Finally, she nodded. 'Okay. We'll try.'

'That's all I'm asking.'

They sat side by side on the edge of the platform, their legs hanging over, close enough that their thighs touched.

The wood was still warm beneath them, holding the last of the day's heat.

'When we came here as kids, the boys would dangle over the edge or hang off of it,' she said quietly. 'Once or twice someone fell and rolled down the hill. Luckily, it only ever resulted in a few broken bones.'

'Young and invincible. I remember the feeling.' His voice was thoughtful. He was acutely aware of how close she was. A strand of her hair came loose and moved slightly in the evening breeze. 'Not so now?' she asked.

'No. I've grown up. I'm not as adventurous as I once was.' He paused, and when he spoke again his voice dropped lower. 'These days, moments like this are more important.'

She shuffled where she sat and suddenly turned to him, feeling the weight of his eyes on her. For a moment they just stared at each other, and he watched her lips part slightly. Then his hand reached up, almost of its own accord, and stroked her face. Her skin was soft and warm, and he felt her lean into his touch, that small surrender that made his breath catch. 'I promised myself I wouldn't let this happen, but...' The words died in his throat because she was looking at him with such open longing that whatever resolve he had simply dissolved.

When her hand rested on his shoulder, tentative but certain, he drew her closer. He held her face in his hands, his thumbs tracing along her cheekbones, memorising the feel of her, and his lips pressed gently down on hers. The kiss was soft at first, questioning, and when she kissed him back, he felt her body move in close to his. He wrapped his arms around her, pulling her against him. His kisses deepened, warm and searching, and she responded with an intensity that made his head spin. When they finally parted, she took deep breaths.

His voice was deep and husky, full of raw emotion. 'I really like you, Ella. I can't think of anything else except you. You're filling my head, every minute of every day.'

She giggled, a sweet mixture of fun and excitement and relief. 'As much as I've tried to fight it, I love seeing you. And this...' She touched his face, her fingers tracing the line of his jaw, feeling the stubble there. 'This is special.'

'Special doesn't even come close.' He kissed her forehead, her temple, the corner of her mouth, unable to stop touching her now that he'd started. 'I thought I was going mad. Every time I saw you, I wanted to do this, but I kept telling myself to back off, that you probably didn't feel the same way.'

'I felt the same way.' Her voice was soft, almost wondrous. 'I kept telling myself you were just some bloke from Melbourne who'd turn around and leave, and I shouldn't get attached. But then you'd look at me, and I'd forget every sensible thought I'd ever had.'

He laughed, low and warm, and kissed her again. This time there was nothing tentative about it. His mouth moved over hers with a hunger that had been building for weeks, and she responded with equal fervour, her hands pulling him closer, her body pressing against his. They kissed until the world around them seemed to fade into insignificance.

When they finally broke apart, gasping and grinning at each other, the sky had transformed completely. They looked out across the vast plains together, his arm around her shoulders holding her close against his side. The red sun had disappeared behind the hills and horizon, leaving a blaze of glory in its wake. There was bushfire smoke rising out to the west and the bottom of the sky was covered in a smoky haze. Tones of red, pink and orange filled the sky, bleeding up into a darkening deep blue above.

'Wow,' he breathed. 'An outback sunset. The sky is huge. I've never seen anything like it.' He turned to look at her. She was bathed in that golden-red light, her hair glowing, her eyes luminous. 'You're beautiful,' he said, and meant it more than he'd ever meant anything.

'Pretty spectacular,' she agreed, but she was looking at him when she said it. Then she turned back to the view, leaning into him, fitting perfectly against his side. 'It doesn't get much better than that. We picked a good afternoon to come here.'

'The best afternoon.' He kissed the top of her head, breathing in the scent of her hair, feeling like his world had shifted. Everything that had seemed complicated before, the property, the history, his plans or lack thereof, all of it seemed to fall into place. This was where he was supposed to be. With her.

When he stood up, he reached down to help her up, and when she took his hands he pulled her to her feet and straight into his arms. She turned and they stood together, watching the last light fade into the dusty grounds below, her back against his chest, his arms wrapped around her waist. Flocks of galahs flew overhead, heading for the thicker bush of the hills behind where they stood, their pink and grey bodies dark against the brilliant sky. Their calls echoed across the valley, wild and raucous. In the distance, the lights of Matfield were visible through the haze, tiny pinpricks of civilisation in all that emptiness, and the first stars became visible in the darkening blue directly above.

She turned in his arms to face him, and she felt small beside him, his body toned from all the years of work, strong and firm as he drew her to him. Her body quivered as they melded together, fitting perfectly, and when his lips came down on hers, she kissed him back passionately, every part of her body tingling with awareness. His hands moved over her back, her waist, pulling her closer. She could feel his heart beating against hers, and the barely restrained intensity in the way he held her.

When they finally pulled apart, a kookaburra's call sounded from the trees further down the hill. The noise rebounded off the gully near them and then echoed out over the plains, that distinctive laughing call that seemed to mock and celebrate in equal measure.

'The echo of the outback,' he whispered as his hands caressed her shoulders where she stood in front of him, both gazing out across the darkening valley. More stars were emerging properly now, and the sky was a gradient of colours, from deep purple, to navy, to black. 'I could stay here forever.'

'We should go,' she said reluctantly, but she made no move to step away from him. Instead she turned again and kissed him once more. 'I think we've seen what we came for.'

'Have we?' His voice was teasing, his hands still on her waist. 'Because I'm pretty sure I could stay here looking at you for several more hours.'

She laughed and pushed gently at his chest. 'Charmer.

Come on, before it gets properly dark and we end up breaking our necks on the way down.'

But as they walked back down the track, his hand firmly holding hers, neither of them was in any hurry. They stopped twice more to kiss, unable to help themselves, laughing between kisses like teenagers. When they reached the ute and he opened her door for her, she pulled him close one more time.

'This changes things,' she said, and it wasn't a question.

'Yeah.' He tucked that loose strand of hair behind her ear, his fingers lingering on her cheek. 'Is that okay?'

'I can't believe I'm saying this...' She kissed him again, quick and certain. 'But it's more than okay.'

He grinned, that slow smile that transformed his whole face. 'Good. Because I wasn't planning on letting you go anyway.'

'Confident, aren't you?'

'Only when I know what I want.' He kissed her forehead, then her nose, then her lips again. 'And I want you, Ella Patterson. Have since the moment I saw you glaring at me in the pub.'

'I wasn't glaring.'

'You absolutely were. You looked like you wanted to throw me out on my ear.' He was laughing now, pulling her close. 'It was terrifying and incredibly attractive.'

'You're ridiculous.' But she was smiling as her arms wrapped around his waist, her head resting against his chest.

'Yeah, but you like me anyway.'

'Unfortunately.' She pulled back to look at him, suddenly serious. 'Dusty, I need you to know something. I'm going to be difficult about this. I'm going to panic and second-guess everything and probably try to push you away when things get too real.'

'I know.' He cupped her face in his hands. 'And I'm going to be patient and stubborn and refuse to let you push me away. We've already had this conversation, remember?'

'I just want to make sure you know what you're getting into.'

'I know exactly what I'm getting into.' He kissed her again, soft and lingering. 'A stubborn, brilliant, beautiful woman who's scared of getting hurt, but brave enough to try anyway. That's what I'm getting into, and I wouldn't have it any other way.'

She felt tears pricking her eyes, unexpected and overwhelming. 'How do you do that?'

'Do what?'

'Say exactly the right thing.'

He laughed, a warm sound that she felt through his chest. 'Trust me, this is a first. Usually I say completely the wrong thing and end up with my foot in my mouth. You're just making me look good.'

They stood there for another moment, holding each other as the darkness settled completely around them. The stars were brilliant now, thousands of them scattered across the sky in a way that never happened in cities. The Milky Way was a bright band across the darkness, and the Southern Cross hung low on the horizon.

'We really should go,' Ella said again, but still didn't move.

'We should.' He didn't move either.

Finally, she pulled away with obvious reluctance. 'Come on. Before someone sends out a search party.'

'In Matfield? Everyone probably already knows we're out here together.' He helped her into the ute, then walked around to the driver's side, grinning. 'Small towns, remember? No secrets.'

'Oh God, you're right.' She groaned, covering her face with her hands. 'Cass is going to be unbearable. She's been trying to set us up since you arrived.'

'Smart woman, Cass.' He started the engine, then reached over and took her hand. 'Worth listening to, obviously.'

As they drove back towards town, the headlights cutting through the darkness, they talked easily about everything and nothing. Plans for the week, stories from their pasts, dreams for the future that they were both tentatively starting to include each other in. When they reached the edge of Matfield and the streetlights started appearing, Dusty squeezed her hand.

'So, what now?' he asked.

'Now?' She looked at their joined hands, then back at his face. 'Now we figure this out as we go. Together.'

'Together.' He liked the sound of that. 'I can work with together.'

When he pulled up outside her cottage, neither of them moved immediately. The porch sensor light was on, casting a warm glow across the small front garden, and somewhere down the street someone's television was blaring through an open window.

'I had a really good time today,' she said, and then laughed at how inadequate that sounded. 'That's an understatement. Today was...'

'Perfect?' he suggested.

'Yeah. Perfect.' She leaned across and kissed him one more time, slow and sweet. 'Thank you. For everything.'

'Thank you for finding those photos.' He cupped her face gently. 'You've given me more than you know.'

She climbed out of the ute but leaned back in through the window. 'See you tomorrow?'

'Absolutely. Though I should warn you, now that I don't have to pretend I'm not crazy about you, I'm probably going to be around a lot more.'

'Good.' She grinned at him. 'I'd be disappointed if you weren't.'

He watched her walk up to her door, waited until she was safely inside, then drove the short distance back to his cottage. When he got inside, Eli was sprawled on the couch watching football. He looked up with a knowing smirk.

'So,' Eli said. 'How was the lookout?'

'Shut up.' But Dusty was grinning.

'That good, huh?' Eli threw a cushion at him. 'About bloody time, mate. I was starting to think you'd never work up the courage.'

'It wasn't about courage. It was about timing.'

'Right. Timing.' Eli's grin widened. 'Is that what we're calling it now?'

Dusty ignored him and headed to his room, still grinning like an idiot. He pulled out his phone and looked at the photos of his grandparents, at Mina standing on that same lookout where he'd just kissed Ella. His grandmother had stood there looking out at her future, not knowing what lay ahead, not knowing the grief that would come. But she'd had moments of beauty too, moments of hope and love.

He understood now what she'd meant about echoes. The good ones, the ones worth making. Today had created one of those echoes. And tomorrow, and all the days after, he'd work on making more of them. With Ella.

He sent her a quick text: *Thank you for today. Sleep well.*

Her reply came almost immediately: *You too. And Dusty? I'm glad you're stubborn.*

He laughed and fell back on his bed, still grinning. Yeah, he was definitely staying in Matfield.

CHAPTER 31

It hadn't taken Tyson long to catch on that today Ella was different. She hadn't realised she'd been whistling as she restacked the shelves, or that she was walking with a spring in her step. But Tyson did.

'Oi. What's got into you?' Tyson looked up from his paperwork, genuine curiosity in his expression. 'I haven't seen you look this happy in ages.'

She stopped restocking and walked up to where he sat at the counter, the bench covered in invoices and paperwork that he'd been avoiding for days. She pulled up a stool and leaned on her elbows, her hands resting under her chin, a smile playing at the corners of her mouth. She couldn't help but feel the elation bubbling over, that giddy excitement that demanded to be shared. She was dying to tell someone, and Tyson was the perfect confidant. 'I'm just going to be upfront about this. I'm mad keen on Dusty.' She watched his face for a reaction. 'The builder working on the pub. Liam's boss.'

That made Tyson sit up straight, his eyes wide with

surprise. 'I know who Dusty is.' His face split into a grin. 'You're joking, right? After all this time you've finally worked it out. He's a great fella. Look at all he's done for Liam and the town.' He shook his head, leaned over and ruffled her hair like she was still ten years old. 'Ella. Did you stay over his place last night?'

'Jesus, Tyson. No! We've just worked out that we like each other. Give it a break. Nothing like that.'

He picked up his pen and an invoice, trying to look casual. 'Oh. No. Okay. I just thought you seemed really happy, and I wondered if that might have been how it started.'

'Put your manners back in,' she laughed. 'Besides, this is different. It's not a fling or a one-night stand. It's more than that.'

'Whoa. This sounds serious. Tell me you have at least kissed. Like, not just a peck on the cheek, friend type kiss. Like a serious, snogging pash.'

She pinged a rubber band at him that hit him square in the forehead. 'You're disgusting. I don't think anyone says snog or pash anymore. We might have shared a passionate kiss though.' She batted her eyelids at him.

'I was joking. You're right, no one uses those words anymore. Just trying to stir you up and get some spicy info.' He raised his eyebrows up and down, clearly enjoying himself. 'I thought you didn't trust him, especially in relation to these blocks of land. You know, the one your eternal life dream has always been about.'

She stood up and stretched, flicking some strands of lucerne from her shirt. Picking up her hat, she pushed her shoulders back and moved her head from side to side, stretching out the tight muscles in her neck. ' Well, now I trust him. He's filled me in on a lot of the family history, and I understand the situation better. He's promised me that nothing substantial or horrendous is going to go on this block next door. It sounds like they're planning a project that fits in with the town's character. You know, maybe a rustic café or gift shop, or even a gallery. Something that will complement what's already here. It will be in line with the town's building codes apparently, and he seemed genuine when he said it.'

Tyson ducked his head down and peered through the large open doors that opened up to the side of the building. 'Maybe you could go and interrogate the surveyors over there?' He pointed. 'They've been there for an hour or so already. You might get some inside information. But then again, if you trust him, I guess he'll tell you anyway. He must know what's going on there.'

She stood upright and plonked her hat on her head. 'Right, I'll go and just chat to them anyway. I mean, it's still important. We don't want them building right on the fence line. It's a large block, so hopefully they'll position it taking into account where our buildings are. I mean we've been here forever. I don't want to feel hemmed in.'

* * *

TYSON WAS STILL STUDYING the accounts when she returned half an hour later. Sweat beaded on her forehead as she took her hat off, throwing it on a chair with enough force that it bounced and hit the floor with a soft thud. Grabbing a hand towel nearby, she wiped her face roughly, shaking her head. The anger bubbled inside her like a kettle about to boil over, the pressure building with each breath she took. 'You don't look happy,' Tyson said hesitantly. 'No whistling or skipping? What's the verdict?'

He's lied to me. Outright, blatant lies.' Her voice was tight with fury, each word clipped and precise. 'They didn't say exactly what will be built there, but they're scoping out for a building that will take up most of the block. No room for trees, hardly any garden space, and large areas designated for parking. Concrete building, concrete car park, concrete retaining walls. Even some of the fences will be concrete! Concrete, concrete, and more concrete! It sounds like a huge industrial building to me, and it's going to be right next to us. 'Hardly in keeping with our town planning. Everything is timber here. It's the outback, not the city.'

'I tried to keep my cool and get as much as I could out of them, but it was almost as if they'd been warned not to reveal anything.' She was pacing now, unable to stand still. 'One of them did mention a façade on the building that would blend in with the current heritage rules for the town. But the building itself is bloody huge, Tyson. The side wall will be just the other side of the fence there. They're getting relaxation exemptions from the council. The buildings are going to go right up to the back fence. With the parking area, it'll take up the entire block. That's nearly an acre of concrete. No open space, no trees and no gardens. What's the use of all the work we've put in here to make those front gardens appear green even through the drought? This old building Dad has spent so much money on will be dwarfed by some monstrosity. We could have pulled it down years ago and gone for the big shed or concrete bunker, but we didn't. Because that's not what Matfield is about.'

'I'm with you, Ella. I hate large concrete buildings. Why did Dusty tell you it wasn't going to be that when it is?'

'And,' she continued, her voice rising, 'they hinted that once they'd finished surveying this block, they're heading out to the other one out of town. Only early days for that one, but there's an even bigger plan for it. That's if they can get it through council.'

'What does that mean? I thought you said he was all about preserving the memory of his grandparents.'

'Well, I've changed my mind now, and I can tell you if I ever speak to him again I'll tell him that. What a traitor.' She picked up her hat from the floor and slammed it back on her head. 'I was such an idiot. One kiss and I forgot everything I knew about not trusting good-looking men who say all the right things.'

'Ella, maybe there's an explanation. Maybe you should talk to him before you…'

'Before I what? Before I make assumptions? Funny, that's exactly what he accused me of doing when I first met him.' She laughed, but there was no humour in it. 'Turns out my first instincts were right. He's just another city developer who came here to make a quick buck and doesn't care what he destroys in the process. It's even worse now because he's not just working for the developer, he's it!'

'That doesn't sound like the bloke I know,' Tyson said carefully. 'The one who's been so patient with Liam, and volunteered for that charity thing, being nothing but respectful to everyone in town.'

'Yeah, well, people can reel you in and surprise you.' She turned away, trying not to let Tyson see the hurt in her eyes beneath the anger. 'And not in a good way. Sometimes what you see is not what you get.'

'Just talk to him, Ella. Give him a chance to explain.'

'Why should I? He had plenty of chances to be honest with me. He knew how important this was, and what Dad wanted to do with that block.' Her voice cracked slightly. 'He looked me in the eye yesterday and told me to trust him. And like an idiot, I did.'

She walked to the back of the store, needing space, needing to think and breathe without Tyson watching her with those sympathetic eyes. The familiar smell of grain and timber usually calmed her frayed nerves, but today it just reminded her of Dusty. Of sawdust clinging to his work clothes, that soap scent on his skin and the way he'd held her last night at the lookout, strong arms wrapped around her as if he'd never let go. The way she'd felt safe in his arms, protected and understood, she'd thought maybe he was someone who truly saw her. Someone who got what this place meant to her, who valued the same things she did. God, she was such a fool. Such a complete and utter fool for believing that fairy tale. Her phone buzzed in her pocket. She pulled it out and saw Dusty's name on the screen: *Good morning. Can't stop thinking about last night. Dinner tonight?*

She stared at the message, her thumb hovering over the keyboard, indecision warring inside her chest. Part of her wanted to call him immediately, to hear his voice, to demand answers, to give him a chance to explain as Tyson suggested. To let him prove her wrong about him, because she so wanted to be wrong about him. But the larger part of her, the part that had been hurt before and had built walls precisely to prevent this kind of pain, the part that remembered every broken promise and every lie disguised as love, that part just felt betrayed. Utterly and completely betrayed. She typed back: *We need to talk. But not dinner. Meet me at the store at five.*

His reply came almost immediately: *Everything okay?*

She didn't respond. Let him wonder. Let him feel a fraction of the uncertainty and hurt that was currently tearing through her chest. She shoved the phone back in her pocket and returned to work, throwing herself into the physical labour of restacking shelves and hauling bags, anything to stop thinking about dark eyes and gentle hands, and promises that apparently meant nothing.

By the time four-thirty rolled around, she'd worked herself into a state of cold fury that Tyson wisely stayed well clear of. She'd rehearsed what she was going to say and how she'd confront him with the facts, and watch him try to explain his way out of lying to her. There would be no tears or weakness. Just the cold, hard truth that he was exactly what she always suspected. He was someone who couldn't be trusted.

At five o'clock exactly, she heard his ute pull up outside. Through the window she watched him climb out, and even from this distance she could see the worry on his face. Good. He should be concerned.

The bell above the door chimed as he entered and she forced herself to stay behind the counter, to maintain that physical barrier between them. If he got too close, if he touched her, she might lose her resolve.

'Ella.' His voice was warm, relieved to see her. 'I've been thinking about you all day. Last night was...'

'Was a mistake.' She cut him off, her voice flat. 'We

need to talk about what's really going on with that block next door.'

His expression shifted from warmth to confusion. 'What do you mean?'

'I talked to the surveyors today.' She watched his face carefully. 'Want to tell me what they're planning to build?'

And there it was. A flicker in his eyes. Guilt? Recognition? Whatever it was, it confirmed everything she'd feared.

'Ella, let me explain.'

'So you do know.' Her laugh was bitter. 'Of course you do. You've known all along what they were planning and you lied to me. You stood there yesterday, after we...' She couldn't finish the sentence. 'You told me to trust you. That it wouldn't be some monstrosity. That it would fit with the town.'

'It will fit with the town. The façade will…'

She cut him off. 'I don't care about the bloody façade, Dusty!' Her voice rose despite her best efforts to stay calm. 'It's a concrete bunker that takes up the entire block. No trees, no gardens, parking right up to our fence line. How is that in keeping with Matfield? How is that respecting what this place is?'

'If you'd just let me explain the full plan.'

'Why should I? You've had weeks to explain. Months, actually. Instead, you let me think you were different, that you actually cared about this place and the people in it.' She could feel tears threatening and fought them back furiously. 'You're just like every other developer I've read about. Come in, make your money, destroy what makes a place special, then leave.'

'That's not fair and you know it.' His voice was harder

now, defensive. 'You don't know what you're talking about.'

'Then tell me! Tell me what possible good reason there is for building a concrete industrial monstrosity next to our family business that we've spent a lifetime making sure to keep in line with the heritage aspect of the town. Tell me why you lied about it fitting in with the street. Tell me why I should believe anything you say when you've been deceiving me since the day you arrived!'

They stood there glaring at each other across the counter, all the warmth and connection from the previous night shattered into sharp, cutting pieces. Tyson had wisely disappeared into the back, leaving them to their confrontation.

'I wasn't deceiving you,' Dusty said finally, his jaw tight. 'I was trying to respect my family's privacy until they were ready to make an announcement. There are reasons for the design, good reasons, but I can't explain them yet because it's not just my information to share.'

'How convenient.'

'It's the truth.'

'Is it?' She leaned forward, her hands flat on the counter. 'Because from where I'm standing, it looks like you used me. You used my knowledge of the property, my connection to the town, and got me to trust you and care about you, all while planning something you knew I'd hate.'

'That's not what happened, and you know it.' His voice rose to match hers. 'What happened between us last night was real. What I feel for you is real. This building has nothing to do with that.'

'Everything has to do with that!' She was shouting

now, past caring who heard. 'You can't separate them. You're going to destroy what I love about this place and what my family has worked for generations to preserve. And you think I'm just supposed to be okay with it because we kissed?'

'I think you're supposed to trust me enough to believe I wouldn't do anything to hurt this town, or you. I think you're supposed to give me the benefit of the doubt instead of jumping to the worst possible conclusion, the second things don't go your way.'

'That's rich coming from someone who's been hiding the truth for months.'

'I wasn't hiding it. I was waiting for the right time to explain.'

'And when would that be? After the concrete was poured? After you'd got what you wanted and moved on?'

He flinched at that, and she knew she'd hit a nerve. Good.

'You know what?' He stepped back from the counter. 'You're right. This was a mistake. Not last night, but thinking you'd come to understand what I'm about, that you could see past your own incorrect assumptions long enough to trust me. I should have known better. You made up your mind about me the night we met, and you're determined to find any justification for that decision. You won't listen to anything that will ever change that.'

'Maybe I was right to make up my mind.'

'Maybe you were.' He turned towards the door, then stopped and looked back. 'For what it's worth, what's being built there is what this town desperately needs. But you're so caught up in your own hurt and suspicion that you can't see past the concrete.

'Don't you dare make this about me being unreasonable. You lied.'

'I kept a necessary confidence. There's a difference.' He pulled open the door. 'When you're ready to listen instead of just attacking, you know where to find me. But I'm not going to stand here and be accused of things I didn't do just because you're scared.'

'I'm not scared!'

'You're terrified.' He gave her a look that might have been pity or disappointment. 'And that's the saddest part of all of this.'

The door closed behind him with a definitive click, and Ella stood there shaking with anger, hurt and, dangerously, regret. She could hear Tyson moving cautiously in the back room, probably deciding whether it was safe to emerge yet.

She sank onto the stool, her anger draining away, leaving only exhaustion and a hollow ache in her chest. Maybe she had overreacted. Maybe she should have let him explain. But the betrayal felt too raw, too similar to every other time she'd let her guard down and been hurt.

Her phone buzzed again. Another message from Dusty: *I'm sorry I couldn't tell you everything. But I'm not sorry about last night. That was real, whether you believe it or not.*

She stared at the message for a long time, then turned off her phone and got back to work. Some things, once broken, couldn't be fixed. And maybe it was better to learn that now rather than later, when it would hurt even more.

CHAPTER 32

usty let a couple of days go by, hoping that Ella would ring him or call in to talk, that she'd cool down enough to listen to reason. But she didn't, and he threw himself into his work with single-minded intensity, hoping that the sweat, grind and physical exhaustion would somehow dull the pain that sat like a stone in his chest. Her accusations had hurt more than he wanted to admit, cutting deeper than he'd thought possible from someone he'd known such a short time. But it wasn't really the short time that mattered, was it? It was the intensity of what they'd shared, the connection he'd felt from that first antagonistic meeting. Throwing his tools down, he wiped his brow with the back of his hand. Eli stopped work and looked up at him, concern written across his face.

'Rocky start to the relationship?'

'You might say that.' Dusty leaned against the wall, feeling the weight of the past few days pressing down on him. 'She's bloody stubborn and feisty.'

'But?'

'It doesn't change how I feel about her.'

'Well go and talk to her. Don't let it simmer and turn into a situation worse than it already is. I've seen what happens when people let stuff fester.' Eli set down his hammer. 'You both care about each other. Sort it out before pride ruins everything.'

'That's what I'm about to do.'

He'd driven to the produce store. They needed some more of the brackets they stocked there, so he'd pick them up and some other gear he needed. And he'd talk to her. Maybe Tyson would be there, and he could talk to Ella out the back, or somewhere by themselves. He wanted to sort this out once and for all. He'd give her a chance, but he also needed to draw the line. If she didn't trust him after this, then perhaps it wasn't meant to be.

INSIDE THE STORE, flecks of grain and hay floated in the sunlight that poured in through the large open side of the shed. Dusty looked around, taking it in properly for the first time since this whole mess had started. It was just like it had been in the old days. The same days when his grandfather and Nonna had probably come in here to buy what they needed, standing at that same counter, maybe facing the same kind of suspicious looks from locals who didn't trust foreigners. It was obvious the love and care that had been put into the business and the building over the years, along with the hard work that went into keeping the outside looking fresh and not dry. He understood where she was coming from. If only she'd let him explain.

'G'day mate,' Tyson's voice was loud and gruff, coming from the back of the building. 'If you've come to see her, she's not here.'

'I've come to see Ella. I need to talk to her properly.'

'She's not here. She's pretty cranky and I'll give you a warning, I don't like to cross her when she's in one of those moods. She's the most stubborn person I know. She'll fight to the death for something she's passionate about. And this town and this business are two of those things.'

Dusty stood his ground. 'I get it. I understand where she's coming from, but I asked her to trust me on this one. I'm just not in a position to talk about what we have planned for next door. Not yet.'

'Well, your surveyors certainly filled her in on enough for her to get the picture.'

'Oh, is that why she's angry?' Dusty felt his frustration spike. 'They shouldn't have said anything. They were told to keep quiet until we were ready.'

'They didn't say much, but enough for her to know that some huge concrete conglomeration of building, car parks and walls is going to be right there.' Tyson gestured towards the block next door.

They both looked out through the side of the building. Dusty shook his head. 'She's got the wrong picture in her head. If only she'd come and talked to me instead of jumping to conclusions. She needs to trust me.'

Tyson laughed out loud. 'Unfortunately, she's been there and done that before. She's pretty adamant about not doing that again. Good luck, mate. Because you're going to need it.'

'Where is she?'

'She didn't say, but I've got a fair idea. It's where she always goes when she needs to think.'

'Where?'

'Think about it. I thought she talked to you about a place that meant a lot to her.'

Dusty instantly knew. 'Thanks mate, and for the good luck. I'm going to give this one more go.'

The sun in the middle of the day was strikingly hot, and the heat from the ground rose to meet Dusty as he quickly made his way across the plain, heading to where he hoped to find Ella. She had half an hour's start on him from what Tyson had said, and he walked quickly, looking for any clues that she had walked this way before him. Her car was parked where he thought it would be, and surely she would only head for the same spot where they had been together not that long ago. The spot where everything had felt possible.

There it was. A distinct set of boot prints making their way across the barren ground and tufts of grass, pointing directly to where he was going.

He picked up his pace and pushed his hat down hard on his head. Middle of the day. A heat wave, and windy enough to pick the dust up and swirl it around him, into his eyes and mouth, making him cough. He should have brought more water, but he'd been too focused on finding her to think straight.

* * *

As he neared the spot he slowed down, walking quietly. Before he got too close, he called out so as not to startle her. 'Ella. I've come to talk to you.'

She was sitting staring at the ground, her head between her hands as she perched on her favourite rock. When she looked up, he caught anger and surprise in her gaze, and he readied himself for her onslaught of words.

She stood up instantly when she saw him. 'Apologies. I'm on your land. It won't happen again.'

She went to walk past him but he grabbed her arm and stopped her, feeling her trying to pull away. 'Stop. Just stop and listen to me. Don't apologise. I know this place means as much to you as it does to me. I would never stop you coming here, even if you hate me.'

Her lip quivered and he saw her shoulders sag, as if she was defeated. 'I don't hate you. I just... I just don't understand why you've lied to me.' Her voice was smaller now, less angry and more hurt. 'You know I'm even past caring what does get built. It's your business. But why not be upfront with me.'

'I just spoke to Tyson. I know you've talked to the surveyors and they've told you some of the details. I asked you to trust me and I said I'd fill you in when I could. When my family was ready.'

'I know, but it's too late now.' She looked away, unable to meet his eyes. 'I'm confused because I thought I really liked you but it's hard when what you want for the town is so different to what I want. I'm not sure I could live with those differences. You're a developer. You want big things and to make money.' She pulled her arm away. 'I'm the opposite. I like simple. The heritage of the town and the quality of life for people living here are more important to me than making money. We come from two different worlds.'

He put his hands on his hips and blocked her way, refusing to let her run again. 'We do. Very different worlds, but you've assumed the wrong thing again. I'm not interested in money over people. People come first with me. Look at the family I come from. Everyone has devoted their lives to helping people. You might think I'm just a builder or someone who just wants to construct and develop, but I'm way more than that. The people and community always come first with me.'

He could tell the quiet resignation she had started with was now being overtaken by a defiant attitude. Her chin lifted and her eyes flashed. 'Then why would you erect a building on that block that is going to be ugly and destroy the look of the town? And why would you also be planning a major development for out here? You never even mentioned that to me.'

'I never mentioned it because I only thought of it after we talked. It's a pie in the sky dream and I've only got them to do some prelim marking out here to see if it's feasible. Just give me a chance, will you? We have something, you and me. You know that. You felt it also. Don't throw it away because you're scared.'

She folded her arms and looked down at the ground. When she looked up he thought he saw tears in her eyes. 'Why would you build anything large or out of character out here? Look at it. It's sacred, with echoes of the past all around us. It's an amazing property. Why would you spoil that?'

'Give me one chance and I'll explain everything, show you all the plans. Let me show you what we're actually planning instead of what you've imagined in your head based on incomplete information from surveyors who don't understand the full picture.'

'I've got to get back. Tyson will wonder where I am.'

'Ella, please. Just give me a chance. Come over to my place tonight. I'll cook you dinner and explain everything. If after that you're still not sure, then so be it. I can't do any more, but please give me that chance. Trust me. I promise you won't regret it.'

He pleaded with his eyes, his stomach churning at the thought of losing her after only just getting together and realising how much they meant to each other. The thought of going back to how things were before that sunset kiss felt unbearable.

'Seven o'clock. Don't bring anything.'

Her face was stony and she gave him one hard look before turning and making her way down the hillside. His eyes followed her until she was only a tiny figure in the distance. Every bone in his body wanted to run after her and plead some more, but he was nearly out of patience. He couldn't make her want to be with him or trust him. If she didn't turn up tonight, then he was going to accept it was over. Over before it had even really started.

He stood there for a long moment, the heat pressing down on him, looking at the small memorial to his grandmother's lost baby. So much grief in this place, so much loss. He didn't want to add his own broken heart to the echoes that already haunted this land.

CHAPTER 34

At six thirty that evening, Dusty stood in his small kitchen, stirring pasta sauce and trying not to check his phone every thirty seconds. He'd cleaned the cottage properly for the first time since moving in. He'd bought fresh bread from the bakery, made sure there was cold beer and wine in the fridge, and attempted to cook a meal that wouldn't embarrass him or give her food poisoning. The pasta sauce was his mother's recipe, the one thing he could make from scratch rather than coming out of a jar or a tin. It was the one dish he'd mastered through years of Sunday family dinners.

Eli had wisely made himself scarce, claiming he had plans with Cass, although Dusty suspected his mate was just giving them privacy. The cottage felt too quiet without his usual banter.

Six forty-five. Still no sign of her.

He checked the sauce again, adjusted the heat, and wiped down counters that didn't need wiping. His nerves were on edge. What if she didn't come? What if she'd decided it wasn't worth the risk and that her assumptions about him were easier to live with than the truth?

Seven o'clock. The knock on the door made him jump. She stood on his doorstep looking uncertain, her hair down around her shoulders and wearing a simple dress he'd never seen before. She'd made an effort, and that gave him hope. 'Come in,' he said, stepping back to let her pass, relief flooding through him so intensely his knees felt weak. She'd come. Despite everything, despite the anger and hurt, she'd shown up. That had to mean something.

'It smells good,' she said, and he could hear the nervousness in her voice.

'Mum's recipe. If this doesn't work, I've got nothing.' He was trying for light, trying to ease the tension, but his hands were shaking slightly as he poured her a glass of wine.

They sat at the small kitchen table where she'd shown him the photos of his grandparents. It felt like a lifetime ago now, although it had only been days. 'Ella,' he started, then stopped, not sure where to begin.

'Just tell me,' she said. 'Tell me what you're planning. All of it.'

So he did. He told her about the medical centre his family wanted to build, the state-of-the-art facilities that would bring proper healthcare to Matfield for the first time in the town's history. He explained why it needed to be substantial, why the size wasn't about ego or profit but about having enough space for proper examination rooms, consultation spaces, maybe even minor surgery capabilities. He walked her through why the car park was necessary for ambulances and patient access, particularly elderly patients, or those with mobility issues, and why the concrete was unavoidable for a building that had to meet strict medical standards and health regulations. He showed her the actual plans on his laptop, pointing out how the facade would blend with the town's heritage, how they'd included gardens despite the constraints, and how it would save lives.

'There's no other block in town that suits better than this one. It ticks all the boxes, especially because of how big it is and being central to everything.' He paused, his voice rough when he continued. 'My grandmother's baby died because there was no proper medical care out here, Ella. She died because help came once a month if you were lucky, and that month the luck ran out. They had to watch her get sicker and sicker, knowing something was wrong but having no one to help, no one who could save her. This medical centre means that never happens again to anyone. It means when someone's baby gets sick, or when an elderly person has a fall, or when there's an accident, there's help right there. Not two hours away in one of the coastal towns, not via the flying doctor that might take hours to arrive, but right here in Matfield. Minutes away instead of hours.'

Ella was quiet for a long time, staring at the plans. When she finally looked up, her eyes were wet.

'Why didn't you just tell me?' Her voice was soft now, all the anger drained away, replaced by understanding and guilt. 'Why didn't you just say that from the beginning? I would have understood. I would have supported it.'

Because it wasn't my story to tell yet. My family wanted to make the announcement properly, through the right channels. They didn't want word getting out before all the approvals were in place.' He reached across the table and took her hand. 'But I should have told you anyway. I should have trusted you not to say anything. I'm sorry.'

'I'm sorry too.' Her voice was small. 'I jumped to conclusions. Again. I assumed the worst instead of trusting you.'

'You've been hurt before. I get it.'

'That's not an excuse.' She squeezed his hand. 'You asked me to trust you and I didn't. That's on me. I guess we both should have trusted each other.'

They sat there in silence for a moment, holding hands across the table, the pasta sauce bubbling forgotten on the stove.

'There's more,' he finally said.

She looked up. 'More?'

'Yes. It looks like the block on the other side might be willing to sell us the back part.'

'You mean Kenny's Butcher's?'

'Yes. He only uses the front part for the store. It's on two titles. He's agreed to sell us that back section.'

'More car parking spaces?'

'No. Room for a men's shed. It can work in conjunction with the medical centre, sort of like a mental health support space for blokes who might not walk into a doctor's office but will pick up a hammer and talk while they work. It would be good to have a place for women also, but one step at a time. I think once my family gets further into this, there could be more to come. We've all wanted to do something like this for years. And I'm going to ask your father to be involved in all of that. There are finer details that still need to be worked out, but that's the plan.'

Ella's breath caught. 'A men's shed? You're building Dad's men's shed?' Her voice cracked. 'He's wanted that for years. He's talked about it forever, about giving the local blokes a place to gather, to work with their hands, to talk without it feeling like therapy.' She pressed her hand to her mouth. 'You're really doing that?'

'With your father's involvement. He should run it, design it, make it his. We're just providing the space and funding.' Dusty squeezed her hand. 'It's what this town needs. What blokes who might be struggling need. A place to belong.'

'I don't know what to say.' Her voice came out as barely a whisper, overwhelmed by the scope of what he was describing. 'Dusty, this is... this is incredible. Your family is going to change lives here, save lives. And I accused you of...' She couldn't finish, shame washing over her in waves.

'There's no need to say anything. I understand why you reacted the way you did.' He squeezed her hand. 'There is a large family trust backing all of this, Ella. Money from my grandparents' estate, and from my parents and siblings who've all contributed. Between them all, and a large inheritance from our other grand-parents, there's plenty of money to do a lot of good in places like this. And there's going to be endless possibili-ties that we'll be able to accommodate over time. This is just the beginning. And I'm going to ask your father to be involved in all of that when he returns. His knowledge of the community and what's needed here will be invaluable.

There are finer details that still need to be worked out, but that's the plan.'

'Your grandparents ended up wealthy by the sounds of it. Is that another reason why they never sold out here? They didn't need to?'

'Yes. Nannu teamed up with his brothers once they moved to Melbourne and they were lucky enough to buy land at the right time. They owned several properties in inner Melbourne and hung onto them. Worth a fortune now.'

'What about the property out of town?' she asked finally. 'What are you planning there?'

He took a breath. 'That actual property will be mine. I've already bought it from the family trust.' He hesitated, then began again. 'One day I'd like to build an observatory there. Not anything fancy at first, just a small dome with a decent telescope, maybe a twelve or fourteen-inch reflector. I want one with enough aperture to really see the deep sky objects properly. The darkness out there is incredible. You'd get views of the Milky Way that people in cities can only dream about.'

He was warming to the subject now, his passion evident. 'I've been thinking about it for months. We could set up proper viewing platforms and maybe some basic accommodation for visiting astronomy groups. Nothing commercial at first, just somewhere locals can come to understand what's above them. And for anyone who's interested in astrophotography, the viewing conditions out there would be exceptional. No light pollution, stable air, clear skies most of the year. We could even do school camps out there. It's limitless.'

'It's a beautiful idea,' she whispered, understanding immediately what he was envisioning.

'Nanna loved it when I showed her anything about the stars and night sky. She would have loved to sit back out here and see everything so clearly. I feel like it would be bringing more of those echoes to life, sharing what she never got to fully experience.'

Ella stood up and walked around the table, and he stood to meet her. When she wrapped her arms around him, his chest finally unclenched.

'I'm sorry,' she said against his chest. 'I'm sorry I didn't trust you. I'm sorry I let my past get in the way of seeing who you really are.'

'I'm sorry too,' he murmured into her hair. 'I should have told you all of this sooner.'

They stood there for a long moment, just holding each other, and Dusty felt the fear and tension of the past few days finally start to drain away.

'The pasta's burning,' Ella said eventually, and he could hear the smile in her voice.

'Shit.' He pulled away and rushed to the stove, stirring frantically while she laughed.

'Some romantic dinner this is turning out to be.'

'Hey, I tried.' He grinned at her over his shoulder. 'Not my fault, you distract me.'

They ate dinner together, talking and laughing and slowly rebuilding what had nearly been broken. It wasn't perfect, and there would be more challenges ahead, but they would face them together now. And that, Dusty thought as he watched Ella gesture animatedly while telling a story, was all that really mattered.

Later, as he walked her back to her cottage, their hands linked, she stopped and looked up at him.

'Thank you for not giving up on me,' she said.

'Thank you for showing up and listening,' he replied, and kissed her under the streetlight, not caring who saw.

This time, when he watched her walk to her door, there was no uncertainty. Just the knowledge that they'd figured an important step out together, and that whatever came next, they'd face it together.

CHAPTER 35

The tables were all set up and the school fete was well underway. A large canopy hosted the contestants in the baking competition, the white fabric flapping slightly in the hot breeze. There was much laughter and banter as the bakers stood behind their entries, arranged on tables covered in checkered cloths. A trio of judges walked up and down in front of the tables, asking questions of the bakers and writing notes in their notepads with the kind of serious concentration usually reserved for judging Olympic events.

'Serious business,' Dusty whispered to Patricia who stood near to him, arms crossed and watching the proceedings with obvious amusement.

'Always,' she replied. 'See Cecily at the end there, she wins every year. Nothing can beat her custard tarts. People come from all over the state for them. She makes them at the bakery. It's her speciality. Won so many ribbons over the years she could wallpaper a room with them.'

He looked down at his Nanna's biscuits, arranged carefully on an old serving plate. 'You think they're better than these, or your lattice slice?'

Patricia laughed. 'It's not just about the taste. They have a judging criteria, you know. Texture, appearance, presentation, authenticity. It's quite complex actually.'

'Shhh. Here comes Ella,' Patricia whispered to him, her eyes dancing with mischief. 'Look smart now.'

He tried to keep a straight face as Ella and the other two judges approached his area. The other two were old timers, both women who were also known for their winning entries in the past. Myrtle, the older woman with steel-grey hair pulled back in a severe bun, looked him in the eye, her pencil poised for writing down his answers. 'So young man, can you tell me the story behind these biscuits?'

Ella smirked a little and he twisted his mouth to stop from smiling too much at her obvious enjoyment of his discomfort. 'This recipe has been passed down to me directly from my grandmother, who came to this area in the fifties. She was the descendant of Afghan cameleers and this recipe was passed down to her, and it has become an important one for my family. It's one of the few connections we still have to that side of our heritage.'

He could tell Myrtle was impressed, her eyebrows rising. 'Afghan cameleers. Were both her mother and father from Afghanistan?'

'No. Her mother was an Aboriginal woman, Dawn. She came from around the Marree area.'

He waited for the response, watching Myrtle's face carefully. 'Oh dear. That's unusual and oh my goodness...' She sniffled and shook her head a little as if trying to clear cobwebs from her mind. 'That would have been very frowned upon back in those days. They must have been brave, and might I say very determined to continue with that relationship in the face of such prejudice.'

'They were, and then when my grandmother married a Maltese man who came out here after the war, and also ended up near Marree, it caused even more trouble. They left that area and ended up here in Matfield. They faced many hardships, not only because of where they came from, but also because of the language barrier and just being seen as outsiders.'

'Oh, my goodness,' Myrtle said, her hand going to her chest. 'I grew up in Sydney. My grandfather was from Malta, also. We called him Nannu.' She rubbed her hand across her other arm. 'Hence the olive skin, and I have a penchant for good food and loud family gatherings. Well, I must say after tasting these previously at the tasting table, I can state that I'm very glad you're continuing with such an important tradition. These deserve recognition.' She scribbled in her notebook and nodded to Ella and the other lady. 'Let's move on.'

Ella winked at him as she passed, her hand brushing against his arm briefly in a gesture small enough that only he noticed. She was only an assistant judge. Myrtle was the one who did the questioning and no doubt, would make the final decision.

He watched as they passed along the line of entries, stopping at Patricia's lattice slice and spending considerable time examining Cecily's famous custard tarts. What he wouldn't give to eat one of Patricia's slices right at this minute. Being an entry in the baking competition was hard work, and he was starving.

CHAPTER 36

That night at the pub was fabulous. By now Dusty knew most of the townspeople who gathered there, and he took the jokes and banter about his baking skills well. He hadn't won. Cecily, the lady who always won, had taken out first prize, her custard tarts maintaining their legendary status. He had, however, been awarded a special medallion for maintaining traditions, and Myrtle had made such a big deal about the story behind the biscuits when she awarded the prizes that she'd talked for nearly ten minutes. In fact, she'd talked so much about his entry that the winner had frowned and rolled her eyes from side to side, clearly wondering when she'd get her moment. Eventually, after a modest thank you, Dusty had merged back into the crowd, the medallion in his pocket.

Now, amidst the animated noise of the pub's main room, he was surrounded by friends, and he really felt like he belonged here. At a nearby table, Eli sat with his arm around Cass, who was giggling at something he'd whispered in her ear. They looked completely absorbed in each other, oblivious to the crowd around them. When Cass caught Ella watching, she mouthed 'Thank you' and blew her a kiss.

He felt like all the stars had aligned and he was the luckiest man on Earth. Even more so because next to him was Ella. She must have decided that she wasn't pretending anymore, or hiding what was between them. She held his hand openly, pressed up next to him when they stood at the bar, and even gave him a kiss before handing him a beer, completely unconcerned about who saw. It was as if the grin couldn't leave his face, a permanent fixture that made his cheeks ache.

* * *

DUSTY WASN'T the only one feeling pleased with the way everything was working out. Colin and Helen Patterson stood near the bar, tanned and relaxed from their travels, taking in the sight of their daughter laughing with the dark-haired builder they'd heard so much about from Tyson.

'So that's him,' Helen murmured to her husband.

Colin watched as Dusty said something that made Ella throw her head back and laugh, that genuine laugh they hadn't heard enough of since she'd come home. 'That's him.' He smiled. 'And look at her face. When was the last time we saw her looking that happy?'

'Not since before Melbourne.' Helen squeezed his arm. 'Before everything with Trent.'

'This fella's different,' Colin observed. 'You can see it in the way he looks at her. Like she's the whole world.'

'Should we interrupt?' Helen asked, already knowing the answer.

'Give them a minute. Let's watch our girl being happy first.'

* * *

Later, when most of the crowd had thinned, Dusty and Ella said their goodnights. It seemed like half the town wanted a word. They chatted to Cass and Eli, Oscar and Patricia, and to her parents, who'd pulled Dusty aside for a warm greeting and a promise of dinner soon. Eventually, they walked back to her cottage through the quiet streets, the air finally cool, stars blazing overhead in that way they only did in places far from city lights.

'Come in?' she asked at her gate, and there was a question in her voice that went beyond simple hospitality.

'Yeah,' he said. 'I'd like that.'

Inside, she poured them both wine, and they sat on her small couch, close together, chatting in low voices about everything and nothing. They talked about the fete, the town, and their plans for tomorrow. But underneath it all was an awareness, a tension that had been building since that sunset kiss on the lookout.

'Dusty,' she said eventually, setting down her glass and turning to face him. 'I don't want to waste any more time being scared or careful, or pretending I don't want this.'

'What do you want?' His voice was rough, thick with emotion and barely restrained desire.

'You. All of you. Here, with me.' She took his hand. 'Is that okay?'

In answer, he pulled her close and kissed her, slow and

deep and full of everything he'd been holding back. She responded with equal intensity, her hands moving to his shoulders, his neck, threading through his hair with gentle urgency. When they finally broke apart, both breathing hard, their hearts pounding in unison, he rested his forehead against hers.

'Are you sure?' he asked.

'I've never been more sure of anything.' She stood and held out her hand. 'Come to bed with me.'

He followed her to her bedroom, his heart pounding. She turned on a small lamp on the bedside table, the dim light casting gentle shadows across the walls. When she turned to face him, there was no hesitation in her eyes, no doubt. Just want and trust, and something that looked a lot like love.

They undressed slowly, taking their time, no rushing or awkwardness between them. Hands gentle, voices soft, they explored each other, committing every detail to memory. Every touch felt precious, deliberate, and when they finally made love, it was with a tenderness and powerful urgency that surprised them both, a connection that went beyond the physical into something neither had experienced before.

* * *

AFTERWARDS, they lay tangled together, skin against skin, hearts still racing. Dusty traced patterns on her shoulder, her back, noticing everything in detail. The way her hair spread across the pillow. The small freckle on her collarbone. The way she fit perfectly against him as though she'd always belonged there.

'What are you thinking?' she whispered, her fingers caressing his chest.

That I'm the luckiest man alive.' He pressed a kiss to her forehead, breathing in the scent of her hair. 'And wondering what I would have done if you hadn't shown up at my house that night when I explained everything? I don't think I could have just walked away. I would have kept trying, kept fighting for this, for us.'

She propped herself up on her elbow and looked down into his face, her hair falling forward onto his body. 'Don't. Let's just put all that behind us. I do warn you though that I am very stubborn. That won't change. I'll probably drive you mad sometimes.'

He drew her back down into his arms, their bodies fitting together perfectly, naturally, as if they'd been designed for exactly this. 'I don't want to change anything about you. I love you just the way you are. Stubbornness and all.'

She went very still, and he realised what he'd just said. The words had slipped out naturally, easily, as though they'd been waiting there all along.

'You love me?' Her voice was small, wondering.

Yeah.' He cupped her face in his hands, his thumbs gently stroking her cheeks. 'I love you, Ella. Have for a while now, if I'm being honest. Probably since that first night when you glared at me in the pub and I couldn't stop thinking about you.

Her smile was radiant in the soft lamplight, her eyes shining with unshed happy tears. 'I love you too.' Her voice caught with emotion. 'I think I have since that night at the quiz, even when I was pretending to hate you and doing a terrible job of it. I just want us to be together,

Dusty. Really together, no more walls, no more fear. Just us.'

'I'm going to stay out here, you know.' He said it seriously, wanting her to understand the weight of the decision. 'I'm going to settle in Matfield permanently. This is home now.'

She leaned down and kissed him, slow and sweet. 'We'll be here together then. You and I. Building a life that lasts, creating memories worth keeping.'

'Together,' he agreed, pulling her closer. 'Always together.'

They made love again, slower this time, taking their time to explore and discover. Between kisses, they whispered plans and promises, building a future with words and touch. Outside, the night deepened and the stars wheeled overhead in their ancient patterns, and in that small cottage in an outback town, two people found themselves in each other.

When they finally fell asleep, tangled together and exhausted, Dusty thought of his nanna. She'd sent him here to lay her grief to rest, to make the echoes good, to transform pain into something beautiful. He'd done that, but he'd found so much more than he'd ever imagined possible.

And tomorrow, when the burning sun would rise over the dusty earth and paint the countryside with its golden hues, he and Ella would wake together and begin building that life. A life built on honesty and trust, on hard-won understanding, freely given in love. A life where painful echoes would be transformed into beautiful memories. His promise to his grandmother had led him to a woman who understood what it meant to fight for the places and people you loved.

The outback had given him Ella. Matfield had given him purpose and belonging. This small town, with its weathered buildings and friendly people, with its harsh beauty and unforgiving summers, had given him what he'd been searching for all along without knowing it. It had given him home.

Together, in each other's arms, warm and safe in the darkness, they had both finally found where they were meant to be.

~~~
~~~

Rhonda Forrest is an Australian author who juggles writing and publishing, alongside teaching high school students. She writes captivating contemporary fiction and historical romance about relationships, family life and social issues, set amidst beautiful and uniquely Australian landscapes.

After bringing up three daughters and traversing several careers, Rhonda went on to teach creative writing, English and history. Her passion for literacy, history and travelling around Australia fuels her novels. Along with her husband, she divides her time between Tamborine Mountain and a century-old cottage with a rambling garden overlooking the waters of the Whitsundays.

Recent novels bring to life the remarkable characters and settings that make up the unique Australian heritage and take the reader on a journey from bush to beach, with steamy romances, riveting history and eclectic characters.

Some books are available in audio and large print and you can also find some titles available in Portuguese, Publisher- Leabhar Books Brazil.

If you enjoyed this book or any of Rhonda's other books, you can make a big difference by writing a review, or leaving a star rating on Amazon, Goodreads or Bookbub. A personal recommendation to family, friends, libraries and book clubs is another great way to share the books with others. You can also follow Rhonda on Facebook, Instagram, Goodreads and Bookbub.

Author's favourite - for your enjoyment, sample chapters from *Nothing Without You* are in the back of this book.

Website - https://www.rhondaforrest.com/

ALSO BY RHONDA FORREST

OUTBACK QUEENSLAND ROMANCE SERIES

With a cast of eclectic characters and set amidst the rugged outback of Australia, the **Outback Queensland Romance Series** will introduce you to stories of friendship, resilience, and loving relationships that come together to triumph over obstacles defined by the past.

Two Heartbeats (Book 1) is followed by the sequel, *Time Will Tell* (Book 2)

Turn Left (Book 3), *A New Start* (Book 4), *Outback Magic* (Book 5) and *Echoes of the Outback* (Book 6) are stand-alone books with some links to the other books in this series.

SALTWATER ROMANCE SERIES

SALTWATER ROMANCE SERIES

From the wild freedom of 1970s Australia to the tangled emotions of the present day, the Saltwater Romance Series delivers three powerful love stories.

Set against the rainforests of North Queensland, the Whitsundays, and the golden shores of Stradbroke Island, these novels explore first love, rebellion, second chances and the journeys that lead us back to ourselves, and to the ones we can't forget.

***Sample chapters from Nothing Without You are in the back of this book. Enjoy!

'A dingo howls, a star falls.
Don't worry for me, I'll be home soon.'

We'll Meet Again trilogy is an epic World War II saga that will take you from outback Queensland to the jungles of New Britain, then back to the peaceful hinterland regions of the Sunshine Coast and Tamborine Mountain. Based on actual events that include the invasion of Rabaul, and the tragic sinking of the Montevideo Maru, these are emotional stories of love, survival, and the resilience of the families who waited for their loved ones to return.

SILKWORM SECRETS SERIES (Book 1 and 2)

Growing up next door to each other in 1960s suburban Brisbane, Ruby and Bobby should have an idyllic childhood. However, Bobby's home life is vastly different than the loving security of Ruby's family, and not even the sanctuary of their shared treehouse set high in a mulberry tree can offer him the safety he needs. Emotional and layered, *Silkworm Secrets* is a moving story about the secrets children keep, the power of friendship, and a love that overcomes the hardships of the past.

Forever More, continues the story of Bobby and Ruby and reminds us of the good and bad in people and that a loving family can come in many different forms.

BINDARRA CREEK ROMANCE

Bindarra Creek Romance

BEYOND THE GATE - Mystery Romance at Bindarra Creek

CHRISTMAS AT FORREST GLEN - A Bindarra Creek Romance

A MAGICAL SUMMER - A Bindarra Creek Small Town Christmas Romance

A WINTER'S PROMISE - A Bindarra Creek Christmas in July Romance

ALSO AVAILABLE IN A BOX SET - CLICK HERE!

WHITSUNDAY ROMANCE - YOU MAY NEVER WANT TO LEAVE!

Love by the Jewel Sea - Book 1

Summer by the Jewel Sea - Book 2

The Lure of the Jewel Sea - Book 3

THE SHACK BY THE BAY - Whitsunday Historical Romance

Romantic and purely Australian, *The Shack by the Bay* captures the pristine beauty of the Whitsundays and the wartime memories of older Australians while introducing an eclectic blend of friends and family.

ALL MY HEART - A Tranquil Bay Romance

A small town and school - She only had to last six months.

KICK THE DUST - Contemporary Romance

'If I close my eyes, it's easier to hold onto a memory. When I open them, I think it might really be there in front of me.'

SAMPLE CHAPTERS - NOTHING WITHOUT YOU

Beaudesert – 1977

*P*rologue

Evie sucked on a lolly as she lingered in the doorway of her mother's bedroom, her gaze moving from one end of the room to the other. The sweet chocolate filled her mouth as she bit down, her teeth crunching the orange coating of a Jaffa. She strolled into the room, picking up some items of interest before helping herself to a couple of her mother's possessions.

A thread of guilt ran through her, but she justified her actions. It wasn't really stealing; it was just sharing family belongings. She secreted the items into the pockets of her school uniform, her mind flitting between the stolen treasures and the impending life-changing events scheduled for that evening.

She swore as she dropped the last Jaffa meant for her mouth, the lolly bouncing on the timber floor before rolling under her mother's bed. No one else in the house ate lollies, and the last thing she needed was for anyone to suspect she had been in this room and home on a school day. The consequence of wagging would be a grounding, which she did not need on the eve of the most important night of her fifteen-year-old life.

She bent down to see if she could rescue the lolly, no doubt its coating now covered in dust. As her eyes landed on it, the sound of a key sliding into a lock, followed by the creak of the front door opening, made her heart pound and she froze where she stood.

Her mother's laughter echoed along the hallway. A man said something she couldn't understand. Confused for a split second before moving into action, she slid under the bed and pressed herself against the wall. Wriggling under as far as she could, she held her breath as her mother and a man whose voice she knew but had trouble identifying, entered the bedroom.

CHAPTER **One**

Beaudesert 1968

Evie first laid eyes on Chris McIntosh on her very first day of primary school in 1968. She remembered it vividly because on that particular day—and that day alone—her mother walked her up the dirt road that ran past their house, turned left, and holding Evie's hand tightly, guided her through the main entrance of Beaudesert State School.

A large wooden archway with the school's name emblazoned on its gable left Evie feeling as tiny as the insects clustered on top of a dead cockroach near her shoe. She sidestepped a group of yellow ants that wriggled and scurried around the larger insect, a few working together to drag the bug somewhere else. Perhaps they were trying to get it out of the line of mothers and children streaming into the school.

She wanted to stop and watch what happened to it, but her mother tugged at her hand, pulling her under and through the archway into the school grounds. She looked up at the sign that declared the school's name and a number, which she later learned said 'Established 1887'.

When they stopped for a moment, Mother undid the hair clip in Evie's hair and adjusted it to where she thought it should go. She tugged gently at Evie's plaits, squinting at them to ensure they were even. Father had stopped Mother from cutting Evie's hair the week before. 'Leave it be, Maya,' he said, using his firm voice. 'It's beautiful and nearly down to her waist.'

Mother had continued to brush it. 'It's a pity she didn't inherit my blonde colour or your black hair. She's in the middle. Dark brown. Definitely got your eyebrows, though.' Father had won, and Evie's plaits remained neat and long.

At last, Mother was satisfied with them, although she must have noticed a stray hair in Evie's eyebrows because she licked her finger and then ran it over the top of both. Lick. Left one. Flatten. Lick. Right one. Flatten.

When Evie jutted out her chin and pulled her head back from her mother's hand, she received a head shake in return. 'Stand still, Evie. Let me check how you look.'

Her feet hurt and she scuffed them in the dust, annoyed that she had to wear the new shoes her mother had bought. She wasn't used to anything on her feet, and she noticed that some of the other kids had bare feet and weren't wearing stiff, black shoes that pinched their toes. 'Why do I have to wear these shoes?' she asked her mother, pointing to an older girl who walked past them. 'She doesn't have any on.'

Her mother made that tut-tutting noise that meant she wouldn't answer the question. Instead, she pulled on Evie's hand before walking quickly up the path to where a group of mothers, similarly holding fast to their children's hands, were listening to a lady. The lady, who she later came to know as Mrs Montrose, was her year one teacher.

Evie scrunched her toes inside her shoes, the confines of the leather restrictive and tight. It was as though her feet were in jail, and she didn't like that she had to do something she didn't want to do. She stomped her foot, then tapped the toe end on the ground, scuffing the leather. Her mother made a growling noise and propelled her forward as Mrs Montrose started to call out names from a list she held in her hand. A boy beside Mrs Montrose held other pieces of paper, passing the teacher a page when she asked for them.

'Thank you, Chris,' the teacher said. 'I don't know what I'd do without you.'

Evie stared at the boy, and he must have felt her eyes on him because he stared back, unsmiling, as he shuffled his bare feet on the concrete pathway. He wasn't much taller than her, his blonde hair short and neat. Like the other boys, he wore shorts and a T-shirt, his skinny legs moving up and down as he struggled to stand still.

'He doesn't have shoes on,' Evie said. She must have

spoken too loudly because her mother yanked her hand and told her to be quiet. Her complaints continued about wearing shoes, but she stopped when the boy poked his tongue out at her. It was an automatic response to poke hers back at him, and for a while they exchanged looks, their tongues poking out and then quickly back in when Mrs Montrose spoke again.

'Thank you, Chris. You can go.' No one seemed to notice the tongue-poking-out exchange; they were all too busy talking. The boy glanced at Evie again and poked his tongue out one more time, before turning on his heel and walking away. She watched him as he moved along the path, joining another group of boys gathered around the racks where the bicycles were kept.

Her attention was drawn back to the people around her, and she stared intently at the other kids starting year one. At least they were suffering the same shoe problem as her, each wearing some sort of footwear. A girl standing nearby offered a friendly smile. She wore brown sandals with silver buckles that kept them in place. At least she hadn't poked her tongue out. Evie smiled back.

As an only child, Evie didn't have the company or security of brothers and sisters to look after her. Some of her friends who lived on her street were attending the same school, but they were either a few years older or a bit younger than she was.

There had been discussions at home about making friends. 'Just tell them your name and say you want to be their friend,' her father advised, tweaking her plaits and sweeping her up in his arms. He cuddled her tight. He had a sweet, warm smell that she loved. When she pushed her head into his chest and closed her eyes, the familiar scent of his aftershave lingered in her nostrils and sometimes she could still smell it on her clothes a long time after he held her. The smell always comforted her, as did his voice, his words spoken quickly but softly, with an accent different from anyone else she knew. Sometimes, he reverted to his native language, Italian. This usually happened when he was excited, sad, or argued with Mother. Father was a calm man though, so fortunately arguments didn't happen very often. The best thing about him was he always told her he loved her. Mother never said those words, but Father said them to her at least once a day, sometimes more.

All the love she needed came from him. He said his love for Evie came all the way from Italy. 'It's from your nonnas and pappas. Even though you can't see them and they can't hug you, they are sending their love.'

Carlo migrated to Australia in the 1950s, travelling alone and leaving behind his entire family and friends. 'I wanted a new life. I had dreams for this land of opportunity I had heard about,' he told Evie. 'I cut cane in North Queensland and met new friends. There were mosquitos as big as bumblebees and snakes longer than my body. *Fa molto caldo.* They call it humidity here. The heat was something else. We worked hard though, and made good money. When I came to Brisbane on a holiday, I met your mother. She was beautiful and made me laugh back then.' His face fell with a wistful look, as if he wanted those old times back again. 'She was looking for a husband, and I a wife. We bought this house, and I soon became Queensland's top vacuum cleaner salesman.'

She loved that story, even if she had heard it a hundred times before. Father's voice was smooth, and his pronunciation of words differed from others because he spoke in his second language, English. Some people laughed at his accent and made fun of how he talked. Once she had even heard some people in the corner store say bad words about her father. He had been at the counter asking for milk while Evie dawdled behind. She had slid her feet along the shiny lino floor as she looked at the food on the shelves for sale. Father moved to the cash register, and she smiled as she listened to him talking while he paid. His words were eloquent, and he even threw in one of his own words, '*Graci*', to thank the young girl behind the counter.

A lady and man were in front of Evie as she looked longingly at the chewing gum display, the imagined taste of Juicy Fruit rolling around her mouth.

The woman looked up and stared at Father, her face scrunched up in a nasty smirk as she twisted her mouth and nearly spat her words out. 'Bloody wogs. Can't even speak English. They'll take over the country if we're not careful.'

The man with the lady added more mean words, and the two of them muttered about 'Ities' and 'filthy migrants'. Evie had heard the slang word 'Ities' before and she knew they were talking about her father. A nearby empty trolley was a valuable weapon for her vengeance, and she grabbed it without another thought, ramming it into the lady's broad backside. 'I'm so sorry,' Evie apologised before pushing it harder, pretending she was trying to steer it in another direction.

The lady shrieked as she stumbled forward, a bottle of milk in her hand falling to the ground and shattering. The white liquid splashed back up over the lady's clothes and across the groceries in her trolley.

Without a backward glance, Evie continued down the aisle. She left the trolley near the front counter before skipping through the exit and quickly joining her father, who was waiting for her on the pavement outside.

'Where were you? I only needed to get milk.' He bent down and straightened her jumper. 'Chewing gum? Was that what you were looking at? Maybe next time, my little bambino. Let's go.'

Evie giggled, imagining the mess left behind and how annoyed the lady would be. It served her right, she thought. How dare they talk about her father in that way! Most people loved him and the way he spoke, especially the women who entered the vacuum cleaner shop where he worked. They hung off every word he said and fluttered their eyelids as he drew them into his sales pitch. They would then, without exception, purchase whatever vacuum cleaner he promoted that month.

It wasn't just his smooth words or interesting accent that drew people in. Father looked different to a lot of the men who lived around them. He had a neatly trimmed moustache, the short, dark hairs tickling when she pressed her cheek to his lips. His black hair was slicked back, with never a strand out of place, and he wore collared shirts in various colours, thin dark ties, and black formal trousers that matched his shiny leather black or brown shoes. Even his socks were of the finest quality. The trips he made to Sydney were not only for selling vacuum cleaners and meeting up with other salesmen from around Australia, but he also spent time at the big department stores, seeking out the newest attire imported from Europe.

Even at five years old, she knew that her father loved her, more than he loved her mother. If she had something important to ask or a secret to tell, it was her father she turned to. He never told her he was too busy, or laughed at what she said. Instead, he asked for even more information, and made her feel like a grown-up with something important to say. Mother was always busy cleaning, cooking or dusting. Even if she was sitting down having a cup of tea or just staring out the window, she wasn't really interested in what Evie had to say. 'I just need some time to myself, Evie,' she would say. 'Go and talk to your father.'

Father said the reason her mother didn't want to listen to her stories and needed to sometimes be alone, was that she had grown up in a household with a stern, strict, and argumentative father. Mother pulled a face when Evie asked her about her family. 'Think yourself lucky that your father and I may not always agree, but we don't fight or yell at each other. We always end up agreeing on what's best for you.'

The only time Mother wasn't serious or busy, was when Father gave her a second glass of wine with dinner. When the three of them sat around the yellow and white laminate table and ate their dinner together, her father would talk about his day at the shop. Mother would listen, usually not adding too much, but seeming to enjoy the conversation. What she did love was Father's wine. After a couple of glasses, she would take her blonde hair out of the bun she usually wore. Shaking her head, she'd ruffle her hair with her hands and wiggle her shoulders, as if she had been set free. Set free from what, Evie wondered, but she had no idea.

Unlike any of her friends' houses, there was a rack that held bottles of wine. Father had a drink of wine with Mother each night with dinner, and that was when everyone seemed to relax. It was as if her mother had become a different person. Mother said the kitchen made her happy. The bright yellow cupboards and drawers that lined one wall made her feel like she was sitting in the sun. Father had built wide shelves and brightly coloured canisters sat on them. They had yellow lids and flower patterns on the front and had been a present he brought back from one of his Sydney trips.

After the first glass, Father would start telling jokes, or he and Mother would talk about places they had lived before. Mother would laugh, her shoulders bouncing up and down, sometimes even happy tears running down her cheeks. A little more wine would be poured into her glass, and sometimes Father poured a small amount for Evie to try. Some nights Father showed Evie how to wind the spaghetti around her fork and suck it into her mouth. Once, her mother joined in the sucking contest, and the three of them competed for who could suck the longest piece of spaghetti the quickest. Her mother's eyes had sparkled that night, and Evie noticed the looks exchanged between her parents. They were a family, just the three of them. Mother was beautiful, and in love with Father.

On nights like that, Evie's world was complete. It was as though she had the most perfect family in the world. The trouble was, those nights didn't happen that often.

Evie thought back to the night of the spaghetti sucking competition, and how beautiful her mother had looked.

Now though, on Evie's first day of school, Mother seemed as nervous as Evie felt. Her face wore its typically serious expression, and Evie pulled her hand away from her tight grip. She wiped it on her school uniform; her palm was sweaty and red from being held so tight. The girl next to her smiled and copied Evie, also prising her hand free.

The two mothers began talking. They seemed to know each other and before she knew it, the girl came up beside Evie. 'My name is Layla.'

'My name is Evie,' she answered back, admiring Layla's long blonde hair, which was tied up in two bouncy pony-tails. Layla held out her hand, and she put hers into it. Both hands felt warm, but they weren't sweaty, and neither squeezed hard.

Evie's mother bent down and spoke to Layla. 'You two can be friends. Sit together and look after each other.' It was a surprise to hear how kind her mother could sound. Usually, her directions were short and swift. The kind words and soft cuddles were what her father was for.

Evie had thought it would have been better if Father had come with her on the first day of school. But he was away on business. 'Sydney. He's gone to Sydney for a week,' her mother replied when Evie asked where he was. Her mother frowned, like she often did when she asked more questions. 'You don't need to know everything, Evie. He's in Sydney. Selling vacuum cleaners. That's all. Now remember, keep your words and questions to yourself. Children are meant to be seen, not heard.'

Chapter Two

Layla and Evie became best friends on that first day at

school. Luckily, they lived not too far away, which meant that Layla and her older sisters, Patrina and Emily, could wait for Evie on the corner of her street every morning to ride their bikes to school together. Layla's mother's name was Yvette, and she knew Mother through the tennis club. The arrangements made between the two mothers on that first morning of school stayed in place for the next seven years. Come rain, hail or shine, Evie and Layla rode together.

After Layla's sisters left and started at the high school that was further away, requiring a bus trip, the two girls continued to meet every morning and make their way to school together. Some days they were early, so there was time to dawdle and stop at the horse paddock. An old piebald mare that loved the tuna sandwich Layla's mother made for her lunch, waited each morning at the fence. The girls giggled as the mare stretched her neck over the barbed wire and nuzzled their school bags, until they gave her what she was looking for.

At first, Mother was surprised Evie needed two sandwiches each day, and queried that she wanted to have the same jam on both. After a while though, she stopped questioning. She was just glad that Evie appeared to have settled into school, made some friends and expected less and less of her precious time. Layla became used to the shared sandwiches and felt lucky to be rid of the tuna, instead enjoying the sticky sweet jam that covered thick butter on crusty brown bread.

During lunch break, Evie and Layla always sat in the same spot. A gentle sloping area under the shade of tall pine trees was a perfect place to observe others, share the jam sandwiches and tell their secrets.

It was where they were sitting on the last day of grade five when Evie had her first conversation with Chris McIntosh. There were always groups of boys playing football down on the flat grassed area in front of them, and a couple of times Evie had noticed the boy who had poked his tongue out at her on her first day of school. He was older than she was, so she had not had anything to do with him over the previous years, only noticing when he got an award or won a ribbon on sports day. Today, he jogged towards them. His football had landed nearby, and Layla snatched it up as it bounced close to her, hiding it under her jumper.

'Give us the ball, please,' he said, holding out his hand.

Layla giggled. 'What ball?'

'I'm not stupid. It's under your jumper.'

Evie was impressed with Layla's certainty around older kids. Her self-confidence and larger, stronger build were good reasons, along with her fun personality, to have her as a friend. There was a feeling of safety in her presence. Today, however, perhaps she was pushing her luck. Layla wrapped her hands around her stomach. 'You need to pay to get it back.'

'It's my ball. Give it back.'

'Nope.'

Another boy appeared behind Chris, his glare showing that he was not happy. 'Give us the ball back.' This boy's name was Adam and he was taller than Chris.

'You gotta pay me,' Layla said.

'With what?' Adam asked. 'We've got no money.'

'You have to kiss me then,' Layla said.

Evie's face must have mirrored the horror she felt at

Layla's suggestion, and she blinked hard when Chris replied, 'I'm not kissing anyone. Now give the ball back.'

Layla clutched her stomach tighter. 'No. Someone has to kiss me.'

By now Evie had heard enough. 'Layla! Give them the ball back.'

No one spoke. It's a standoff, Evie thought. Suddenly, Adam bent down and kissed Layla on the cheek, wrestling the ball from her. She fell backwards laughing, kicking her legs in the air as the two boys ran off.

'My first kiss!' she shrieked. 'And with Adam Pearson! A year seven boy! Wait 'til I tell my sisters!'

Chapter Three

Layla had always been braver and more adventurous than Evie. By the time they reached the end of year seven, her best friend had kissed more boys than Evie could count. The kissing always took place where no one would see; behind the groundsman's shed near the oval, under the stairs in the double-storey year seven block, and even behind a tree on their way to school.

'You just need to ask one of them to kiss you,' Layla told Evie. 'You're missing out.'

She was horrified. 'No way. My dad said not to let any boys kiss me. They're only ever after one thing, and to stay away from them.'

'He's just telling you that because he doesn't want you to have fun.'

The two girls sat away from prying eyes in their usual hideout, an old shed near the back fence of Evie's property. It was musty and dim inside, and every so often a mouse scurried out from under the timber orange crates stored on the shelves. The tiny marsupial's scampering movements and twitching nose sent the girls shrieking and jumping up onto the nearest chair. They persisted in using the shed though, as it was their own space, where no one bothered or nagged them about picking up their mess.

Today, Evie brought a few books her mother had recently given her. One was called *Guide Through Teen Years – A Reliable Sex Education Booklet for Girls 12-14.*

'That's us,' Layla said. The two girls giggled as they looked at the illustrations. Layla read some of the words out loud, thrusting her hips back and forth as she imitated the descriptions in the book.

'Oh, my goodness,' Evie whispered. 'Look at these pictures of a rooster and a hen doing it.' She turned the pages, her eyes wide. 'Where are the birds and the bees?'

Layla grabbed the book from her. 'You idiot. That's just what grownups say to us kids. It's not real. Here, look at this one: Mothercraft. Check out the girl on the front cover. She's so dressed up, like she's going to church.'

Adorning the front was a black and white photo of an attractive young woman, beautifully dressed and wearing oven mittens, taking a cake out of the oven.

'This book is so old fashioned,' Layla said as she grabbed it off Evie and opened it at what she had decided was her favourite page. As she read the words, she changed her voice to sound like a very posh adult. 'A young woman should ensure that her husband's dinner is ready for him each evening.' She paused and wiggled her chest, pretending to have large breasts, and then held her hand out as if she were holding a cigarette. Placing the pretend cigarette into her mouth, she drew back, pursing her lips to blow the invisible smoke into the air as she continued. 'The good wife should ensure that she always greets her husband at the door when he returns from work and that she is looking her best. No man wants to come home to a wife who doesn't look good.' She rolled her eyes before closing them, fluttering her eyelashes when she eventually opened them again.

'Stop being so dramatic,' Evie said. 'Hurry up, I want to know what happens next. Is there any sex stuff in there?'

'Not likely. Listen to this. Always be punctual with dinners cooked and your husband's slippers warmed by the fire or heater. When you open the door to greet him after his hard day at work, take his coat and help him remove his shoes, slipping his feet straight into his warm slippers.'

Layla put her finger down her throat and pretended to vomit. 'No way. This is bullshit.'

Evie peered around, checking through the window to make sure no adults were making their way towards the shed. 'Shh, don't swear. You'll get us in trouble.'

'I'm not going to pander to any boy. I'm an equal and no one will tell me what to do,' Layla said as she turned the page. 'We think differently in my house, because we're all girls. We talk a lot about the different paths our lives might take. We're going to make our own choices.'

'Do you miss your dad?' Evie asked, a sad tone in her voice.

'No. I don't. Mum does though. I was only two when he died, so I don't remember him. It was because of the war. He had things wrong with him from injuries he got in New Guinea. Mum said so. She's been our mum and dad all in one. She says women can do anything if they put their minds to it.' Evie stuffed the books back in her bag. 'Does your dad boss your mum around?'

'No way,' Evie said, as she took the book back from her friend and tried to straighten the cover where Layla had bent it. 'Dad's the softie in our family.' She thought hard. 'They do their own thing. Dad lets Mum do what she wants and Mum's the same, although she does get cranky when Dad goes to Sydney for work so much.'

'Sounds like it's fair in your house.' Layla sighed and ran her hands over her legs. 'Look at them. Beautiful and smooth.'

Evie pouted. 'I'm not allowed to shave mine until I start high school next year. How embarrassing. Mine needs doing more than yours. At least your hair's blonde. The hairs on my legs and eyebrows are darker than what's on my head.'

'You should just do it. Shave. Forget what your parents say.'

'I only have to wait a bit longer. On the school holidays we're going to Stradbroke Island, and Mum said I can shave them before we go. I can't wait.'

'I want that Adam boy from the high school to run his hand over my legs and then,' Layla pulled a crazy face, 'and then I want him to touch me here.' She put her hand between her legs.

Evie was alarmed and sat up straight, her eyes wide. 'Layla! Why would you let him do that?'

'I read my sister's diary. She writes all the stuff about what her boyfriend Matt does to her. She loves it. They have sex in all different places.'

'What do you mean?'

'They do it in Grandma's house when she goes away on holidays, they did it in the hay down in the stables behind the racetrack, and once last week, standing up in his bedroom when his parents were at church.'

Evie was intrigued. 'Standing up? How does that work?'

Layla lifted her eyebrows up and down continually, her eyes wide. 'I'm not sure and it didn't show that in those books, but if I could get Adam to touch me, I reckon I could work it out.'

The conversation continued for a long time, only stopping when Evie's father called to them from the back veranda of the house. 'Dinner time, my little bambinos. It's time for you to go home, Layla. It will be dark soon. Here, take these tomatoes and capsicums home for your mother. She's a good woman. She works hard.'

'Thank you, Mr Romano,' Layla said, accepting the brown paper bag full of the fruit Carlo loved to grow. 'She loves your tomatoes and the free vacuum cleaner you gave her.'

He waved his hands in the air, 'It was nothing. Demo model. Make sure you are a good girl and help your mother.'

Evie stood on the veranda with Father, his arm around her shoulders as they waved goodbye to Layla.

'She's a good girl, your friend Layla,' he said. 'A very good girl.'

Evie went to say something else but then thought it better not to. If her parents knew what Layla was really like, they wouldn't want her to be friends with her. There was a certain limit to what she told them, and the conversation she'd just had in the shed with her friend was not suitable to share, especially with her dad.

There had been a change in Layla's attitude in the last couple of months, and Evie struggled to keep up with her knowledge and desire to do different things. Evie was also jealous because Layla had her periods. She was a woman. Well, that's what Layla said. All the boys liked Layla, but Evie wasn't sure that reading her sister's diary and hoping to do similar things when she was still only in year seven was such a good idea. Most of the boys in their grade were noisy, silly, and not interested in girls. Some of them still even thought girls had germs. That's why Layla liked the boys from the high school. She said they were more mature; one of them had asked her to go to the show in town the next week.

Evie washed her hands and face, ready for dinner. She ran her fingers over her eyebrows, the dark hairs much thicker than Layla's. Her mother said she would pluck them for her once she started shaving her legs. A pimple on her chin stood out and she squeezed it between her fingers, rubbing her hand over her skin where the little whitehead had been. There were so many aspects of life that were changing—some good and some not so good.

She liked that sometimes on weekends, her father took her with him when he went to work. A desk had been allotted to her and she was given some alphabetical filing to do. Glenys, the lady he worked with, fussed over Evie and told her she was pretty and looked like someone called Sophia Loren. At morning tea, she sat and had a cup of tea with Glenys and her dad, listening to them talking about the newest vacuum cleaners that had arrived that week, and how everyone in town was putting in orders.

They treated her like a grown-up, and Glenys even asked her if she had a boyfriend. Shaking her head, she could feel her face burning. 'No boys,' her dad said, shaking his pointer finger back and forth in the air. 'No boys until she is finished high school.'

Another day, her dad had taken her into the city. She wore her best dress with a yellow spotted bodice. It was tight and her mother said it showed off her slim waist. The skirt section came to above her knees and she was excited to wear a pair of knee-high white boots that laced up from the bottom to the top. They had been in a hand-me-down bag of clothes that Glenys had given her, and matched some of the other dresses that belonged to Glenys's daughters. As she brushed her long brown hair, then smeared Vaseline on her lips to make them look shiny, she silently thanked her father for some of her features.

Although her legs weren't that long, and it always felt like her backside was enormous compared to Layla's, she thought other parts of her body were satisfactory. When she sat in the front seat of her father's car on one of their trips into the city, she felt as though she was so grown up. She crossed her legs at her knees and made sure her dress didn't get crushed. They parked alongside the Brisbane River, and her dad held her hand as they walked along the pathway. He pointed out buildings he knew the names of and the different places he had gone to hold vacuum demonstrations. 'Lots of carpet in those offices,' he remarked. 'That means lots of vacuums for the cleaners.'

On one trip to Brisbane, her father needed to buy

some new clothes. They went to a shop that sold suits and other formal clothes, and she sat in a plush leather chair, trying to look as grown up as she could as he tried on a variety of stiff-collared shirts and brightly coloured ties. His appearance was another thing she loved about him. His black hair was slicked back with Brylcreem, and he looked like a movie star to Evie. When he wore a dark suit and his moustache was newly trimmed, he resembled the man in the cigarette ad on television that said, 'Blow in her face and she'll follow you anywhere.'

Neither of her parents wanted to explain the meaning of that line, and she wondered why anyone would wish to have cigarette smoke blown in their face.

Her dad looked more glamorous than the man in the ad. He had darker skin and whiter teeth and wore a large gold ring with a black stone in the middle. Even her friends at school told her he was handsome. Now, as he led her to a café that was hidden away in an arcade that branched off Queen Street, she held tight to his hand, hoping he would sit for a long time and drink the tiny cups of coffee that he loved, as well as take her into more shops.

When he pulled her chair out for her to sit down, she could feel the eyes of those around her watching. A lady and a man at the table next to them smiled. The man leaned over and spoke to her father. 'You'll soon be chasing the boys away from your front door,' he said.

Her father laughed and placed his hand on her shoulder. When he looked at her like that, she thought her heart would explode. She was lucky to have a loving father and mother, even though Mother was different and not so patient. Coming to the city with her was very different from what she was experiencing with Father today.

Trips with Mother involved a crowded bus ride to and from home, and usually not a window seat where she could watch the trams glide past or see the newspaperman on the corner of the street calling out for people to buy his papers. Instead of a café and coffee, it would be a pie, chips and gravy at the Coles cafeteria, the metal seats cold and hard, the lights bright, and the room filled with noisy people who pushed past, trying to find an empty table and chairs. Mother didn't usually allow time to look in the shops afterwards either; instead, she headed straight for where she needed to go, only purchasing what she wanted before heading back to the bus for home. Those days were no comparison to the outings with her father. He was, quite simply, the best parent in the world.